Tamara Wilding was born and brought up in England, in the Shires. This is her fourth outing into darkly humorous fantasy, a genre she has enjoyed for many years.

By Tamara Wilding

In the Graeffenland Series

The World Unseeing
A King in Graeffenland
Princess of Bones
Metacosmoclypse
Once A Knight
Hand & Eye
Jaeson Smith, Private Eye
Jaeson Smith, Deja Vue

Metacosmoclypse

Tamara Wilding

This paperback edition first published 2015.

Copyright 2015 by Tamara Wilding.
Second Edition October 2016

The moral right of the author has been asserted.

All characters and events in this publication, other than those clearly in the public domain, are fictitious and any resemblance to actual persons, living or dead, is purely coincidental.

All rights reserved. No part of this publication may be reproduced, stored in a retrieval system, or transmitted, in any form or by any means without the prior written permission of the author, nor be otherwise circulated in any form of binding or cover other than that in which it is published and without a similar condition being imposed on the subsequent buyer.

Cover based on an acrylic painting by Tamara Wilding, copy right 2015.

Chapter One – A Priestly Predicament.

Berythus Naechos closed the door to the Temple of Libraria behind him. It was a stout door, hard dark wood inlaid with great metal bands, lacquered with paint, and many, many, layers of grime.

It was not the main door, they lay on the other side of the building, and opened onto Quill Street, but the 'tradesmen's entrance', that led onto Leavings Alley. Apparently it had been named for an old orphanage, now long gone.

He turned his head, gazing furtively up and down the alley. This was a man afraid. Not a big man, nor especially a short man either, his robes, hood drawn up against the cold dank mists, hid a thin face with a small nose, and a thin scholarly body, used to the indoor life.

He hunched, a little against the cold, but more to present a smaller target, should trouble appear. Perhaps he even sought to hide behind the wisps of mist and smoke drifting through the night. His lantern, small and hooded, bar for an aperture at the front, its beam shining an orange shaft through the grey mirk.

He carefully pointed it this way and that, his caution almost painful to behold. He stepped out his nose wrinkling and his free hand rising involuntarily to his face, as if to ward off the ever present stench, of indescribable foulness, that smote his senses. No sea breeze reached these alleys, so tall were the surrounding buildings.

He took another step as fearfully gazing downwards now at the unnameable, lumps of matter that littered his path. Actually, looking a little too close at one lump in particular, some things were all too nameable, thus was the disadvantage of an education brought home to him.

He stepped on, gingerly, tentatively, listening now, his ears not spared their measure of fear and anxiety. His lantern light, lit upon graffiti. It too was unspeakable, well, perhaps in fact, more unpronounceable, and as a scholar he felt slightly put out by that fact. He knew a dozen languages. Old, new and arcane, and yet here was a patois he did not understand. Some of the diagrams were a bit more obvious. He reddened, shivered and moved on a little quicker. He knew he couldn't hang around, but he knew he mustn't fall foul of the people of night.

He walked steadily now, his feet picking their way quietly through the night, strange and not so strange noises, sometimes from the buildings either side. Many of these were derelict, their fairly stout outer walls hiding the crumbly flaky ruins within.

This not to say they were abandoned. The poor, the wild, the mad, and the criminal, were their usual denizens. He hated what Carseport had become. He remembered what the city had been like before King Xagigg had been crowned. Xagigg had been a man then, now of course rumour was he had become some undead fiend, some sort of Lich.

People carried on regardless, some people had profited. Death did not stop people from working. Xagigg's dark magick stopped all but the most wealthy from resting peacefully in their graves. Zombie factories arose, making some few merchant families rich beyond their wildest dreams, for awhile. There was even a little boom, as the countries damaged by the dragon strikes recovered. This did not last long, as the darkness fell in the southlands, cities, gone dark, their people turned into dark eyed horrors, living only to destroy and recruit into their own numbers.

He shuddered again, he pulled his hood up around his head once more, a needless nervous action, as it settled back, almost immediately to its accustomed position. His cloak flapped around him as he moved, as swiftly as he dared down the alley way, the chill misty night air stabbed cold clammy fingers at his face, and the backs of his hands, ran wet. Was it the mist or was it sweat? Perhaps it was both.

The alley curved, and bent. He slowed. His thoughts presenting him an image from long ago, the marching liveried Bone Legion, rank upon rank of newly raised zombie troops, accoutred with spears and shields, bows and daggers, helms and chainmail. He remembered watching them march onto the ships, bound for the South, the salvation of a place far away, he knew only from maps.

That was years ago, and the Bone Legion was still there. Trade had all but dried up. People did not like zombie made goods, and despite the Wall, despite the Iron Legion, and later he had learned, the mighty war machines of the Gnomes, agents of the Dreaded Devourer had slipped through.

Countries, weakened already by the Dragon strikes of old, now fell to internal strife, bandits, warlords and monsters had made the continent a place of misery. Famine and plagues had followed.

Carseport had declined. He had kept studying, hoping for the best, after all it couldn't last forever, could it?

He turned the corner, cautiously, his lantern hooded fully. He let the light out gently. No one was to be seen. Good, he carried on.

Yes, he thought, his studies. He had read most books and tomes in the Temple. Libraria was a goddess of knowledge, after all, and he as her priest, devoted his time to worship, through books. As the years passed he wondered if there might be some help, some solution to the nightmare, recorded in one of the old Tomes. Yes, he thought in the end there is nothing new under heaven.

Plucking up his courage, he had opened the locks on the Forbidden Section, works so dangerous to mind and sanity, that none should read them, unless of course they had a will of adamantine and no internal critic. These books, chaotically written by human or inhuman hands or appendages, had never been properly edited. In fact a weak minded individual would risk his or her own mind being edited by the book itself, such was the disturbing, mind wrangling shenanigans invested in the heinous eldritch tomes.

Eldritch as in very old indeed, certainly thousands of years old in their original, one or two said to have existed before the world began. How that would work he didn't like to think. Perhaps they came from a different world, an older world, or perhaps it was just out and out lies. Who knew?

He giggled as he thought of it. He had worked for months. Long, long days and nights he had huddled, just candlelight for company, as he had perused the darkling works.

He had translated and digested some of the oldest and the worst, of the rather large and horrible collection. Now, as he stepped lightly, cautiously, almost catlike, if such a cat, was a little drunk, or hampered by an exceptionally ferocious mouse clinging for dear life to a rear leg. Yes, now as he made his way through the nightbound accursed city (some people regarded Carseport as accursed, and some didn't, it's a matter of perspective), his mind squirmed and wriggled, beating at the eggshell thin bone of his puny braincase, with it's urge to scream howling into a void of eternal oblivion.

But he had done it. He had his scroll, his personal magnum opus. He must deliver it, before beating his brains out joyously upon the cobble stones of Caresport.
He had learnt much. He knew how the Devourer could be re imprisoned. Destroyed or slain, too much to hope for, and the maddening hints of strange unearthly powers, that might just do that, when appeased in ghastly fashion, remained elusive and tormenting.

He had found out how, and the bare bones, with no unnecessary elaboration, he had written down, clearly so any might read and know the way.

He knew how and the finding of it had shredded his reason. He had but one last, one final mission, and then peaceful oblivion.

He hurried through the alleys, by day he knew the ancient tottering city of Carseport, like the back of his hand. He was a native, Carseport, born and bred.

Yes, he remembered Carseport, back when it had Kings and Regents, when the corruption was just the normal corruption of greed, lust, and envy.

Sloth was only latterly a problem. The workers who had grafted in factories, now discarded in favour of zombies, were reduced to petty crime and panhandling. The Zombiemation of the factories, had created bumper profits, for the already rich mill owners, and despair for their former employees.

He laughed, then cringed. It had carried through the mists of the night, dully thudding off the night air.

He walked on, a little slower, ready to hide or flee, if need be. Oh, accursed city! Rightly nick named the Necropolis of Xa, after Xagigg, the Lich King, Master of the realm of Graeffenland, and via his Bone Legions, leader of the 'free' world.

He laughed again, tittering inanely at the thought.

A Lich King, protecting the 'free world'!

He stopped. He had heard something. Just what it was, he was not sure. A muted sound, like a scuffle, or dragging noise, perhaps, down a side alley, just ahead.

He patted his pocket where the scroll resided. It was there. Good! He mustn't lose that.

On he crept, using his lantern as little as he possibly could. What lay in the shadows? These days it might be anything. Reality too, was broken, decaying, fading and frayed at the edges.

Where old houses and courtyards had been, sometimes they no longer were. Great holes had appeared. Though they were not holes as such, usually mercifully masked by mists. Lord Biphel, Mayor of the City, had reacted quickly when the first 'gaps' had appeared, walling off the affected areas, and King Xagigg himself, had worked a great magick, that so far, had held at bay any further, absences.

Yes, absences. Those looking beyond the mists, reported back nothing but blackness, and stars. Strange colourful stars, that moved and warped before the eyes, as though thro the bottom of a swirling lens. That, of course, was if they reported back at all. Many times such viewers, would vanish, in body, and sometimes just in mind. The new Asylum, run by the Sisters of Despair, was looking after hundreds of casualties. In a city where Zombies did most of the work, madness was a growth industry.

Holes in reality, oh yes, he'd read the forbidden words and dark texts, they too had read him, their dry, rustlingly, crackling voices, whispered in the corners of his whirling mind. They mocked him, told him all would soon be nothing, consumed, devoured, voided.

He wept and laughed. He had written it down. The answer, an answer, a solution to the insoluble nightmare of the Devourer. He giggled, and caught himself, clapping his hands to his mouth in fear and nervous hilarity.

The noise, he had heard it again. It was closer, it was shuffling even now, as he listened, it was edging nearer. Nearer to him!

He moved, quicker now, less caring of noise. It was too late for stealth. His feet flapped on the cobbles, which despite the city's rundown and dilapidated nature, were swept daily, by zombie care takers. Most people ignored them now, the malaise was solely one of hardship on the destitute living, and the callous fantasy land of the rich mill owners.

Yes, the zombie factory owners were, mostly, still rich, but none of their wealth reached the ordinary people. He was probably now being stalked by a footpad, one of those driven by extremis, to steal from any, however little they had.

His hand brushed a door on his left, he paused and gently pushed. The door swung inwards softly shushing dust back into the chamber beyond. This was lucky! So many buildings were empty now abandoned and boarded up, their only residents the homeless, and the rats.

He closed the door to. Now, the rich did not need the people, the people were left to fend for themselves, in a declining spiral of misery and growing poverty.

Rumours of strange cults at large in the city, preying on the vulnerable, the desperate and the unlucky. He put his back to the door and listened. Someone, or perhaps something, stumbled by, it's breathing came in muffled gasps. Somewhere, within the smallish room, there was a scratching, rustling, scraping noise. Just rats, probably. Some strange rats had been seen in the city, though. He shivered. Yes, just the rats. Even in Carseport, Xagigg's Capital, even in the zombie city, rats thrived, and some had grown strange indeed.

He risked a little light. The room he was in, was grey and mildewed. Rotted fabric hung at the boarded up window. Two figures were prone, covered with rags and scraps of......

He looked no closer. Six pairs of glittering rodent eyes, had looked up at him. He closed the lantern. Turning back to the door he listened. Nothing, except perhaps the sigh of the wind.

He pulled the door slowly open. Cool darkness beyond. The seasons were all messed up too, these days.

These strange unholy days, and dark twisted nights. He put his hand over his mouth, muffling the traitor sounds.

Calm again, he stepped lightly, and slowly, out. Turning left, he crept down the alley. He had to deliver the message, at any cost! Well, time wasn't really of the essence. Even a year or two might not matter. Maybe it was already too late?

Who would know if he failed? He remembered the way now, left that's it, down the passage, ah, a little starlight, the strange green stars were the worst. They moved, differently, sometimes visible by day.

In the green-white starlight the alley was clear. He rushed on, and suddenly.
"Alright, what's the rush?"
The surly voice belonged to a surly man, whose thin cloaked figure, lifted away from the alcove of a doorway, just to his right.

He froze.

"Good evening?" He ventured, knowing it was not good, nor in fact he immediately realised, was it evening. He suddenly felt sure the man in front of him didn't care.

"I'd say good night but we've only just met." Said the man, sarcasm in his voice.

Berythus could feel the evil grin more than see it, he knew he was being sized up.

"You can have my money, gods know it's little I have, and......" A thought struck him.

"Yes, I can do better than that, you help me get safely to the Temple of Arn Triumphant, and I'll pay you twenty pieces of silver. That's more than is in my purse by a long way."

"You don't say...."
Surprise, gave him pause, and he stood quietly mulling it over. He tucked away something that had been in his hand. "Say I believe you, it's dangerous out here at night. Why do you want to go wandering about?"

He stepped closer, staring fixedly at Berythus's face. He had spoken with genuinely mystified curiosity.
"It is vital I get there. Everyone's lives could depend on it."

Berythus put a hand over his own mouth to stop the giggling. He mustn't think I'm crazy!
"Vital? Right, right. What you giggling and snorting for? You drunk? You're bloody having me on!"

He moved slightly, menacingly, mists rolled in the alleyway, brushing coldly, and clammily around the two figures.

"I get nervous when I'm terrified! We must go now!" He whispered to the footpad.

"My name is Kristoph." Said the thin man, slowly extending his hand. His eyes were still narrowed, but what had he got to lose.

"Good! I'm Berythus! Let's get out of here."

Chapter 2 - Above it all.

The world glittered below them as they stood, on the bridge of understanding.

Down they gazed, at the forests, the cities, the mountains, the seas, the deserts, the ruins, the swirling starry absences.

"Leave with me. There are other worlds, we can make new homes on any of them."

The tall glowing figure, more or less youthful, human and male in appearance, put his hand to his cheek, and smiled indulgently down, at the smaller, similarly shimmering figure.

This one, was, in appearance, an old white haired, bearded man, with a pink crown of coral, and strangely, a great fishy tail instead of legs. He floated, next to the other more ordinary, shimmering man.

He hovered, or swished 'water,' apparently in mid air, just above the bridge.

"I still have worshippers, and they are immune to this accursed Devourer's unwholesome influence! Why would I abandon them? Really, Jim, why would you abandon your people?"

The great god Jim, for it was he, adjusted his pale blue robes. He sighed.

"The writing is on the wall. Jam himself, faded, his last true worshippers dead or converted. Jam and I never saw eye to eye, but I wouldn't wish that on anyone."

The twin gods of Jim and Jam, had sprung into existence, due to a schism, spelling mistake or editorial error, and, separated initially by distance, and then by dogma, two separate cults arose, and with them, two separate deities, where only one had been before.

The two gods had been friendly, mainly embarrassed rivals, from the word go. Their worshippers, and priests, of course, took it all very seriously, even coming to blows upon occasion. As otherwise written, in the defence of Carseport, the priests of Jim and Jam, settled their differences, and died to a man, defending their city, against the children of the mother of millions, a terrible, ancient, alien evil, unwittingly released from its ancient bonds. The talisman of Jim or Jam, even proved proof against the evil creatures, at least, that fragment directly behind the talisman, was safe.

Now, when the great god Jim, gazed down upon the world, he saw two small towns, in northern Uleafea, where he still had worshippers. It was time to bail out.

The old sea god looked up, narrowing his eyes.

"Yes, no one really believes in Jam today, or tomorrow, anymore."

He scratched his chin.

"It is getting quiet around here."

He looked around. The world above, the higher plane some called it, had been full of the exotic pied a terre's of the gods, and other allied spirits, now it was sparsely occupied.

The buildings that remained, were mainly just fading, misty shadows of their former selves, or gone entirely, with their late masters.

Kershaggulumphie, Lord of the Oceans, gazed down at the world, and then looked up again, at Jim, survivor of the pair of gods, whose cult had schismed all those centuries ago.

"How can you leave this world? After all you have been through here?" He said.

"Precisely, I have enough stored energy to start again, somewhere less doomed."

He actually laughed. The old sea god stared at him mutely.

"Why do you care what happens to these petty, feuding, greedy little creatures?" Jim relaxed his face into a benign smile.

The old sea god looked away. Jim's smile, was a really annoying smile. He thought quickly.

"The stakes are so high, if you stay, and we win, we will be two of the last gods in this world. Does that not appeal to you? We can rebuild this world any way we like."

Jim sighed, and shook his head sadly.

"You will fall to oblivion. No, fighting the elder horror does not appeal to me. You might remember fighting them first time around, but I wasn't here then, and, well, I'm a lover not a fighter."

Kershaggulumphie, Lord of the Oceans, did not remember. Yes, he was ancient, but the Spirits whom the old Shamen worshipped, were all gone. All gone, except, for their Relics. He looked down, at the spark that marked one Relic in particular.

The old Shamen, their Spirits, and the early Mages, had made weapons. Weapons that worked.

He smiled. He thought he had an idea.

"I shall stay, but, we have been friends so long won't you gift me a part of your stored energy so I can truly make my last stand a blaze of glory?"

Surprise crossed Jim's face.

His smile faded. A serious look crossed his face.

"Of course, but I wish you would reconsider. You will die here. There is no fighting this horror."

He looked thoughtful, and extended his hand palm up. In his palm a swirling sparkling light appeared. It rotated, gyrated, sparkled, in greens, blues, reds and yellows. It seemed alive.

The old sea god reached out, and it passed to him, fading into his hand as he took hold of it.

"Thank you, old friend."

He smiled. His plan might work. Maybe it was madness to stay, but perhaps it would work.

The great god Jim gazed at him and smiled.

"I wish you a glorious death, my old friend. I go now though, so I will not see it. Farewell!"

He turned, an oval, shimmering patch appeared in the air beside him, and with a slight smile, and a look almost but not quite of regret, he left.

Gone from the world. Whether his remaining priests or worshippers noticed, who knew?

The old seagod looked back down, he gazed at the islands and ports, where his worshippers dwelt. His worshippers held firm, indeed they had had their victories over the servants of the dread Devourer of Souls. This was in no small part due to their adoption of a curious ceremonial tattoo, intended to show devotion or initiation and ward off evil. In fact the tattoo, executed correctly, genuinely did prevent possession and the evil eye. You learn something new everyday. It wasn't even his idea, it was an island custom, adopted by his priests. Quite likely, it was originally a shamanic practice.

Perhaps another lucky break could come his way too.

He gazed around the upper world, the world of the gods, of the ether, the world above the rainbow, it had had many names.

Libraria's halls still stood undimmed. She was little worshipped, and that little seemed enough, as always.

He swam through the ether, passed from the Bridge of Understanding, through the blue litten, shadowy Cavern of Ignorance, and out passed the Rocks of Frustration and Happenstance, into sight of his Palace of Waves, or Realm of the Fluidity of Taste. That last was not a name he had chosen, the other gods had voted it in, back in the day, mainly he suspected, because he did not like white marble or pillars.

They had been a conservative lot, marble, marble every where. He would have named their pied-a-terre's the Tombstones of Reason or perhaps the Teeth of Mediocrity. He laughed.

He drew closer to his home of the ages, where in he had dwelt so many years now. Blue green light flickered through it as its very structure ebbed and flowed, back and forth. As bright and real as ever, his servants and aides, gathered to his side.

"Lyrinsos, I need you to go over to Libraria's Hall, and ask for a peek in her reference section. I'm looking for anything about Zonthas."

Lyrinsos, was a Merman, blue, no ears or hair, finely muscled, gills, but in his current state, legs. The legs or fishy tail aspect of Merman culture was of endless fascination to humans. Merman did not like to talk about it. It was complicated.

He nodded, his blue robe, swishing gently. He turned and headed for the passageways of travel. The 'easy' route, directly through the 'lands of consciousness', were a bit too fraught for most non divine's, and as a Spirit, albeit an old and wise one, he wished not to be lost in thought, or subsumed into the unconscious of the world.

For this very reason, the passageways of travel had been made by an old messenger god, long since defunct, to expedite communication betwixt gods, and to allow the occasional visitor from the middle land, the world in which Graeffenland itself was a part.

Upon these roads he hastened, avoiding the blackened twisted remains of some of the paths to the middle land.

Chapter Three - Lost in the Mists.

Jaeson Smith had now lived in Boston, two years. He rented a small office suite up on the second floor of a tatty old commercial building.

His name was emblazoned on the glass top panel of the door, and the half frosted glass stud wall, sent shadows in the stairwell, and revealed ghostly shapes as people walked by.

He'd left New York, he'd left in a hurry, after, certain things had happened. Certain, strange, horrible things, that he had encountered, things he could not explain, yet alone, end, with the sharp retort of his service revolver.

He couldn't explain it, but then, the witnesses had all vanished. The evidence vanished. All that remained was a gray green stain on the paving behind that old tobacconists. Nothing more.

His precinct hadn't cared, in fact, his lieutenant had told him to forget it. What about those people? He had asked, to be met with a blank stare, and, what people?

Missing persons reports went missing, files vanished, angry relatives were ignored, or shown the door.

He'd worked on in secret, in his own time, snatching moments to search, to inquire. He found out, certain things. Dark little snippets, rumours, gossip, and directions to the harbour. He was determined, he was keen, he worked tirelessly night and day. His health had suffered, dark rings appeared about his sharp grey eyes. He became gaunt, eating less, drinking more, and smoking, too.

People talked. His colleagues at the precinct look at him askance. He found the Herbalist, an old Chinese man, who just smiled and nodded at his talk of dark secrets and dread things.

Herbs he had bought, seeking inspiration, seeking dreams, seeking solace and tranquillity. Some he ate, some he burnt, some he smoked, and some did give him visions. Visions of strange worlds, and stranger people. Odd dreams he had then, and terrible nightmares.

He gave up the herbs, for larger doses of malt liquor, even though it was prohibition, many of his colleagues drank, and his new enthusiasm for the drink they took as a good sign. Until he talked. The things he spoke of they did not like, and soon he spoke no more, and only drank alone.

He was fired. They warned him. Finally, the Captain ordered him into his office, and sacked him. It could only have been a mere matter of months after the event, the things he had seen. He hadn't cared. He'd sold his possessions and taken the motor coach out of town.

Boston happened. More by chance than planning. A retired friend of his, O'Hearne had invited him down. He'd heard his troubles. O'Hearne had heard things, rumours, unexplained things himself, and had watched some good men crack.

He had been glad to retire, and hearing his old friends predicament, he'd got in touch. Boston was good to Jaeson Smith. O'Hearne helped him set up an agency, well, it was their two man band.

Smith and O'Hearne, Private Investigations. Barely had they settled into their new office, with the name plate freshly screwed beside the door, gleaming brass, with dark lettering, and his new partner was gunned down by an angry spouse.

That was it. Jaeson threw himself into his work, one meaningless domestic dispute, errant husband, wayward wife, crooked business partner, after another.

Now, this case. Here he was, pacing the pavements of Boston Harbour, scouring every lowlife joint, for a hint of this man's whereabouts.

Arthur Frederick Crabushin, rich businessman, philanthropist, upstanding member of the community, had vanished. His chauffeur, Charles, knew nothing. His new young wife Elanor de Desperro, knew even less, but had cried piteously in his office, whilst insisting, he was the man for the job.

She was blonde, her red dress suited her pale complexion, her red lips sucked feverishly at the cigarette he had offered her. The smoke hung in the air around her like a ghostly shawl. Had she had the old man murdered? She wouldn't be the first and she wouldn't be the last either.

He'd taken the job, a hundred dollars a day plus expenses, he wouldn't turn that down. It would settle some bills, buy some liquor, maybe get his suit cleaned, or another suit. Maybe two.

Who could say how long the case would last?

So, here he was, walking in the cold clammy mists of a Boston summers evening. It shouldn't be this cold, this quiet, or this damn cobblely.

Cobbles, how quaint, he liked it. It was dark except for the coldly gleaming stars, and the odd eye twisting dark patches, here and there in the sky.

He'd drank, just a finger of rye, at each dive. He hadn't gambled, nor had he whored. He'd bribed, spent good scratch, and had got little. Mr A F Crabushin, had been around, every so often. He was known, and yet never made a big splash. A quiet man, he drank little, gambled a little, whored, well, not at all. Always impeccably dressed, and, well, always wearing his hat, light brown, Austrian, in style, with a feather on the left. He also always wore his thin scarf.

He was sensitive about his hair. He was, bar a few straggly scraps, bald. He had bad skin too, and well, a bad odour, like, rotting fish. None of this was offered by Elanor. As far as she was concerned, he was the perfect gent.

The perfect, rich, old sugar daddy. She never mentioned how he'd made his money. Somewhere in Europe, before the War. She knew nothing of his business either, or his Clubs, or much about his hobbies. She was a classic blonde, in so many ways. He guessed, she worked, she had previously worked, in a Night Club, maybe, even as a singer. She had the looks, maybe the voice, too. She didn't say.

Now he walked, through these silent, gloomy alleys. The noise and lights of the city, the harbour, the people, all gone, snuffed out like a candle, with less than a wisp of smoke as a memory of their ever having been.

Mist, heh, there was always mist. A chill stole over him, and ahead, a shadow moved.

He paused. He watched. No fear stole silently into his heart. Not since, the event, those years ago.

He waited and he didn't have to wait long.

Two figures, men, well 'humen,' and, not, the 'other,' approached.

They spoke. For a moment, they sounded foreign, speaking in an unknown language. Something pinged, and his stomach flipped, and, they were speaking English, albeit English, full of fear.

They feared him, their surroundings, the night itself. He could almost taste it. Something also smelled, it could be this old alleyway.

"We don't want any trouble. We're just headed for our temple."

This was said by the shadowed figure to the right, who was wearing a long coat, or was that a robe?

'Temple,' oh, he had heard correct. He barely suppressed a shudder. His hand was on his gun, but still within his coat.

Could it be true? Were they here as well?

His mind jumped back all those years ago………

Chapter Four – Happy Home on the Road

It had been almost a year now, since Nirnadel, erstwhile Princess of the Kingdom (or should that be, Lichdom?) of Graeffenland, had been reunited with her mother Rhian, and her grand mother Lyra.

A whole new world had been opened up to her. Not only was the food in the gypsy camp, the best she had ever eaten, (including the fare she enjoyed in the restaurants and inns of Gnomgart). Life as a Princess in King Xagigg's Court was frugal bordering on starvation, indeed, she realised, she had been little more than a bird in a gilded cage.

The People of the Wagons were so different! Friendly, genuinely honest (with each other), helpful (with each other), and they lived, better than Kings. At least, better than King Xagigg did, although, technically, he did not live at all, as he was Undead.

Of course, nearly everyone in Xagiggs Court, was in fact dead, Zombies, intelligent, unimaginative, Zombies. A handful of living men, trusted retainers, did certain jobs, Zombie maintenance, for example. Everyone else, had been Undead.

Now, there are many tales of Zombies, but these Zombies, were raised by a Master Necromancer, which King

Xagigg was, having existed, one way, or another for centuries, before, taking possession of a hapless knight, who just happened to be vaguely in line for the throne, at a time when other heirs had been crisped by Dragons, slain by Horrors, or simply slain, by opportunistic mercenaries.

Xagigg, did also have the considerable advantage, of a fresh army of Zombies, no other challengers, and the gratitude, however conditional, of the City's populace.

The Zombies, did not crave brains. They were still reasonably bright, at least, if they had been bright to start with. They remembered, they still had their old skills, indeed, they still had their old souls........

Most of this, Nirnadel knew, and her mother, who had fallen in love, or lust with the gorgeously handsome new body possessed by Xagigg, did not actually know the body was possessed at the time, and only found out, years later, when someone actually addressed Xagigg, by the bodies original name.

Xagigg had been, and still was, a relatively benign King. He did not bother with Taxes. The Merchants volunteered to assist with projects when needed.

He left the people, more or less, to do what they pleased. The Merchants did just that. Nirnadel, had seen virtually nothing of the cultural life of Carseport, all she knew came from books, and musical performances, by Zombie bards.

The Undead Courtiers went through the motions of Court life, and this had seemed completely natural to her at the time. Now, she knew better, and was making up for lost time. She had forever sworn off sandwiches, especially egg and cress.

Her father, who she now knew to be a Lich, (he had been assassinated, but did not let that slow him down), had not yet come after her. Perhaps, he was happy enough that she was safe with her mother's people, and they certainly moved around, only spending a few weeks in each place.

The day after her arrival, they had broken camp, and the People of the Wagons (they had dropped bird moniker's, her family, were originally called 'the people of the Magpies,' but after merging with so many other families, and survivors of other groups, they decided to be more inclusive) had begun their travels north east, following the roads, and trails, towards the city states and towns, of the Wernobergian League.

Many of the families had suffered terribly during the dark years, her mothers people least of all, because, in no small part, of Rhian's involvement with Xagigg.

Indeed, Rhian had run off to be Xagigg's Queen, as otherwise told, back when Xagigg not only had a pulse, but could send pulses racing too.

In the end Lyra had led her people, and the survivors of the other gypsies, to the continent. There, of course, they struggled, against bandits, warlords, goblins, and other horrors. They survived, making allies, and learning the lay of the land.

They had, spent much time in the Vondrvehre, a great forest, near the northern coast, and the pirate city of Vondrberg. The city had now fallen into to ruins, bar for the Castle, held by a self appointed Baron.

Nirnadel liked life on the road. She had never felt so free. Even sharing a wagon with her mother, was still better than her old tower, back at the Palace.

Men, were something else. She had had her eyes opened there. The People of the Wagons, were a matriarchy. The women, ruled, in all things, including choosing their mates.

Clothes were another thing, she had put on weight. Quite a bit of weight. She hadn't realised just how thin she was until, her mother struggled to find her any spare clothes. She had arrived with no luggage, after a long and arduous journey, with several near death, or indeed, near things that should be dead, in any sane world, experiences.

She had brought, a mysterious glowing blue flask with her. Apparently it was highly magical, and a gift, or a trade, that her grandmother had expected.

Lyra, Head Woman, Wise Woman, and Soothsayer, of the People of the Wagons, was old now, grey and white hair wrapped in a colourful red and green scarf. A great patterned woollen robe covered her small form, she still stood up straight, but she had become frail. The burdens of leadership had weighed heavily upon her.

Lyra had something Rhian had never really had. Lyra knew magick, the old magick, that had bound faeries, back when only those with the gift could see them. Bound them in bonds of magick that they could not defy. With the great change in the world, and the release of the first Horror, magick changed, the normally invisible faeries became visible to all, and the rules of magick had changed.

Princess Nirnadel had learnt Necromancy from her father and then from his library, she had inherited the Gift, as it used to be called, and she could appreciate Lore in all its forms. Her Grandmother's Art she found fascinating and yet, the elderly Wise Woman would not share, fending of requests for knowledge, leading questions, subtle enquiries, and avoiding discreet espionage.

In fact Lyra found all this quite amusing, not having the heart to tell Nirnadel that most of her Art had ceased to work when the change in the World had come.

She repulsed all enquires, and offers of knowledge, on the whole necromancy and magecraft, were not valued highly by the People. Zombies, well, were not at all welcome, and she was advised, well, told quite sternly that reanimations, were forbidden.

She complied, a small price to pay, in fact she felt happier than she had ever been, and had quite enough to keep her occupied. She would find out soon enough what the glowing bottle was for. Oh it was important, she was assured.

Chapter Five – Memories and Nightmares

All those years ago. He'd been so proud to make it to Detective. It wasn't easy, he worked hard, socialised hard, and had made all the right friends.

It was his curiosity almost cost him the promotion, looking the wrong way, asking the wrong question, but his smile and ready wit pulled his fat from the fire.

He'd misunderstood, he said. No, he wasn't angling for a cut, a piece of the action, he was a good guy, he'd watch his brothers backs. They said they'd watch him.

He smiled more, bought more than his fair share of rounds, despite, the prohibition in full swing, and laughed at everyone's jokes. Things got back on course, except, some of the guys, still watched him askance.

They didn't know him well enough.

He got the promotion and his new Lieutenant, Lucowsky, a thin, tall, middle aged pugilist, who believed, not so much in the Law, as, in the squad, started him off easy.

Soon enough though, he was on homicide, and there were plenty of those to go around. He did what he was told, he did what was expected. He smiled less, and drank a little more. Little bonuses would come his way. Some he stashed, some he blew, and the world got that bit darker.

It was another grey, dull day in Autumn. There'd been some trouble, gang trouble, everyone thought, a group of young men causing trouble.

The Duty Sergeant had asked them to take a look at it. No one wanted a gang war, even a small one, made every one look bad. Especially to the Press. No one wanted the Press running stories.

So, he'd drawn the short straw, make some enquires, find out what was behind it all, and then something could be done.

Except, that wild eyed lad, was he Polish? He was never sure. He'd found out at the timed, but his memory, was not quite what it used to be. He was dark haired, with dyed white streaks, some weird foreign fashion probably, or gang insignia, and he was by turns violently angry, and morosely grief stricken.

Yes, that angry young man, George, Georgan, Georgiou, something like that, again, his memory, not what it was, thankfully. Anyway, this youth, said his sister had been kidnapped. He, his friends and cousins, said they knew where, they were sure, and they had had to be arrested, had to be thrown in the cells, to cool off.

It was an old house, some old colonial relic of a bygone age, curiously out of place in the vast stew of styles of twenties New York. They said she'd been seen, seen going in there, with some old, old man.

The old house, nestled amidst brick walk ups, and they had all but broken down its antique oak doors, before the cops had arrived.

The tobacconist, hearing the ruckus in the back alley, had called the Police.

Mister Van den Kloofen, Ernest, he was sure, he'd said his name was, was almost as old as the shop he worked in. Or was he the owner? He wore his years well, in a dim light he would pass for thirty, but on closer inspection, he seemed quite elderly. Elderly, but spry, with a curious glitter in his slate grey eyes.

He didn't know who lived there, he said, smiling wistfully, where was he from? Oh, he had come over to America, years back, from Eindhoven. It was long ago, and he had made a little life for himself, or obtained a little life for himself, strange turn of phrase, strange quirky smile.

He'd found like minded friends, he said, and chuckled.

The youths were cautioned, warned off, descriptions of the girl were dutifully taken, though, no search would take place for some days, if it happened at all.

He'd taken the job on, held on to the details, but that very night, the night of the youths release, trouble sparked again.

This time, passers by, alarmed by shrieks and screams, had called on New York's finest.

They'd arrived, he was called by the Duty Sergeant, and arrived after the initial furore, about twenty minutes after, he'd run part of the way, his rough apartment, with shared telephone, was not far.

He got there, and it was quiet, just one bored patrolman, distractedly counting lamps along the road.

He'd been there awhile. No, he wasn't first on the scene, no he hadn't waited specially for him, his partner had gone off, and he was waiting for him to return.

Few people walked by, no one seemed to know anything. They just hurried by, irritation, or concern shown, when he spoke, he was in plain clothes after all, and had to wave his shield to get the time of day.

The lamp staring patrolman didn't know who had called it in, he'd just heard whistles. No, he didn't know who had whistled. It was probably the wind. He'd looked at him then, as though really just seeing him for the first time.

The wind, he had said, the wind's a funny thing, when it blows and glows. Blows and glows! The Patrolman stood there, and turned back to counting street lights.

Jaeson Smith had then felt bewildered. He had stared across the street, the alley, the tobacconist, were there, dark, closed, quietly wrapped in the shadows of the lamp lit twilight.

He'd walked across, into the alley, into..... he couldn't think what, he'd slipped, his feet sliding from under him. He'd slipped on a great puddle, a pool of grey green slime, slime that stank on his trousers, where it had splashed on his legs.

Ahead, he could see the house. There it was, nestling amongst the brick walk ups, glowing. At first he thought its lights were on, well, they must be. Well, he couldn't see the source, it just gleamed, a silvery moonlit glow.

Its oak doors, if oak they were, were wide open. Voices, voices spoke, indistinctly, spoke or sang, sang or chanted.

He walked up to the old metal rails, touched them, they were slick with goo, some greasy oily residue.

He'd snatched his hands away, and cautiously stepped up the stairs to the doorway.

The silvery grey light showed a hall beyond. He stepped through the door, and light blazed, orange light, bright red light, and green light, showed, what lay beyond, tapestries, men, where none had been before, men in golden robes, their ancient lined faces turned to look at him, with expressions of irony, joy or sadness.

The sound was gone, as though his ears were deafened, yet they spoke, laughed and shouted at him. He counted at least nine robed priests, he was sure that was what they were.

His strength was gone, and yet he still stood, limply, his pistol in its holster, within his nice new jacket.

The priests stared at him, he knew not if it was hatred, surprise or admiration. Their faces rippled in ways that hurt his eyes, his eyes that seemed to drown in the bright yellow light.

Two of them closed in upon him each taking an arm. In the deafening silence, that roared through his head, they turned him, and walked him, to the black, starry hole, flanked by the damaged oaken doors. They cast him soundlessly screaming into the black.

He fell upon his face. Unconsciously, he touched a little cut, on his chin, the cobbles were rough here. The silvery light had faded, and he had numbly staggered back to the lighted street, through the dark alley.

He still dreamt of that walk, the endless walk, in the roaring dark. His hands clapped to his ears to hold out the explosion of city noise.

He had staggered home, the noise was slowing dying down, and now it was normal, after a block or two, or his ears were normal. For weeks after he would look at his ears, they weren't different, the mirror sowed no change.

He had gone back, that morning, and the alley was there, the grey green stain, fading more each day, the strange old house, was, well, just a strange old abandoned warehouse.

The tobacconist was closed, and never reopened. The youths were gone, no one ever found them or word of where they had gone, likewise the girl.

The patrolmen, well, three had gone missing, and missing person reports surged, all people who might walk that way, of an evening.

He'd built a file, a dossier, but everything was a dead end, and now, two weird priests, stood in front of him, stood there and spoke to him.

His gun was in his hand, it would be the work of moments to shoot them both down.

Chapter Six - Mountain High

The Dragonridge Mountains ran almost coast to coast across the Great Continent. Their heights varied, from only two thousand, or so feet, up to almost six thousand feet.

They border many states and countries, and locally were known by many different names. They were intermittently crossed by many passes, tunnels, and even one or two well made roads.

This changed, along with most of the local names for the mountain range, barely twenty years ago, when, after their long imprisonment, and release from servitude as a Mage death from above strike force, the old dragons moved back in.

Dragonridge, Dragon Peaks, and Don't Go There, in various dialects, languages, and symbolisms, soon became the new names of choice.

They didn't cause any particular trouble, at least not at first. Unless, you herded Goats. Goats, it appeared, were a chief staple of the Dragon diet. They didn't take many goats, especially considering the rather huge size of these Dragons, some reaching over two hundred feet snout to tail tip.

The trouble in the South begn, and soon became a tidal wave of refugees, and horror mad people. Arshan, the Fist of the Devourer had come, at the head of a growing horde of the possessed, destroying or converting all in his path, all in the name of some dark dread Great Big One. His power, the power of his arms, were without doubt. The Kingdoms, Republics and City States of the Southlands all fell before his horde, their cities burnt, and turned into unspeakable ruins, festering in the shadows.

Their Cities ruined, trade ceased, farming ceased, the countries of the South ceased to exist except on old maps, and in the memories of those who were not there, or who had fled in time.

The countries to the North of the Dragonridge mountains quailed with each report, mobilised for war, some more peaceful lands, had not known war for centuries.

The Dragons closed all the passes. They broke the tunnels, at least all the ones they knew of, and for creatures of the peaks and upper airs, they seemed to know an awful lot about tunnels. Or at least someone did. Those who enjoyed Dragon watching, and their were a few of these, with their little notebooks, sketch pads, and in some cases, fancy glass viewing scopes, some in double, held with both hands, some in singular long tubes, with eyepieces, or reflectors onto white fabric screens.

Alchemists and philosophical mechanics were kept busy, by the Duckers, as they were called. It was a name they had adopted or been christened with, early on, due to their habit of hiding, whenever a Dragon seemed to be flying their way.

The Duckers, nearly all reported the Dragons flying South, flying South for preference. All wondered why, no one seemed to be sure. No one seemed willing to try to ask either.

Funnily, when the Dragons had first returned, folks had wondered who would be the first great Knight, to ride out against them, and into legends. The lands that were Republics, smiled and gazed askance at their Aristocratic neighbours, all of whom seemed to agree, that actual Knighthood, chivalry, and charging two hundred foot long monsters, in plate armour on an expensive charger, with just a wooden lance, was outdated, lacked finesse, and was a particularly stupid idea in the first place.

Interestingly, one alchemist in particular, a Master Macquai, of Heidelheimberg, came out with a mass producible metal tube with a wooden stock, which using his patented bang powder, would fire, a rounded metal lump (patent pending), several hundred yards, through plate armour, and potentially through Dragon Scale too.

His Macquette's became very popular in one State in particular, who after some initial teething troubles, and lost fingers, from misapplied bang powder, had established their first brigade of Macquettemen, though shooting Dragons was the last thing on their mind. They were thinking, in the main, of Arshan's Horde, and, incidentally, their neighbours.

Their test in the field against any enemy, would have to wait. Arshan, the terrible warrior mystic servant of the Devourer, Arshan the dreaded six foot muscle bound warrior, whom was said to be faceless, whether due to a mask, or some other more horrible possibility, turned away from the mountains, or was forced back from, the mountains, and headed his horde, for the coast, which had no Dragons, but would find itself stymied for other reasons.

The people north of the mountains continued though, to look up with fear when Dragons flew by, until the years passed, and, no Dragons attacked towns in the north. Years before, long before, Dragons had struck, appearing from nowhere, apparently at random, out of clear blue skies, and razing to the ground many of the Great Cities of the world, and many minor ones.

So the people felt they had good reason to fear the Dragons. Occasionally, brave, reckless men, (who may also have been Duckers), would enter the mountains, climbing up to see the Dragons roosts. Tales and legends spoke of golden treasures to be had wherever Dragons slept. Some people believed such tales.

Other than goats bones, trees branches woven into vast matted nests, they found nothing.

Occasionally, a Dragon would be present , but after gazing for a few moments with it's catlike eyes, they would be ignored. A tall tale told by one Ducker in particular, was that one even posed, whilst he sketched it in his notebook.

In truth, a typical human warrior, however knightly, magickal arms or not, could not stand against a Dragon. These Dragons, could be two hundred feet long, nose to tail, scales like adamantine, breath like a blast furnace, and claws that could gouge granite.

So the Dragons were not worried. Not in the least.

And one day, an adventurous young mountaineer, ventured up one of the busiest peaks, formerly known as Pleasant Snows Peak, in the local dialect, now known as Dragons Dance, or Flaming Dragons Nuisance, by local farmers who had had to deal with a surge in melt water, including needing a new bridge, not to far down stream. Snow was not much of a feature on the Peak these days.

He climbed up, he was, indeed is, (so far in this tale he is still around), a passably good mountaineer, one of the easier more direct approaches. Higher and higher on the Peak, ignoring the drizzling rain, and winds, blowing firmly west, until he came to a great shelf of rock, a shelf seeming cut into the very mountain itself, and mostly on the south aspect. This was new, in that, tales he had heard of the peak, from old veteran climbers, did not include any mention of a vast shelf. It was vast. A village could be built on it, and with a visionary moment, he almost could see such there, in his minds eye, perhaps with some special roped carriage that could be drawn up and let down the mountain side.

His musings did not last long, the cold stone under his gloved hands had been scratched by many claws, ridged and pitted, and bracing himself against the wind his stood up upon it and moving in towards the mountainside, he gazed around.

In the near distance and facing firmly south stood a great stone chair, in fact a throne, high backed, and crudely carved.

He stood, his form highlighted against the blue afternoon skies, dark clouds scudding, and swirling, passed, and wondered.

Erik Hauengris, young, muscled, adjusted his thick green felt hat, smoothed down his thick khaki climbing jacket, and stuck his hands in his pockets. This was the Peak, and there was no one here, except a great chair. This he walked towards, and around to see the front and the view it gazed upon.

To his surprise, it wasn't empty..

On the great stone throne, sat a great stone statue. It appeared to be a man, nine feet tall, maybe, wrapped in detailed stone furs, great bushy stone beard, muscled arms, and a gleaming hammer, glowing in a most unstonelike fashion, resting on his lap.

Erik walked around, and stepped up to the seated statue. He whistled softly through his teeth, the detail was amazing!

He fell over backwards, flat on the stone, as the great figure's head turned, and his eyes fell upon him, the glow in them striking him, and pinning him to the floor with an immeasurable weight.

Erik stared his mouth open and his mind reeling. Not a statue, just dust, just a giant covered in dust, and debris! He couldn't move, all the strength had gone from his limbs, but not from his mouth.

Erik spoke: "Oh, great master of the Peak! I did not mean to wake you from your slumber! Pray thee release me from your gaze, and I will be gone soonest!"

Erik felt more amazement than fear, the dusty being stood, shook himself, and returned his gaze south.

"I don't sleep. I haven't slept for years."

The voice came from the giant, but softly, seeming to come from the rocks as well.

"Thank you!" Yelled Erik. His limbs released from whatever power had pinned them, he was up and heading for the way back down, whence he had come, sliding to his hands and knees again as he reached the edge of the great rock shelf. He swung over and began his descent, seeing above him a great Dragon swooping in, it landed soon after, the vibrations through the rock surprising, but not loosening his hold.

He moved down in haste. To die on the slopes below, or in the belly of Dragon or Giant, did not appeal.

The great Dragon watched him move, painfully slowly down the rock face. He turned to the giant.

"Shall I slay the Mortal?" Spoke Lamluca, for such was the great Dragon's name. Erik did not hear this, for Lamluca, used telepathy, an ordinary skill of the great Dragons, and spoke thusly to the giant, with no other audience.

"No, he does not matter." Thought Adan, a man, not a giant, though tall, and yet no longer a man. He had changed much and many times over the years.

His attention though, had been diverted, and the Devourer, had, shifted, slightly, he wasn't sure how, it's location was the same, but it had altered itself, perhaps lessened, in just those moments he had looked away.

He felt irritated. All these years locked in silent, epic mental struggle, and what had he achieved?

Lamluca's thoughts reached him, "You slowed it down."

"I should have taken Kershaggulumphies offer."

Adan looked down wistfully, and stared at the great steel coloured enruned hammer, glowing relic of a bygone age, that he still gripped in his right hand.

It had served him, and it had consumed him. Its essences had sustained him, and transformed him, empowered him, or he empowered it, he wasn't sure.

It had grown and changed as he had grown and changed. He no longer drank or ate of the viands of the lands of Summer. The people of that land, had retreated, back to it, with the Devourers appearance. Disappointing, he had hoped they might stand against it with him, what with their pretensions of Brotherhood, and family.

They had scrammed back to their happy home dimension, or world or afterlife, whatever it was. He could see them, feasting and playing eternally, if he concentrated. The Hammer had given him power.

He held it firmly, its runes glowed, and he cast his vision, southwards, crossing the thousands of miles, to the Citadel, the Ziggurat of the Devourer, where the great dark shadow of horror yet hid, and felt it recoil and writhe, bracing itself against his will, once again.

Lamluca watched him, standing rigid, his mind locked on the alien horror, grappling it, constraining it, and the ancient Dragon mulled. There must be a better way.

Lamluca gazed up, he too could see into other worlds, if he wished, though, often there wasn't much to see, just repeats, history repeating itself, time and again.

He gazed into the Upper World, realm of the gods, definitely with a small 'g', for they had done nothing useful, as far as he could see, in recent times. He searched, there the Lord of the Oceans Palace, waterlike, a rippling, busy, full of blue people, merfolk, he supposed. His attention was noticed, a squinting Dragon, gazing between worlds, tends to get noticed. A merman, his blue-purple scaled mail glistening, and his shell like helm dipping as he looked down, saw Lamluca, heard his message, and hurried away.

Adan, it would appear, would get his chance to reconsider Kershaggulumphies offer.

Hours later, Erik Hauengris, reached Tumenca, a small Village in the foothills of the mountains, in the Inn, the Barons Tumble, so named, after an ancient nobles accident, a fall of some sort.

In the Inn, he took considerable refreshment, becoming by stages, slightly, moderately, and extremely, refreshed. His progression attracted considerable attention all the more so, when he spun his tale of Dragons, and a fearsome giant.

This was laughed at by all, until he mentioned the hammer. His description, wiped the smile off the face of an otherwise jolly gnome, a traveller, he would say, a spy he actually was.

Hammers, enruned and relicy, was serious news. The Alt Konig, the Gnome King, would want to know this. This was important. The gnome himself, was under two feet tall, and had been sitting at the bar, on a high chair, with built in steps, and had been merrily guzzling a small beer, in a larger glass.

This he put down, and he straightened his red hat. It was a tall conical hat, standing proudly in stark contrast to his warm grey woollen jacket, and heavy weave trews.

He slipped away, ducking out the back towards the water closets. He ducked in one, but his business was more esoteric. Once out of sight, he gestured, muttered and focussed his mind.

A shimmering Portal appeared, he stepped through. The Portal closed behind him.

He stood, in a large hall, with a high ceiling, rows of desks, and dozens of gnomes hurried to an thro, or sat writing, making notes, taking messages, annotating maps. Oh yes, there were many maps, on walls, on floors, small ones on some of the desks, and they were constantly being updated, altered, adjusted as new reports came in.

Gnome agents portalled in and out as he watched. He rushed across to the Watch Secretary. This was an old white haired, long bearded gnome, in a dark office suit. He sat behind, what was once a very fine grand old desk, but which had been battered, dented and stained by hard use.

Edgar Frise, Watch Secretary looked up. Cotrill Wesker stood before him, glowing with excitement, a broad grin struggling to contain itself amidst ruddy cheeks and the smell of beer.

"This, had better be good." He said raising both eyebrows.

"The Hammer! The Dragon Master! I've found him!"

Edgar Frise's mouth fell open. If it was true it was excellent news.

Chapter Betwixt Six & Seven - High On The Trail.

Nirnadel was flying. Well, her mind was flying, soaring over the forests, fields, and mountains. The scenery whizzed by. She braced herself, she knew what lay ahead.

There it was, amidst the a ruined and deserted land, far beyond the mountains. The great stone citadel. She knew it had been built by the Devourer and its horde of minions.

She focussed her mind, and over the ramparts, empty ramparts, no black eyed guards marched, this time.

Oh yes, she had learned about the servants and slaves of the Devourer. Those possessed by the Devourer came in two sorts. The consumed, as the People of the Wagons, called them, were like robots, will less, unintelligent, and, fairly obvious if you looked at their eyes.

Their eyes, were completely black, as though the pupils extended over the whole eyeball. The others, seemed to have made some unholy bargain with the Devourer, their eyes were changed, and yet, they retained their minds, their intelligence, and possibly their will.

She still thought of them as mystics, the one she had encountered, on her only sea voyage, (so far), years before, had masqueraded as a blind mystic and seer.

This time no minions seemed to be present, and she was falling, dropping down, towards the pyramidal roof, through the roof, into a great dark hole, filled with weird stars, two great yellow glowing ones, grabbed her attention, like twin magnets, in the void.

Two huge glowing stars that looked back at her. She shivered, chilled to the bone, and pulled away. It stared into her, and she, unwilling stared back.

Yield, it seemed to say. You cannot defy me!

The potion, the herbs she had taken, fortified her. She knew she was asleep, she knew her dreaming mind had been drawn to this creatures lair.

Why not? She stabbed the question at It.

She felt it stumble, and re-gather. It was distracted.

You're weak, you are vulnerable! Be a part of something greater than you, all will be consumed!

She thrust at It, focussing her mind with all her strength.

It was surprised, its great glowing yellow eyes, flared, and it slapped her mentally. She clawed at it, and saw something. It had slipped, it did know fear, and a memory had leaked. She caught it with both mental hands, as she hurtled, as she hurtled back to her body where she reposed upon her bed in her mothers Wagon.

The memory, a man, brown and tattooed, naked but for a loincloth, holding out before him, an iron or steel coloured sheet, with runes etched and glowing upon it.

The dark, whorl tattooed, (great blue designs, enmeshed, and illustrated his whole visible body) shaman, held up the sheet, and spoke one word.

"Codex." He said.

She awoke. She jumped out of bed, and scrabbled out of the wagon, and half fell, half ran into the camp. The fire was out, that's odd, she thought. Everyone was up, up and standing around, dressed in grey, grey robes, not their usual brightly coloured attire. No patterned trews, no ornate jackets, no pretty headscarves, or boots with beautiful buckles.

They all converged upon her.

She opened her mouth to scream as their vacant black eyes locked on hers.

She was being shaken.

"No!" She mumble yelled.

"Wake up, dear!" Rhian's voice sounded softly close to her face.

A horrible fierce smell assailed her and was just as suddenly gone. She opened her eyes, wide awake now.

Her mother, dark hair half covering her face, was clicking a stopper back on a vial of green liquid.

"What have you been taking?" She asked, looking pointedly at the potion residue in Nirnadel's mug.

"Quick! A pen! Some paper!" Nirnadel spoke, urgency in her eyes.

Rhian opened a small cabinet, found some charcoal, and a piece of brown parchment.

"Really?" Nirnadel took the meagre offerings, and hastily drew. She drew the symbols she had seen, and then wrote 'Codex' at the bottom.

"What? What is this?" Rhian took the parchment from her and stared at it.

"I didn't wear my amulet, but I went prepared!" Nirnadel said.

"Its mind is on many things or it could perhaps have ended in disaster, but I took or got, a memory from it. A memory it feared. I think it could have been a memory of the Shaman who defeated it."

For years now, Nirnadel had been forced to wear an Amulet of Protection, especially when asleep. Somehow, the Devourer itself could reach her, magically, when she was unprotected. It knew she was the daughter of its greatest foe, King Xagigg.

Rhian brushed her hair aside with one hand, and gazed at the drawing.

"A Codex is a book, a tome, an encyclopaedia, of knowledge. The shaman's knowledge is recorded somewhere, and the secret to defeat that cursed monster is recorded within it!" Rhian exclaimed.

Nirnadel carefully lifted, and placed her amulet back around her neck. No more risks this night, she thought.

"But how do we find such a book, such an ancient tome?"

She shook her head slowly.

"It could be anywhere!"

"Well, Xagigg, your father, he would have had an idea, but I'm not sure we can trust him. Thing is, he could even have that book in his library!"

"No, no tomes with steel pages, nor any religious works. Father, you know, was really just into one or two sorts of magick." Nirnadel sighed.

"Most of the other Master Mages are dead, hah, I helped slay them!" Rhian said ruefully, but with a slight smile.

"They had it coming, though."

Indeed, they had. The Council of Mages had unleashed the Dragons, for reasons Nirnadel and Rhian were still not sure of, and had devastated towns and cities almost at random, across the world.

Rhian had helped Xagigg, back when he was just a Necromancer and Master Mage, to encompass their destruction and, free the Dragons from their control.

Now, now they needed to find a Mage, and not just any Mage, they needed a good one.

Chapter Seven – Blam! Blam!

The thin wiry figure cloaked more in shadows than actual cloth started drawing out something shiny.

Crack! The shot echoed through the narrow alley.

Jaeson Smiths revolver had flashed, its bullet sliced the air between them, its grooved tip, spinning, then drilling through skin, blood vessels, bone, its metal slowly splaying out in the fractions of time it hurtled through the soft inner tissues, smashing all before it until, disc like now, it erupted out of the back of the mans head, in a spray of blood, bone, and brains.

The body, life falling from it, like an old rain soaked cloak, flew backwards, thudding, and squelching on the cobbles.

"I didn't want to do that, but your friend was drawing on me."

He stated, coldly glaring at the remaining man, who seemed to cringe within his strange, and tatty robes.

"Ulp." Berythus Naechos managed. He was well read, intelligent, would have been a wit at parties, were he to have ever been invited to any, and modesty permitting, had a certain gift of the gab. Alas, his life experience had not prepared him for hulking Mages with magical talismans that spat death, at a moments notice.

He trembled, and he wondered if this man was an Alchemist. He'd heard all kinds of stories about what the Alchemists Guilds were developing, alongside the usually unpopular Guild of Philosophical Mechanicians, which seemed to have been enjoying a spectacular renaissance in recent years.

Gone were the water clocks, and imaginative spring operated toys and wonders, in were armaments and devices of war.

War was a great motivator.

He couldn't help himself, he opened his lantern a little wider and directed its light downwards.

His gorge rose. His erstwhile travelling companion, of the last few minutes, was a bloody mess. Bits everywhere. It was horrible. Why he thought, can't wizards, do subtle magick? Magick that was less violent, less messy, and less lethal.

He thought of Xagigg. He shuddered again. Maybe not, King Xagigg, was of the Ancient School, of kill first, resurrect and ask questions later, if necessary, which usually it wasn't.

It was said, even the stones of the city would report to Xagigg, did the Liche King know what he had found out?

Was this man in front of him one of Xagiggs enforcers, here to take him to some dread doom?

"I'll only ask once more, who are you? No sudden moves now, or you'll be joining your friend."

The strange robed figure had looked down, and shuddered, and shuddered some more.

"Yeah, I know, dum dums, illegal, but for some opponents, you need every edge you can get."

He couldn't leave this robed guy as a witness, but he seemed no threat to anyone. On the surface, he remembered the Tobacconist, the harmless ancient old Dutchman. Yeah, harmless. He raised his gun, and held a steady aim.

The timid priest, felt more than saw the motion, and scrabbling, for time, his mind and thoughts falling one over another, yelled.

"Wait! I'm on a quest! It's life or death! The whole future of existence depends upon it!"

The thin robed figure shook with fear. This puzzled Jaeson, his Detective instincts told him this man was not a threat, except perhaps to himself, and the seating on public transport.

He put his gun away.

"Go on." He whispered. A dark menace growling in the back of his throat.

"An unspeakable evil has become loose in the world, and I think I have found out how to stop it!"

Unhelpfully, his nervous titter arose just at that moment.

The cynical old Private Eye, he felt he was aging a year for every month these days, was impressed. This guy was going for the big sell, going for the grand plot, and as a means of saving his skin, he'd chosen well. What others would have laughed at, Jaeson felt no doubt about at all.

"Alright then, say I believe you, so why are you hanging around in dark alleys, with hoods?"

"Ah! Well, I'm on my way to the...." He paused, trailing off as he remembered how badly the thick set figure standing before him had reacted to the word temple, last time.

"I'm on my way to meet with the rest of my, erm, group, my team. I need their help, at the very least, to implement the solution."

He felt pleased. He'd re-gathered his thoughts, thought on his feet, been on the ball, got what was going, and the man was still glaring at him.

"Okay, I'll help you get there, in Boston is it?"

The long words had confused him a little, what's an implement, sounds like a farming expression, he thought, but he had caught the overall gist of the conversation.

The nervous priest had no idea what, or where, or even who, a Boston was, or may be, but nodded enthusiastically, nonetheless.

"They are in this city, they are actually not that far away, but it is dangerous to be out at night, or in fact, during the day."

The strong looking figure before him looked dangerous, he could get him where he needed to go. So long as he didn't go mad, or just turn out to be some kind of evil Mage, out looking for victims.

He shivered again.

"Which way?" Asked the gruff man.

The priest pointed with his lantern, and they walked, cautiously, with many sideways glances, in the direction he had indicated.

Ahead, the cobbles, mist fading in and out gave way to paving. Nicer paving than Berythus was used to. Things must be looking up for Carseport, he thought.

He looked this way and that. He was lost. In fact, he didn't recognise a thing. He ought, he thought, at least to be able to see the masts of the ships in the harbour, hear the sea, the sounds of the city. This city had sounds, sounds of life and people, that, he was quite unused to. Looking around, his heart sank, with every moment that passed, every direction he looked, he was more sure, he was somewhere else.

He walked right, following the street, the avenue. It was ornate and rich beyond imagining, beyond, he was now absolutely certain, anything that had ever existed in Carseport.

They walked on a bit further.

"You know, I'm not sure where I am at the moment." He carefully ventured.

"Is that right?" Said the figure walking beside, and he noted, slightly behind him.

"Yes, you see, in my.....world, we should be at the harbour right now, and less than a hundred yards from my friends. Right now, I'm not even sure what world this is."

The man beside him had stopped.

"Good story. Other worlds. How would you have gotten from here to there, or from there to here?"

He didn't sound incredulous, not even particularly annoyed, he did perhaps, sound disappointed.

"I don't know."

"Well, you can come back to my office."

They walked on, silently, mists falling or rising, the sounds of the city dying away.

"Your costume certainly looks authentic."

In the street light he had been sizing up the skinny priest. His costume was good, if it wasn't real it had to be theatrical, or home made, with a good eye for detail. A detail for the crudely medieval.

The lantern, oil lamp, must be an antique he thought, in good condition, for all that in was battered, and dented.

The fog thickened, and then started to thin, the pavement ran out and they were stumbling on rock.

"What the hell!" He shouted.

The evening, giving way to night, of Boston, had been replaced by broad daylight.

Broad daylight.

Broad daylight, in what for all the world looked like a quarry, a large quarry. No way had they just stumbled into it.

He grabbed the scrawny priest.

"What did you do?"

"I? Nothing! I swear, I swear by all the gods, this is not my doing!"

They both looked around. There was no city, no sea, barely a cloud in the sky, just some blackened or crystallised bushes or trees in the distance.

In was virtually an empty stone desert for miles, just broken by rocky ridges and boulders.

"Reality is breaking down." Berythus offered.

"It must be affecting more worlds than just my own." He continued.

Jaeson gazed around in wonder, his initial surprise and fear, replaced by curiosity. Maybe, after all these years, he would get to the bottom of what was really going on in the, for want of a better term, the world. He actually smiled.

"A quest then. Let's go!"

He marched forward.

They had been walking for more than a mile, only for a few minutes really, when their ears were assailed by a terrible sound.

It sounded, like a donkey, was being slowly strangled, in a big echoey cavern. The noise washed in and out, they both crouched down, Jaeson's gun appeared in his hand, almost instinctively, cocked and ready.

Berythus just crouched down and stared around at the sky.

And then it appeared. A terrible blue cabinet, tall yet barely two men wide, doors and windows, of mind twistingly improbable dimensions, and of all things, a little light flashing on the top.

The dreadful braying cacophony ceased, a door opened inwards, and a man jumped out.

Dressed in what could only be some kind of dress dinner suit, or some stage magicians outfit, he yelled, whilst waving a weirdling metal wand, that hummed and glowed as he spun about seemingly looking for a target to latch on to.

"It's very important you listen to what I say..." He began.

"Hell, no." Said Jaeson.

His gun fired, his aim deadly. The capering apparition, threw up his arms, a spray of reddish ichor, decorating the quarry floor.

"Well, that's one of your devils done for." Jaeson said.

He blew the end of his barrel.

"Do, do you shoot, is that the right word, yes, do you shoot everyone in the face who jumps out at you?" Berythus, was aghast.

He wondered if perhaps the Mage of the blue cabinet, had arranged their arrival. He hoped not.

He considered prayer. He wondered if a quick death would be too unreasonable a request.

The door of the blue cabinet was still open.

"Shall we have a look? Inside? You know whilst were here and nothing else is happening?"

"No." Said Jaeson.

"Anything could happen."

"Isn't anything just what is happening?" Berythus seemed annoyed.

"Okay, you look."

Berythus approached the entrance to the cabinet. He skirted around the ruins of its former occupant, and peered in.

He staggered back, turned and running through the unfortunate previous occupant, stopped by the watching Detective.

"It's a nightmare of glowing lights, steel beams, and, it's huge! Far bigger on the inside than the outside!"

He exclaimed.

Jaeson Smith looked at it thoughtfully awhile.

"Nah, let's go. It just looks like trouble to me."

They walked passed it, up a rise, and on for about an hour, across the rocks...........

In the distance, a mist was rolling towards them.

Chapter Eight – Eriks Odyssey.

Erik came to. The smell of stale beer assailed his nostrils, his senses reeled, and his stomach heaved.

His head hurt, he sat up slowly, slowly grasping the table top, it was heavy, dark stained, oaken wood.

He gazed around the gloomy Inn daylight sneaked n through some half curtained windows. One or two other patrons lay, or slumped, around the room. By the gods, it was a dive!

His head hurt, and his mouth was dry. He stumbled to his feet, cautiously and carefully, he walked weaving through, amongst the other tables, up to the bar.

No one was there, so he moved around, behind the counter. Water, he thought, water first.

Water, there was, a jug, as far as he could tell, it was okay, not fresh, but not stale. He splashed it over his face, letting it drip down his clammy neck.

The shock of the cool water, helped clear his mind. He poured a little into a mug, sniffed it, and drank. It was refreshing.

His head still hurt. He checked his pockets, his jacket, and his trews, nothing was missing. He hadn't been robbed, that at least was something. He was angry. They had laughed at him. He told them of wonders, the things he'd seen, and they had all laughed. They'd bought him drinks, many drinks. They enjoyed his tale, but they did not believe him.

He stepped out, gradually, pulling himself and his thoughts together. He ought to go back home.

No, no, no, he thought. Someone needs to know!

Everyone needs to know! He should go to the city, Heidelheimberg, and he should tell the court, or at least, somebody in authority!

It was too big a story for him to just forget about it. He grinned, and then set his jaw grimly. He had no proof. Still, anyone going there would at least find the shelf, might even find the 'Throne.'

Yes, he would go. He would take the chance on what they might do, what could they do?

Laugh, he thought. Laugh and throw him out.

Yes, he would try anyway.

It started to rain. He shivered and began walking away from the Village of Tumenca, and on towards the road to Heidelheimberg.

Just a few hours later, he realised he should have had breakfast first. He should, he pondered, have bought supplies for the journey. It was, he realised, quite some way to the city. Many miles.

In fact walking it might take him quite a few days, maybe even a week. He cursed his impetuousness. He would find somewhere en route, for supplies, and maybe, breakfast or more likely, lunch.

The hours passed, the dirt road stayed dirt, the weather improved, a little sunshine would streak through the clouds, and then through the leaves of the trees by the roadside.

The occasional cottage, and small farm, appeared, from time to time, generally every few miles. These he approached, and where possible, bought a drink, and items of food. His little knapsack, filled with bits and pieces, and his purse lightened with every mile.

In this at least, he had had some luck, the crops had been good, and people were generous in times of plenty. One farmer tried to get him to marry his daughter, at least, this is how he chose to interpret it, local dialects were a bit odd sometimes. Naturally, he declined, the farmer, a grey haired hulking man, did not seem offended, and proceeded to try to sell him a pig. This too, he declined. He smiled as he thought of evil rituals rumoured to be practiced, with the use of pigs, and wondered what the students of Heidelheimbergs notable university, would pay for a live one. No, he thought, poor pig!

He left the nice little slate roofed farmstead, and walked through the evening.

He counted his blessings, at least he thought, I live in one of the civilized lands. Few bandits, fewer monsters. He paused, other than his climbing pick, he had no arms.

He shrugged, and kept walking. The night was peaceful. Occasional animal noises, the occasional night owl, the shushing of wind through the trees, that was all.

That night he dozed under a tree, just off the road. The morning light woke him, and making a short breakfast of smoked meats, and drinking water from a canteen, he resumed his journey.

Trees lined the dirt road, and an hour into his days walk, he heard the unmistakeable clatter and jingle of a carriage! He smiled, he might be able to catch a ride.

Standing to the side, he waited, and in moments the carriage came into view, four horses, two men up front driving.

He waved, and they slowed, slowly stopping beside him.

"Ho stranger! Whither bound?" Cried the man, liveried in a deep blue long coat, dark high boots, and a tall hat.

Erik waved again, and approached slowly.

"Any chance your headed to Heidelheimberg?" He asked.

The coach was smart, it paintwork, and brasses, well maintained, its chestnut horses fine and handsome beasts.

It was a company carriage. A long carriage, two doors on each side, black and gold paintwork, and, he already knew, four bench seats, within.

"One shilling, and you can ride to Navorny. That's our first stop, and it's as close a we get to the city."

This suited him just fine, he fished a silver shilling from his pocket, and tossed it up. Adroitly caught by the driver, who waved him to get on board.

The little window on the rear door showed an empty bench. He turned the shiny brass handle, climbed in and closed the door.

Plenty of head room, he turned and sat down.

The rest of the carriage, had another seven occupants. One man quietly reading, two dozing, some ladies, well dressed, knitting, reading and chatting in hushed tones, to one side. A pair of soldiers, green and white uniforms, peaking out from under their great grey coats.

One other figure, hooded and with a bandage over his eyes, sat alone, asleep, perhaps, in the corner opposite his.

He settled back, as the jolt of the carriage recommencing its journey, rocked the cabin.

He smiled. His luck had changed. Navorny was nice. He had been there before, a few times. A nice market town. But a few miles south of Heidelheimberg.

He could have a night in a good Inn, get freshened up, a change of clothes even, and make his way to the authorities in a bit more style.

The hooded figure turned its head, almost imperceptibly, as the carriage rocked. A smile crossed its lips too, in the shadows.

Chapter Nine – Referential Quest.

Lyrinsos was a Merman, blue skin, no ears or hair, light scales, like a snakes, but not clammy. He was finely muscled. He had gills, but could also happily cope with air. At this present time, he had legs.

The Merfolk could make that change from fishy tail to legs and vice versa, as many times as they liked. It was, a long drawn out awkward process, which they didn't like to discuss with strangers.

For reasons known only to himself (and indeed it was considered rude to ask), Lyrissos had his legs on.

He also had a mission, an important one. He had had an uneventful career, in many ways, as a guard, then a trader, between the kingdom below the waves, and the few human lands, who would have anything to do with them. The Merfolk, occasionally, saw Humans as food, and this was not seen as an endearing quality.

He'd dropped the ball, and nearly got himself harpooned, in a small fishing village among the lost islands of Perrenios. The islands, are only generally regarded as lost by northern seaman, the islanders, and, practically everyone else, know exactly where they are, even going so far as to have them on their charts.

In deference to the northern sea captains and navigators, they would only show special edited charts, if occasion, demanded it.

Anyhow, his indiscretion, earned him two choices, one unspeakable, the other, the Priesthood. He initially opted for the unspeakable, but the judges could not pronounce sentence, so they forced him into the Priesthood.

Years passed. The Priesthood hated him, and when a vacancy arose upstairs, he was duly despatched to serve the Lord of Oceans directly.

This he did, at first astonished at the honour, then, a bit depressed at the prospect of, well, thousands of years in the Divine Realm.

You see, mortals, even long lived ones, such as the Merfolk, when stuck in the Upper World, cease to age.

Kershaggulumphie, Lord of Oceans, was not a demanding boss, interminable rituals, shoal herding, and oceanic symphonies seemed to be his almost eternal future. Until of course, the disaster of the great dark ones release.

He wasn't musical, but he could hum along to the symphonies, and even, pretend to sing.

Now, he had been singled out by a vindictive universe for a terrible mission.

He was expected to negotiate with the goddess Libraria, so he could search the forbidden section. Everyone knew, those books read their readers. Read them, edited them, critiqued them, and spat them back out on the discard pile, usually insane, dead, or both.

Someone, somewhere did not like him. He could not blame his god, because he had spoken to him that morning, and really, he seemed to like him.

He thought about running away, and then, after the necessary, but never discussed process, swimming away to the ends of the Earth, assuming there was an end. Presumably there was, and if he got there, he would find life had created his own special nasty fate, just there, just for him.

So, he went to Libraria's Halls, crossing by the safe paths from the Lord of Oceans Palace, to the goddesses domain.

The passageways of travel varied enormously, some appeared like bridges, some tunnels through earth, rock, metal, gems, or water, others more like a vortex, you stepped in and whirled straight to the end, no sight or sound or sense of the inbetween at all.

He stepped out onto the pale marble of the steps before the goddess Libraria's great repository.

It was said that one of every book ever written existed within this library, not necessarily properly filed though. Some philosophers even maintained that some kind of connection existed between every library that ever existed.

Most other philosophers regarded this as nonsense, but the rate of banana skin accidents still remained constant, despite, in most cases, the lack of availability of that particular yellow fruit, and in many other cases, strict rules about eating or bringing food into, the library.

Steeling himself for whatever may be beyond, he pushed open the doors. It was as bad as he had been led to believe.

Millions, well, he did not use that word, heaps, mountains, oceanic trenches, full of books, opened before him. A dizzying cyclopean vista of erudition, embodied in paper, parchment, vellum, or stone. Tomes in columns soared into an endless vaulted sky.

"Shit." He said.

It was as terrible as the tales had told. The stench and essence of cat set him sneezing immediately.

He put on the face mask, he'd been given, by a rather apologetic Merman alchemist, it would help, he had said. It did, a bit.

Amongst the terrible stacks, stalked terrible beasts. The feline felons, already eyed him beadily from every direction. They smelt fish.

He was, however, prepared even for this ordeal, this terrible eventuality. He advanced into the stacks slowly, his bodyguard of specially trained attack alligators, followed at his heel, their eyes roving, looking for any catlike transgression.

He was glad he had brought them, for scarcely had he passed the threshold, than a particularly dissolute, flea ridden, rat eared, mangy tom charged his flank.

A swift flash of teeth, and a snap! The darkling horror was duly re-indexed under 'history'.

The alligator spat out the rancid pieces of tom in disgust!

It looked, disapprovingly at Lyrinsos, who smiled beneath the mask. Well done ! He thought.

It did, however, loyally, plod on, guarding its trainer.

Lyrinsos, turned and gazed ahead, there less than a mile away, was a desk. A desk with someone sat behind it.

He would start there. It took some time to get there, the alligators, were a little slow on marble, but they got there.

A middle aged woman, hair in a bun, glasses upon her chubby face, stared at a book open before her, what seemed to be some kind of romance.

He cleared his throat. Not a twitch, or a movement he could see.

"Excuse me, I'm here on urgent message from the Lord of Oceans. Are you listening?"

The woman looked up icily.

"Shh." She said.

Lyrinsos stared at her, seized a book, and began banging it on the table.

Alarm flashed across the woman's face.

"OUT!" She shouted.

"I am Libraria, and I will not be trifled with!"

Lyrinsos just stared at her.

"No, you're not." He said.

"Yes, I am!" She said.

"No, you're really not." He said firmly, but calmly. She, was quite possibly nuts. This was a possibility he had not allowed for. After all, books, as already mentioned, were dangerous.

He looked around, despite the mind bending number of books, Libraria's Hall seemed, especially when compared to the Lord of the Oceans Palace, kind of sad and empty.

It needed clearing out, a good steam clean, pest control for the feral cats, and burning to the ground. Not necessarily in that order.

Gods, there was even a banana skin, stuck betwixt the pages of a book just a yard above his head!

He would never complain about the Lord of Oceans, Sing Songs again.

More quietly, the middle aged woman, spoke:

"I'm her deputy. I have been left in charge, and you should leave now!"

As she spoke the defiance ebbed and flowed in her voice.

"Libraria's not been here for awhile, has she? In fact I bet you don't know where she's gone either. You've never even met her have you?"

Lyrinsos paused. This was a kindred spirit, another sad soul, who has been stepped on by life, time and again, until she finally wound up, alone except for the evil feral cats, lost amidst a gigantic heap of other people's dreams and ideas.

He felt sad.

"Look I just need to know everything about ...."

He stopped himself. He'd forgotten the name.

He smiled nervously.

"Look just point me to the Forbidden Section, I'll find what I need."

She looked at him and softened. She looked hungry. Her hunger went beyond food, he shivered. She smiled. Maybe, blue men would be different she thought.

"I'll show you!" She said.

She seemed immune to the cats, clearly they did not yet regard her as a food item, yet.

She led him down miles of stacks, down stairs, upstairs, through secret passages, then finally out into a great cavern, the far end of which, contained a pair of great black iron gates. They were locked.

"Here it is!" She said.

"Yes. How do we get in?" He asked.

"Oh yes, the key!" She grinned.

She fished around, for rather longer than he cared to think about, finally dragging forth a rather large, black steel key.

She unlocked the gates, and pushed.

The gates swung inwards, and a great icy blast blew outwards. He shivered. She buttoned up her cardigan, which somehow had become unbuttoned. He looked away, dread gnawing at his soul.

"There! Here they are! All the madness and vile evil, from the very beginnings of time itself! Where do you want to start?"

Lyrinsos's mouth fell open, there was a banana skin not ten yards beyond the gates.

Gathering his wits, he looked at the woman.

"I don't suppose there's an index, is there?"

He asked, pessimistically.

Chapter Ten   - Under The Mountains Big and Cold.

The mists closed about them.

"Here we go again." Jaeson Smith gently tapped his gun.

"Please, in the name of the gods, don't shoot anyone else, until we know they need shooting."

Berythus Naechos wrung his hands as the cold and clammy mists wrapped around them.

They walked on, the mists thickening, and then walls, clammy stone chiselled walls, were all about them, hemming them in. Fortunately, Berythus still had his lantern, he turned it up. They were in tunnels, a rough hewn tunnel that stretched behind and ahead of them.

The tunnels smelt. The tunnels smelt disgusting. They smelt of excrement, urine, blood, and smoke.

"Well, what new joy, has the 'gods' set before us?" Jaeson asked, no one in particular.

They walked steadily going down, and down, deeper and deeper into the depths of the Earth.

"Only one way to find out, we go on!" Said the priest.

They walked, cautiously, slowly.

After an hour, a cross tunnel or two later, they heard footsteps, footsteps running towards them. They looked about, a small alcove presented itself, and they crouched back flattening against the tunnel wall.

Figures raced passed. Many, many short armoured figures, and one tall one with a glowing staff, and a bright sword. They went by unseeing.

Behind them though, was a horde whose harsh voices carried down the tunnel.

"Must be goblins!" Berythus offered.

They stepped out into the passage, and like wise hurried down. More cross passages, and intersections followed.They stumbled on, and the pursuit seemed to go off in a different direction.

"Well, I guess we keep going until the mists come and claim us again."

Jaeson Smith was actually starting to enjoy himself. He clearly had gone mad, and this was his imagination delightfully playing with his fears, and phobias. It was quite a trip. He wondered if he would wake up, and where that would be if he did.

They strolled on, Berythus worried, hesitant, Jaeson feeling quietly chilled out. Maybe it was some side effect of the herbs he had been taking? He didn't know, and didn't care.

In the distance he thought he could hear water, and soon their lantern, its dim light stabbing ahead, showed a little under ground lake. It had an island, an island with a little boat or raft moored upon it.

"Well, which way do we go? Or do we wait to see if the mists rise, to carry us off again?" Jaeson Smith started laughing.

Away across the lake, a strange creature stirred, boarded its raft, and began paddling across.

"Anyway, what did you find back there in the passage? I saw you pause and bend over."

"Oh, just this little metal ring. I think it might be gold." Berythus shrugged.

"Look, I'm a priest, but we are a poor sect, and a little gold helps sometimes."

"Yeah, keep it. Enjoy it. If you ever get anywhere were you can spend it, you have a drink on me."

"Oh, thank you, no, I don't really, tend to do that sort of thing. I might buy some books though."

Berythus smiled, it was contagious. This strange man's attitude was catching, perhaps, he was right not to be worried.

Something splashed nearby.

"What are they, mon cherie? What are they doing by moi lac?"

Asked a disembodied voice, emanating from the lake.

"Shine, the light over there." Suggested Jaeson.

Berythus did so. Two large eyes, in a ragged haired head, on a scrawny small body, barely bigger than the small log it rested on stared back blinking, in the light.

"Little pale underground dude, we don't want any trouble, now scram, while we wait for the mists to arise."

Said Jaeson, he felt sorry for the scrawny, ragged creature, he fumbled in his pockets.

"C'est une riddle? Is it a riddle it is asking?" Carried on the quaint little cavern mutant.

"No, please just leave us alone." Said Berythus, nervously fingering his ring.

The strange creature chuckled throatily, clearly it had terrible phlegm, a bad chest, and no sense of danger.

There was a click.

"Oh no, not again." Said Berythus.

"This is my dream, good bye little log monkey." Said Jaeson, aiming carefully.

"What? Mon cherie isn't going anywhere, are we mon cherie?"

Crack!

This echoed quite alarmingly, and the smell of gunpowder filled the damp musty air.

The little figure, slipped in and under the water.

"Well, that's that then." Said Jaeson.

"I wonder why it spoke French?" He pondered aloud.

Berythus just stared at him in the gloom.

"What's French? No, never mind. I don't care. I don't want to know. I do want to know how we're getting out of here! You do know the lantern, won't last forever, it's already burning low. We need to get out of here." He offered, by way of an educated opinion.

"Yeah, don't worry. Just wait, the mists will be along, any time."

Jaeson smiled in the gloom. His was turning out to be his best dream ever!

Idly, as he sat their on the cold stone, he reached into his jacket found some papers, and some herbs, and began rolling.

Chapter Eleven – Wending Winding Ways Whither Wagons Wander.

Rattle, rattle, bump, jingle, rattle, snort, neigh! Nirnadel came back. She'd been sat on the bench, next to Rhian. Rhian, dark black hair greying now, though still attractive in the morning sunshine, holding the reins of their shared wagon.

They were travelling in convoy, quite a large convoy too, stretching along the dirt roads, behind, and ahead. It had stopped.

"Cattle!" Came the call passed back along the line.

Ah, she thought, they would have to wait, until the animals had cleared the way ahead, then they could proceed.

An orange and black dogs head pushed out between them, through the curtained hatch just behind the drivers seat. This, was one of the Faerie dogs, of which the People of the Wagons, had many.

This particular faerie dog was called Fudge, and he was not a beautiful dog, his charcoal coat, was streaked with orange. It was a shiny luminous orange. He had odd eyes, too, One eye glowed green, the other glowed yellow. He had teeth, lots of sharp pointy teeth, and he was two and a half feet tall at the shoulder. His ears, took turns in flopping, in a variety of directions, never the particularly obvious one.

In the last few years, he had added an impressive array of scars, and battle wounds, but for Rhian, he was still her puppy.

His tongue lolled happily out of his mouth as he panted between them. It was quite a warm day, and he was a happy doggy.

"Yo!" Came back the call. It may have started as something else, but, roughly eleven wagons back, "Yo!", was all that came through.

Slowly the wagons ahead began to roll forward, and Rhian, gently nudged the horses on.

Nirnadel, she still held on to that name, though Rhian, and many of the others seemed to think it was a little formal now, tried to concentrate.

They needed to find this book, a great tome, this codex, that kept the secret to banishing, or imprisoning the Devourer, but where to look. They had heard Mages were gathering nearby, in Heidelheimberg, of all places, a peaceful, chocolate box walled city, of spires, towers, artisans, theatres, and enlightenment.

The Burghers of Heidelheimberg had successfully maintained their little country, and expanded it, not through conquest, but through trade, and negotiated defence pacts. It was technically, an aristocracy, but the Burghers had a charter, going back hundreds of years, giving them Rights and Privileges, which they had ferociously defended, and for which now, they were very grateful.

Apparently, they were training Mages, en masse, in a special combat magick. These new Mages, were rumoured to be called Macquettemen, and apparently, looked very smart, in their white and green liveries.

As a place to start, well, it was somewhere. She gazed out across the fields. She could smell the cows now, they must be drawing nearer. Fudge licked her ear.

She wondered, what had happened to Ralph? She'd been separated from him during their shipwreck, just at the harbour of Vondrbeorg. She suspected he wasn't dead, who was his old Master? He'd had one, apparently a Master Mage, possibly one of the old Council of Mages. One of the few survivors, who hadn't been toasted or trampled, by the freed Dragons, which they had bound.

She sighed. How were they supposed to find a tome, that must be many thousands of years old, and although made of steel, or some other metal, of similar colouration it could have been ruined by the ages. Worse, she thought, it could be buried, in some ancient tomb, or some long lost wizards workroom.

She could talk to her father. He would wonder why she hadn't called. He knew, probably, that she had mastered mirror magick, and could enchant just such a device, and thusly could communicate, if she wished. She wondered, was he watching her now?

Her Amulet of Protection would probably protect her from scrying, but, her father had considerable knowledge and power, if anyone could do it, he could.

Now, though, now she knew he was a Lich, no longer a living man, and had been so for many years, would he feel the same way, would he help?

She would have to create an enchanted mirror. She would have to make that call. It would be awkward. Especially, for Rhian, her mother, who although unhappy at her husbands assassination (by poison), was less than pleased, when in fact, he kept on going, ruling as before, his fierce dark arcane spirit, which had only possessed its current body, refusing to let go of it in its death.

She felt cross. He was heartless. She was surprised he hadn't just possessed a new body, and continued from there, except, he was maintaining great magicks, not least the great Bone Legion. Was that why? He didn't want to risk his plots, his stratagems, for the sake of a less musty, leathery, shell, to wear.

She sighed again, necromancy had its dark side, she thought.

Still, she couldn't ignore it, he was still the greatest Mage they could get in touch with.

"Oh look! You can see the Counts castle over there!"

Rhian, was smiling brightly, she pointed vaguely to a mountain spur, a small chain heading north, away from the Dragon Ridge mountains.

There it was, Castle Uis Navorny, sitting proudly above the small market town of Navorny, a place, noted as always being friendly to the People of the Wagons.

The current Count, Bruno Orvull, though a recluse, had maintained friendly relations with the folk, and had indeed, employed them for odd jobs over the years. It was, Lyra, her grandmother, had mentioned, rumoured that at least one of his ancestors had been of the road, though this was largely discounted. Who would give up the freedom of the road, for a dusty Castle?

Apparently, Lyra had hinted, he would see them, he could perhaps, be persuaded to help, in their quest. Something strange, had glinted in Lyra's eyes when she had mentioned the Count. Nirnadel wasn't the most observant, or indeed the most sensitive person, but Lyra, had something she was not sharing.

She had asked Rhian, what it could be? Rhian had looked at her surprised. She didn't know, and was sure what ever Lyra had in mind, would be good for everyone. Well, every member of the People of the Wagons, anyway.

Another hour passed, and the town, hove into view. They would not enter the town walls, no, there was a fairground outside, this they would settle down on, for awhile. Her heart leaped. She had heard so many good things of this town, she was going to explore.

She had no money though, but was sure Rhian, would fund her expedition, and perhaps, come with her. She glowed a little, to go shopping, somewhere civilized with her mother!

Just a year ago, cooped up, in Xagiggs Palace, a cage of gold, she could never have imagined this day, or this much freedom! Alright, it was qualified freedom. She was free to travel with the wagons, where ever they went, and she was now seen as one of the folk of the road, with all the good and bad reactions other people had towards them.

Well, it was this or being a lonely Princess, imprisoned in a deathly palace, in a faltering kingdom.

She sighed and then smiled. Navorny would be fun.

Chapter Twelve - All At Sea

The deck heaved. It rolled. It lunged downwards, and then heaved upwards. If you judged it right, you felt weightless, if you got in wrong, it could bring you to your knees.

Boots, he thought. I need new boots. He had been looking downwards. Especially important on deck, no good tripping over a stray line, or stray object of any sort. The crew were excellent! They so rarely failed to batten down the hatches, tidy up, and generally follow all the health and safety tips he had insisted they follow.

They were the best crew available. The most loyal, some knew him, from when he was a Bartender, all those years ago. Others only knew him as a Sea Captain. He had a powerful reputation, and he paid well. His crew knew he played fair, and took his share of risks, and they thought he was clever, or, at least lucky. For many of them, lucky was good enough.

He reached the wheelhouse. It was a beautiful ship. He had traded up. He had traded up quite a few times. Not by force mind you, by salvage. Many a Mate of his, now had their own ships, simply because he had gone away with one, and come back with two.

The cargoes he rescued, some were fabulous. This is how he put it, rescued. You see since the shadow had been cast over the South Lands, trade had failed, ports and harbour towns had been over run, and the Devourers Horde had no use for material goods. So they left them, in their warehouses, in their ships, and mostly the Towns and Cities were abandoned.

Mostly. On a few occasions, he and his men had had to fight. This they did. They knew the Lord of the Oceans tattoos gave a measure of protection, and now they were all tattooed. First event in any new crew members career, getting their tattoos.

His ships all flew a trident flag, in honour of the Lord of the Oceans. They weren't all his ships, but his ex Mates all followed the same custom, and had entered into the same trade.

It was a trade that was getting a bit more difficult, many of the big easy hauls had been taken now, and now, it was, well, looting, as much as anything else.

He always tried to bring back a balanced cargo. Art treasures, raw materials, common wares, no foodstuffs of course, everything like that had rotted away long before, and always keeping an eye out for the locals. He hoped one day, to actually find survivors, but as yet, where the Horde had been, silence reigned.

Gaining the steps, then the wheel deck, and then out of the spray, in the wheelhouse, he smiled.

Rogerios was there, looking half asleep, but in reality, as wide awake as anyone.

"Go below! It's my turn." He said, grinning.

He always took a turn at everything.

Rogerios, smiling in return through his grey streaked black beard, saluted, and went out.

He checked the wheel, it was fine of course, but it paid to be sure. He rubbed his chin, through his ginger facial hair.

He would love a great fluffy red beard, but alas, all he could manage was a reddish down.

He'd been nearly a dozen years at sea now, and had found him self nicknamed Lucky Red. It would have to do.

No one called him Garim anymore, and he didn't miss it. Captain Red, or Captain Fortune, as some up North had called him, all his ventures turned to gold, you see, would have to do.

It had been a long time since he had studied, and toiled in Edrics Lodge, allegedly learning magick, really learning agriculture and book illustration.

He still liked books, and in his cabin below, he had salvaged tomes from all over the South. Some he could read, some he was learning to read. Languages, were not his forte, but he was always learning, a bit here, a bit there.

Yes, the missions were getting a bit more difficult these days. This trip, he planned, quite simply to sail up a river, well, a great estuary, and see what he find there. His maps showed a great city, old Eghior, surrounded, mostly by deserts, but with a harbour, opening into the estuary. His ship should, he thought, be okay. It was a large vessel, on Earth it's closest comparison would be a Galleon, but a bit longer, a bit taller, a bit wider, designed for oceans, not rivers.

He would have to be careful. He had two hundred men, they would be armed and ready, for trouble, so long as the trouble was small, and taken relatively unawares.

He had given it some thought though, and he had an emergency plan, he had spent a bit of money on, and he thought it would work. As a last resort.

He scratched his side. He was still tall, nearly five foot ten, he was still slim, despite middle age being full upon him, and he was muscly, through hard work, and many battles.

He thought through his plans, and grinned. Sometimes, he wondered what would have happened had he not left the Neophyterium, all those years ago. What would of happened had he stayed a 'monk', stayed working on the land, and had not set out to seek his fortune.

He would probably be dead, he thought. Actually, he would certainly be dead. If not slain by Dragons, then wiped out by the Dread Brush Sprouts of the Mother of Millions. Good grief he thought, what a world to live in.

He wondered what had become of his former colleague, and fellow Neophyte, Adan. They had left together, but shortly thereafter, been split up, until, after incongruous, unexpected, and quite unbelievable events, they had been thrown back together, on a paradisical island called Manaxa, where upon they both ran a Bar, and small holiday resort, until the giant Dragons, and a few other minor issues, had put a damper on the Tourist trade.

He laughed. He was ready for anything.

Or so he thought.

Chapter Fourteen Minus One – Alls Fair.

The fairground at Navorny was huge, acres of good flat (more or less) land just outside the town walls. Like many towns, Navorny had spread beyond its defensive walls, which at twenty feet, stone, brick, and earth embankments, were not insignificant, though overgrown in places, with trees and various climbing plants.

Worth noting, these were just normal plants, not animate in any way beyond that accustomed to any plant, nor particularly poisonous, no more than for example, clematis is, nor particularly ugly. At certain times of the year, flowers, beautiful, yellows and whites, sometimes reds, and purples, adorned them and vicariously, the walls also.

The birds, were a different question. They watched, dark black ravens, huge crows, few other smaller birds. They congregated, upon the walls, upon the trees, upon the roof tops within the walls themselves. They observed, they swooped upon the discarded titbits, forgotten morsels, unobserved trifles, and an open kitchen window, would be a dinner gong, not to be ignored.

They were harmless. Really. To an outsider though, they were, if of a nervous disposition, a sinister icing on the chocolate box appeal of the town.

However, its western edge, had by tradition and long custom been kept free of new buildings, a simple watch house, being the only actual brick and mortar building, on the grounds.

This is not to say, that it was actually empty, for the People of the Wagons were not the only folk of the roads. On this day, many wagons were already in place, and as Nirnadels people arrived, carefully finding a good spot, although somewhat distant from the town gates, some acknowledged them, with friendly word, and wave, and others watched them, watched them darkly.

Pierjin the greyhaired but still tall and strong, gaudily dressed, gold bejewelled, and bandana wearing lieutenant in all but name, to Lyra (the undisputed Matriarch of the clan), took charge, and oversaw the disportment of the caravan, establishing, as subtly as possible, a defensive layout. The faerie dogs dutifully taking up their accustomed positions. Pierjin knew, you could trust no one, and everyone.

Best to be ready for anything.

Nirnadel was learning, she was learning the ways of the world. She knew she had had a sheltered life, but had no idea, just how much she didn't know. Rhian helped of course, she explained Pierjin's ways, that his rule of thumb was, if you cut him open, probably written right through him.

Nonetheless, she was still excited. Rhian found all this amusing, but recalled how she was at that age, grinning when she remembered some of the scrapes she had gotten into, and out of again.

She asked Nirnadel if she could defend herself. Nirnadel, of course, mentioned the word of command, Rhian smiled recalling her own leathers, and, her knives.

She had kept her knives sharp, and often, discreetly, wore them. The world was, in reality, as bad as ever, except for one of the 'bads', this dread monster out of time, an elder darkness, risen to consume the world.

Rhian wondered, could this book, or the knowledge it contained, be found? If it could, what would the world be, beyond its use?

She watched Nirnadel happily helping guide the horses to their grazing. She would need all the help she could get.

Leather, she thought. Leather and knives, and shopping. Rhian went to her clothes chest, and dug out her old outfit, it still fit! More or less.

Stretched out upon the grass, Fudge gazed up . From his vantage point, he watched the Sun in the sky, the birds flying, everywhere except the distant castle. He was happy, this last year had been like the old days, before they had had to flee war and horror, it had almost been normal.

That castle, his senses told him, was not normal. Still, it's over there and we're down here.

A fire sparked into life, and tressle tables were being assembled. Fudges attention was now, fully diverted. The prospect of food, was always interesting.

Nirnadel, her part in the setting up of camp, played, circumnavigated their 'fort'. This is always how she imagined their, sort of, octagonal encampment.

She gazed outwards. The grass, only churned in some places, still had large clear spaces. She gazed, many other wagons were parked, some seemed to have been stuck there for years. Looking a little closer some seemed almost permanent, at least without major renovation they would not be going anywhere.

Her gaze was noticed. Her smile faltered at the hostility in one particular mans gaze. He did not wear the fine clothes of the folk of the roads. His clothes looked quite worn and rough, if they'd had colour, it had long ago faded.

A voice called out to her. She turned, it was one of Pierjins men, well one of his regular companions. Medium tall, and broadly built, grey haired also, colourfully attired, and openly wearing a cutlass, its scabbard gaudily be-ribboned, so that was alright then.

She remembered his name, Borthy, it was.

"Don't go far alone." He whispered, after he'd closed the ground between them.

"This is a civilized land, but there are as many troubles here, as in those lands racked with anarchy, we've seen."

He looked so serious, she giggled, feeling bad immediately, and clapping her hand to her mouth, a blush of embarrassment rising to her cheeks.

He frowned.

"Oh, I've heard your story, and I believe you, but 'civilization' is over rated. They'll ask you to trust them, whilst slitting your purse, or worse your throat."

"It's alright, I know how corrupt people are!"

She exclaimed.

"Trust no one, and trust every one to do what's best, for themselves! I've heard it before, and I'll not forget." She smiled.

"Look, Lyra, and your mother, will have my skin, if anything happens to you, so for my sake, if not your own, stay close to camp for now."

She grinned again.

"Thank you." She said.

She meant it, they genuinely cared, not because they were paid to, but because they wanted to, and that was price less.

He turned, and went off, having seen a detail needing his thoughtful eye.

She headed back to the camp fire, preparations in progress for a small feast. This she could help with, and stay out of trouble.

Chapter Fourteen – Really Fourteen This Time, or On the Front Line.

The City State of Kenovass was, once prosperous, its rolling hills pastures, fine food for herds, mainly cattle, and goats. Its towns, manufacturers of popular pottery and acceptable furniture. It did well from trade, being the main overland route north and west from the Southlands.

The Dragons came, ridden by their Mage pilots, striking seemingly randomly, targets across the world, including the City of Kenovass itself.

No sooner had they began to assess the damage, sweep up the ashes, and begin rebuilding, then the first echoes of the horror in the south, began to reach their ears. Scarcely weeks later, refugees arrived, bringing tales of horror, and a terrible horde led by a great Warlord, Arshan, Fist of the Devourer.

Almost presentiently, ships from Graeffenland, and its defacto King, the Master Mage and Necromancer Xagigg, arrived.

His ships disgorged his Bone Legion, shortly after the first scouts had reported, seeing Arshan's outriders.

Outriders, is the wrong word, and also, the right word. In as much as Arshan had a scout force, seemingly unnecessary for his exalted Horde, a Horde whose mere numbers sent armies fleeing in fear, who could bury any normal sized force, in the weight of their dead, and still be huge in proportions.

Outriders it had. These were folk of the second category, agents of some darker power, not quite the lost soulless, yet no longer amongst the normal run of humanity. They scouted, they spied, they also did ride.

Well, mostly they sat upon, sometimes they stood, sometimes they would recline within a howdah.

You see, what they rode, well, lacked normality, lacked sanity, did not lack imagination, if that imagination was particularly warped, and indeed fecund, of biological possibility, but with sufficient lack of actual biological knowledge, that multiple redundancy of features, for example legs, or arms, or heads, indeed torsos, would not be cause for comment.

Yes, Arshans scouts rode mounts most improbable, mounts most horrible, and sometimes the shock of their appearance, alone, was enough to send opposition reeling and fleeing in terror.

Arshans Composite Cavalry was a thing to behold, if nightmares floated your boat, made you smile, or grin maniacally, or gibber with pleasure. Most people did not like them.

The army of Kenovass, such as it was, and it wasn't bad, fully up to the diplomatic wranglings, border skirmishes, and bandit hunts of the sane world, was no match, nor in any fit state to face Arshan, and it would have blown away like Autumn leaves had not the Bone Legion arrived.

The Bone Legion, armed in the state of the art in zombie weaponry, pikes, swords, cudgels, axes, was fearless, and stiff with resolve (and rigor mortis).

They ranked in their thousands. Disciplined, and led by the battle hardened General Rutger Tostwic, King of a week or two, raised from the dead after the great battle of Carseport, and still as sharp a commander as any could want.

Arshan's initial force was instantly destroyed, it's swarm mentality, falling like wheat, before the legions discipline, and, Arshan paused. He had expected little resistance, and did not seem to have planned for zombies.

You see, Arshans greatest strength, was his agents power to turn, to convert, the humans they met, into Soulless, who frothing and gibbering, would obey his agents, and become an addition to his army. This of course, became understood quickly by the Captains of Kenovass's own army, they quickly fell back to support and sapping roles, digging ditches, building barricades, and towers, blocking roads.

Gradually, the men of Kenovass, began securing their land.

Arshan or his lieutenants, who knew? Mustered a greater force, this he hurled straight for the City itself. A grey mist arose before his force, before they had even reached the earthen ramparts, hastily built just days earlier, and charging into it they died, to a man.

Xagigg had come, and woven a great Death Spell across the battlefield. He was still a living man then, not the Lich he was later to become, and onlookers said he was pale and weak from the effort.

It was not, an unqualified success, for although they died, they did not stop, they were weakened, but something, some dark force, other than necromantic magick, held them up.

Jerkily, awkwardly, they still advanced. Their coordination was gone, and the wrecked creatures attacked everything, animate, inanimate, each other.

Even in this debilitated state, the horrifying force nearly prevailed, simply from numbers, and not all had been weakened by Xagiggs spell.

Fortune favoured Kenovass that day, as, spies having informed the Alt Konig, the great Gnome King, of the attack, reinforcements arrived. The War Mechanicals of the Gnomes, portalled in, stepping through the shimmering doorways from Below, to the very battlefield.

Each was a great thirty to forty foot high mechanical man, great foot plates crushing the ground, sword swinging arms slicing, anything in reach, but more tellingly, the silvery machines, each bore flame rods, great magickal weapons, forged by the Archeus Magnus himself, and directed, by their rather tiny gunners, launching fire globe after fire globe hurtling down upon the chaotic mass of the enemy! This fiery destruction, was enough to turn the tide.

The gnomish forces established their own camp, amongst the joint defenders, and as the years passed, made the difference many times. As the years wore on, they brought the talents of skilled engineers, builders, and architects, to bear on the problems of defense. The city itself, became almost impregnable.

King Xagigg, stopped making personal appearances on the field of battle, entrusting that particular honour to one apprentice, the talented Ten Grief, who, though not as powerful or learned in the dark arts as his master, showed great enthusiasm, for the task at hand.

Now, we see Kenovass after many years have passed. One half of Kenovass exists 'normally,' but with the shadow of daily battles, some times only in the distance, sometimes nearer to the city itself, cast upon it. The other half, a no mans land, a wilderness, battle scarred, and barren, bones of the fallen decorating the landscape.

Arshan, the Fist of the Devourer, never gave up. As the years passed, he employed different strategies, which all failed to gain him any ground.

Ten Grief sat in his suite of rooms in the great south bastion, a relatively new piece of defensive architecture, on the reinforced side of Kenovass. He gazed at the blank mirror, mounted upon a beautiful ebony chest of drawers.

Just his reflection, looked back at him. His tanned face, his shaven head, his third eye tattoo, not actually magickal, but kind of an affectation in honour of his Master Xagigg's great purple gem, set in his forehead.

His tattoo stared back at him, from within its triangle. He smiled. His report had gone well, mighty Xagigg was pleased. He was conversant with Mirror magick, and indeed, many other forms of magick, he could have teleported to King Xagiggs awful presence, but there was no need. Mirror communication was fine.

His eyes looked brown in the candle light, his robes were a tasteful charcoal, embellished with beautiful sigils, runes, and symbols, in silver, gold, and emerald green. He stood, his slim tall form, towering above the enchanted furniture.

He stepped towards the window and gazed south and east. In the distance, the wall, and the picket line, the unending patrols of zombie troops, the occasional War Mechanical, marching up and down the line.

This, he thought, has nearly had its day. Arshans attacks had become fewer, and further between, they had become weaker. Running out of cannon fodder perhaps?

He caught himself and frowned, just what is a cannon? The phrase seemed so appropriate, with sounds of thunder, smoke, and acrid fumes, with the screams of falling multitudes thrown in, but what actually was, a cannon?

It was reality, creaking under the strain. He'd been warned about it, his great master, had been labouring to shore up, the strands of reality for years now. He wondered if Xagiggs version of reality was that accurate, and smiled. He didn't mind.

He liked Xagigg's way, except, with Xagiggs power, what could not a man do? Xagigg contented himself with a small island kingdom, indeed, not even the whole island! He shared Graeffenlands island with Gnomoria, the Alt Konigs place on the Upside, as gnomes like to refer to the lands above, and the Northlands, a small independent Kingdom, no bigger than a small continental barony!

He liked Xagiggs way, but, he could do it better. One day, he would be an Emperor, one day his standard would seen flying across the whole of the world!

He smiled.

That was for later, for now, well, he would need to lay his foundations. From a fold of his robe, he pulled forth a small cameo painting, barely an inch high, of a rather bony girl.

Yes, he thought, firm foundations.

Chapter Fifteen – Into the Maelstrom.

Beep, beep, beep, beep, beep, click! The plastic button stopped glowing, as she released the pressure of her index finger. The white hermetically sealed, sterile walls, of the cabin surrounded her, staterooms on these voyages were austere.

It's not that decoration was not allowed, but most members of the Imperial Reconnaissance Service, felt that it encouraged sloppy thinking, and bad discipline.

She rolled off the couch, into a standing position, pressed another wall stud, the couch slid away, into a hidden compartment, one more stud click, and a sonic shower cubicle opened, little more than a cubby hole, this she stepped into. She was naked, hairless, her slim, toned form, youthful, and athletic, despite its hundred and seventy years.

The sonic shower took moments, its waves removing dead skin cells, dirt, such as there was, and providing a stimulating circulatory massage, all at the same time.

Air filters sucked away the disturbed molecules, and hygiene prevailed.

Exercise routine? No, she thought, nor waste services either, she did not feel the need, and besides, she had been woken early, not an alarm, but, something needed attention.

She turned towards the accessway door. Moving swiftly, and yet unselfconsciously, she pressed another stud, the door panel opened, and leaving the artificial gravity behind, she swung into the access well. Left, was up, that's what the arrows said, and up she went, towards the Bridge, floating freely whilst pulling herself up hand over hand.

She passed six sets of doors, three more Staterooms, the Galley, Science, and Medical. Above her and getting closer, the hatch for the Bridge.

A bit of a grand name, for a small cabin, which, its shielded windows gazing out onto the Stars, had but two couches, Pilot and Navigator.

She opened the hatch, quickly swivelling the circular door release, in the middle of the hatch, it opened downwards, and she pulled herself in, pulling and sealing the hatch behind her.

John was already there, and he switched couches, the low black plastic padded seats common in these ships, climbing back into the Navigators position, as she arrived.

John smiled, his deep green skin glistened slightly in the stellar light.

"Hello, I've been keeping your seat warm! Take a look! We're out of hyperspace."

Pilot Captain Therese Jameson stared at the screens, great banks of monitors, indicating various conditions, states, and local environmentals.

"Well, nothing's wrong, no damage, no alarms, we're just out early. Only minutes in it really, but we are out early."

John was also nude. Clothes, bearing in mind the climate control, and clean environment of the ship, were not used. No need. Safety suits, and enhanced armoured excursion outfits, were in store, if needed, but rarely used.

Of course, they had dress uniforms for shore leave, and at home regular clothes.

"So, what's different, something must be different, lets run diagnostics...."

She quietly began, routine system checks, routine scans, every thing was fine. She looked at the Hyperdrive controls.

"Huh, stellar mass gravity anomaly? But there is nothing out there for parsecs!" She exclaimed.

"No, nothing we can see, or detect. Can there be an invisible star?" John pondered.

"Well, no, maybe, but the other instruments would register something, well, something other than, that."

She pointed at a distant, fluctuating light.

Yes, that. It had been picked up on long range scanners, and scopes, years before, and now, finally, some one had decided to have it checked out. It was, such a large universe, so many anomalies, so many interesting planets, civilizations, and resources, to be explored.

Now, there was this. An oscillating, pulsating changing stellar mass, sprung from nowhere, defying categorisation, and varying considerably day to day. Emitting strange radio signals too, and accompanied by a plethora of satellites, odd bodies of matter, gyrating in no stable orbit around that central, unstable mass.

She could see it. It was odd, and it changed colour, she was sure it did. White, then yellow, red then green, then purple, it was kind of mesmeric.

"Hey!" Some one was clicking their fingers by her ear. John looked at her.

"It doesn't bear watching for too long. I noticed that earlier. It may be its luminant frequency, I don't know, but, we'll have to watch out for that as we get closer, can't lose our heads flying by that thing!"

"We could close the blast shields, and just use colour filtered monitors?" She suggested.

"Yes, let's do that."

John agreed, but as she made no move to the controls, he did it for her.

"Hey, you not going spacey on me are you?"

John asked, looking in mock concern, at her vacant stare.

"No, no I'm alright. By the Founders, I'd swear that thing was alive!"

"Hah! You can't have a living star!" He exclaimed.

John smiled, she was back. You saw it sometimes, people, even experienced Starmen would lose their heads over a beautiful or spectacular sight and would be, for want of a better word away with the faeries, perhaps for minutes, sometimes for hours.

The screens were down, the view outside was now monochrome, and less, hypnotic.

"Well, hyperdrive won't work, we'll have to use maneuever drive to get to the right distance for the standard mapping and analysis. It could take some time."

"How long?" John asked.

"Well, maybe five days, we'll have to accelerate and then decelerate, try and find an acceptable orbital approach, we do not want to get to near until we have a run down of its radioactive spectrum."

She paused.

The IRS's ships were the best in the Empire, they had to be, but, their shielding was only so good. The wrong emissions could, seriously damage or cripple the ship.

"We'll run some tests, long range, as soon as possible maybe, in a day or two. If there's dangerous emissions, we'll want to know before they are wreaking havoc, not during."

She looked at John.

"We still have some of the remote survey packages don't we? They can operate up to point one parsec's away?"

"Yes, I can boost the range, on one of them at least, by raising his power output. It'll reduce it's life span, but, if needed we can check it out more remotely before committing to an approach."

John looked thoughtful. This was a clear, sensible plan. The rest of the crew would probably agree, but the Science Officer might have puppies, if he didn't get his 'close up' of the anomaly. Of course the Flight Crew, had the last word.

Chapter Sixteen - Count your Blessings

Count Bruno Orvull sat on his high backed carved oaken throne, he was not strictly entitled to one, but it had been in his family for centuries and he, very much liked tradition.

He had just had his lunch, and his Butler a tall greying, balding man, called Karles, slim and birdlike, in manner, was clearing away.

He loved the folding table, made of beautiful rosewood, that a town carpenter had made especially for him, some years ago, now. So informal, so handy, much better than sitting at his great long table, alone.

He'd considered eating with the staff, but well, that just wasn't done.

He'd considered eating out. He could certainly afford to do it, but, well, to harness the horses, pull out the carriage, go into town, just for the mediocre fair of the best Inn's in town, well, that was far too much trouble.

He wasn't old, he'd just turned forty. He was not particularly fit or tall, a medium specimen of old aristocracy. His hair, dark brown and coiffed in a fashion that was fashionable back when he was a student at Verdanes.

Oh! He had had such dreams in his youth! Philosophy, astronomy, medicine and meta physics, these subjects were his first love! Stretching the bounds of possibility, pushing back the unknown, doing really cool stuff, and doing it with style.

Magick, of course too. Perhaps, if he had started later, he could have stuck to Hunbogi's course of mail order magick. He could have been a Mage. Well, wrong time, wrong moment, he had made up for it later with his own studies.....

Maybe.

Well, the great Dragon Strikes had put paid to all his formal studies. All his relatives gone, gone in one day, and they hadn't all been in one place.

Navorny and the Castle, was undamaged. It had not been a target. His relatives, always keen to be seen in all the right places, were at them, just at exactly the wrong times.

The Chamberlain of Castle Navorny, dusty unused place that it was, little more than a post office box for correspondence, had written to him to recall him from University, and also let him know, that, as the last man standing, he was now the Count.

Filled with sadness, he had returned to the ancestral pile, pulled the dust sheets off the great chambers, unveiling furniture that had not seen the light of day, in some cases, for many years.

He settled in.

He was also, now, rich.

Considerable assets of his family had been lost, in the chaos and destruction around the continent, but considerable assets remained.

He developed his own projects, his own research's built his own laboratory, and refurbished the Castle's library, extending it, into neighbouring chambers.

He'd bought up books across the remains of the civilized north, and had continued his studies.

For awhile, a short while, as previously mentioned, he had followed Hunbogi's Mail Order course, in magick.

It had worked for him, but it was too basic, so minor, so trivial, so insignificant. He wanted bigger things. Better things. Moving Things.

Personally, well, he had not married, not being the marrying kind, as his father might have said, had he not be scorched to a crisp by Dragon's fire, and squashed by falling masonry.

Heaven's knew he was not handsome, but as a rich single aristocrat in a stable land, he was highly eligible.

Many beauties had vied for his attention and mostly they gave up. Sometimes, their lines of finance had been cut. Sometimes, their country of origin had collapsed. Sometimes, they were cast adrift by coup, or other civil unrest. Some, even found better options elsewhere.

Now, this.

Not only was a certain rare and wonderful substance about to be placed in his very hands, for but a purse or two of gold, but also, a Royal Princess, of Graeffenland, no less, and trained in the darkest arts of all, necromancy, was in his town, and accompanying his much anticipated couriers.

Fortune was smiling upon him again. He would have to win her hand, and her knowledge.

Chapter Seventeen – Hitting the Books

"Bring me a light, um, I'm sorry, what's your name?"

Lyrinsos stood, between the great metal gates, the dark wrought iron, its intricate framework resting back against the walls, and ahead of him, stretched great bookshelves, full of books, tomes, and scrolls, all containing examples of every ineffable story, legend and magickal art, known, unknown, unknowable, and raved madly, by every candle lit wordsmith of doom.

He gazed at the shadowy rows, where the hell was he going to start? He looked down at the banana skin, its yellowy brownieness innocently mocking him, but a few feet away now.

What, he thought, did our yellow fruit munching friend read?

A light appeared. It was bright blue and attached to a magnifying glass, small and square.

He looked at it. What a good idea! He held it out before him, pointing the light at the ground before him, near the banana skin.

"My names Mary Lin," she said.

"You did ask, Mister......?" She paused expectantly, gazing at the back of his blue, fish scaled head.

"Oh, Lyrinsos, just Lyrinsos." He said.

He could see scuff marks, on the floor, he carefully followed the trail....

Yes, and a trail it was, it led, well, nowhere, but it met the wall, rather the book cases, quite a few times first.

So he thought. Someone portalled in, somehow. This individual examined the books, and portalled out again when done. No way to know if anything is missing, but what clues are there?

He gazed carefully at the shelves. Yes, someone had climbed.

The titles on the books squirmed, and grinned at him. He was sure they didn't really, it was just his imagination, wasn't it?

There he thought, the spine of a particular book glistened. He reached up, he could just get it, and pulled it out.

"Look if you need steps just whistle." Mary Lin said, behind him.

"Okay."

He gazed at the book.

"The Poems of ID, by Ralph the Unsteady. Hmm."

He looked at the pages, quickly, just looking for sticky prints.

Two pages were stuck together, he couldn't believe....
He stopped that thought right there. Let's just see what this is first.

The pages prized apart, fairly easily. This, he thought has been recently, well, pawed.

It was a short story.

Apparently at the centre of all reality, a great amorphous, protoplasmic blob existed, writhing its tendrils, and wobbling its reddy brown meaty globes, in time to strange musical nose flutes, played by gigantic squamous, toadlike kitten creatures, who apparently, danced madly around it, in playful kitteny revelry.

He staggered. The image in his mind was just too awful. He pulled himself together. How could such silly words have an effect on him like that?

He read on, cutting through the invocations, the mad gibberish, trying to find the kernels of information amidst the rambling pleas to be eaten first, and not reserved for second serving.

There it was, when the Devourer shall arise, the great Zaza Boggoff, would be free to manifest, at the centre of the multiverse, all reality would be reabsorbed through the Devourer into Zaza Boggoff, and the circle of creation and destruction would be complete.

Zaza Boggoff, was the beginning, the main course, and the dessert, all came from him, and all would return to his tentacular noodliness.

The Devourer! By the gods, the Devourer had come and surely Zaza Boggoff would follow, concluding the cycles of eternity, in one warm squelchy mess.

He whimpered.

He sat on the floor, trying to compose himself. Why bother he thought? We're doomed. The old mad poet and story teller knew what was on the cards, what was fated. There was no escape.

He stood up again, and pushed the book back. What else had been disturbed, other than my mind, he thought, staring and shining the blue light, up and down the rows.

One book stood out, by its absence. Someone had been in a hurry, and had left, part of it there. It was a fly leaf. He pulled it down.

It read "The Multiverse, Quantum Physics and Atheism, by Derrick Raffle Smyth Bones, of the University of" the last bit was torn away.

Multiverse? Quantum Physics, Atheism, clearly the writings of a loon, but Libraria, wherever she was, must have a system, so there must have been something important in that book. He placed the shred of paper in his bag.

The bag was conveniently mounted on the back of an uncomplaining attack alligator. Cracker, gazed up at him, tiredly, but without complaining. He'd walked a long way for an alligator, but did not mind, he served his god too.

Chapter Eighteen - In the Study.

The light glowed. It was tiny, then brightened orange, orange then yellow. It was square, well not exactly square, closer up it was elongated, elongated in the vertical.

A vertical oblong yellow light, and then it dimmed, as something drew across it, filtering it, dampening it down.

Beyond the light and yet within it, a hand. A pale hand not young, old and yet not old, released the fabric it had drawn across the window.

The stone, narrow arched window, its glass, old, lumpen thick, designed to hold back the elements, and hold in the thin air. The stone a honey red colour, at least on the inner side.

The tower room, curving stone steps, leading down, and curving stone steps leading up, wide in diameter, dominated by a table, a table on which, and above which, hovered a spectral blue image, sounds shushing from it.

"Well, let's see what strangeness is happening."

A mellow male voice thought out loud.

The first hand was joined by a second, they touched the table, then gesticulated, the image splintered, colourful, multilayered, glowing dots, a spider web in three dimensions, he focused in on one particular pulsing dot.

"What this then?"

He wondered.

The image grew, grew and expanded. A braying noise, and a chamber, a Wizards workroom.

The watching presence, saw a man, rubbing his cheek, whilst manipulating dials, buttons, knobs and levers.

The watching presence muttered.

"I must think of a word for these remarkable, strange people. Hmm."

One hand scratched a long white bearded chin.

"Yes. I know. I shall call them, Philosophical Alchemical Mechanicians. Yes, PAM. That will do."

The watching presence resumed watching PAM. PAM appeared as a middle aged bald man wearing an ill fitting fancy suit. He looked like he was going to a theatre.

He worked frantically.

The watching presence waved a hand, the sound went up, a few notches.

"Dear, oh dear, oh dear! I've got to stop this! It will be the end of all life as we know it!"

PAM wrung his hand, and looked like he wanted to go both right, left, forward and back, simultaneously.

"What to do? Oh what to do? Every time I try to lock the coordinates they wobble in and out again!"

The watching presence, stroked his beard and prepared to withdraw from observation.

"It's metaphysical! It's a multidimensional problem, facing the whole of reality! The whole metacosmos, all the multiverse!"

The watching presence paused, PAM knew of the multiverse. This could be interesting.

"How? How to adjust for inter meta cosmic wave fluctuations?"

PAM seemed to be banging his fist on his forehead.

"Think! Think! Oh, for an enlightened scientific peer group!"

The watching presence closed the image, placing a mini version of it, in mid air to one side, he set it to 'record' and turned his attention elsewhere.

"So, what are our foolish gods up to?"

Muttered the white bearded Arch Mage.

He gesticulated and another dot in his matrix blossomed into a huge image, with surround sound, and bright colour.

It was a palace, under water, in well, the Upper World, the World Above.

In the image, there seemed to be, a concert going on.

The Lord of Oceans, resplendent with his golden crown, and ceremonial trident, reclined upon and slightly within a great floating, upholstered half shell.

Beautiful mermaid attendants stood at hand, viands and delicacies upon their trays, some had legs, some fishy tails, It didn't seem to matter in the strange watery environment.

Beside him and seated slightly lower on a similar shell, was a nine foot tall, bemuscled, bearded, and fur clad giant.

The giant, who had a great hammer across his lap, looked uncomfortable.

"So, how is it I can breathe here?"

Adan asked again.

"Don't worry! The Upper World is the World of the mind! It's intellectual water, spiritual water, water of the soul!"

Kershaggulumphie, Lord of Oceans smiled indulgently. He was happy. His religion had never been so popular, his star was rising.

Adan, had sat through two and a bit hours of hymns, ballads and shanties.

The sea was the primary theme, in all these tunes and songs.

The Lord of Oceans seemed happy though.

Adan forced a smile as he looked at his host.

His host beamed.

The symphony concluded. Adan watched, confused, then clapped, sort of, in an under intellectual or philosophical water, kind of way.

"Good! Good!" Said the Lord of Oceans.

"Now it is time, you've decided?"

Adan nodded, grimly. He had already been away from the mental battle too long. Best to get this over with.

"I'm ready."

"Hold out your hand, and brace yourself."

Kershaggulumphie reached out his hand, a multi coloured ball of divine energy forming within it.

Adan stretched out his hand.

The energies leapt across, and surged through him.

He felt different and yet the same.

The great hammer beside him, now purred, and it seemed to smirk.

Adan felt the watching presence.

The Arch Mage his gaze and attention fixed on proceedings, suddenly felt a mind reaching for his.

He snapped off the connection.

So, that's a bit more serious. A god that can sense him. A breeze briefly rustled the tower room.

He stood stock still, concentrating furiously.

He relaxed, the probe was blocked, his enchantments still held, but it was a surprise. No one had been able to sense his magick for centuries! No only could someone, but now, this god could potentially track him down, and who knows what else.

Something nagged at the back of his mind.

"I know that hammer!" He exclaimed.

Chapter Nineteen – Worked Hard, Played Hard, Morning After.

Nirnadel sat on the foot plate at the back of her mother's wagon. The early morning air helped. The crisp sharp sweet smell of the dew on chilled mountain air soothed her throbbing head.

She never usually drank so much, she often ate that much, she never danced that much, all in all, it had all been a bit much.

What did her mother say?

Oh yes, test your limits, don't exceed them.

She stuck her tongue out. It was better dressed than she was. She waggled it, and then put it away. She found her water bottle, and poured more cool fluid, into the unknown gravelly desert of her throat. She'd sung too much too. She'd probably sung herself hoarse. She couldn't remember, or hoped she couldn't remember, if those weren't just dreams, she was imagining, she might have to keep her head down for a little bit.

Assuming anyone else could remember. Fudge, strolling nonchalantly in from the field beyond, smiled in doggy fashion at her huddled form. He sat down and gazed up at her.

"Oh you remember everything don't you!" She sighed. She'd never be able to live it down, if Fudge could talk. Luckily, bar to a few of the Gifted (those who were of a particularly natural magical disposition) Faerie Dogs didn't talk much. They did grin a lot though.

She reached back inside the wagon, found a small tin, which she opened, and she withdrew several strips of spiced dried meat. These she offered, one at a time to Fudge, saying:

"You saw nothing, you heard nothing, you remember nothing, and stop grinning!"

Fudge wolfed down the offered titbits. The fine art of circumstantial blackmail was worth the time it took to master, he thought, chewing thoughtfully. He discreetly turned and sat looking away. Sure he wasn't being observed he grinned again, broadly between chews.

"Oh you!"

Nirnadel exclaimed, jumping down off the wagon, and roughly grapple fussing the bulky old faerie dog.

She got up and stretched. She wobbled a bit, could she still be drunk? She didn't know for sure, but suspected that such might be a possibility.

The sky was clear, and the sunshine shadows, throwing the distorted images of the wagons, ragged, jagged grey black streaks, and blobs upon the grass, before her, as she walked across the camp.

In the distance the Castle straddled the low peaks of the mountain spur. It glinted and glimmered in the early Sun. It looked old, and she could see some air of enchantment about it, a faint, but perceptible heat haze, just within and just beyond, the field of her vision.

Her ears picked up the sound of wheels, crunching on the rough dirt road, the jingle of harness, and it was quickly getting louder. She gazed in its direction, towards, and, at the road, as horses and then carriage appeared, the liveried coachmen, who sat upon the seats at the front, looked around at the fairground, and then back towards the open town gates.

Their coach, of course, being a company vehicle, had permission, by previous arrangement, to enter the town proper, and with no pause, nor checks, nor any slowing of pace, rolled straight through the open town gates, and presumably, into the town square.

Nirnadel smiled. Civilization! After all the chaos and horror, of recent years, the simplest things gave her pleasure. She had to see the town proper, hopefully, before market day, she'd heard the farmers market would be in two days, and then the fairground would really fill, as folk from far and wide, travelled in to buy and sell, their wares.

She wanted to see the town before it got really busy, and before she had to join in the trade with the other fair goers. She wasn't sure what Lyra wanted her to do, she hoped it wasn't fortune telling, though if any one wanted to talk to dead relatives, and would bring their remains, well, she could raise the dead all day long, and zombies did remember, fairly well, especially relatives.

Lyra, seemed dead set against the use of Necromancy, or indeed, actual real magick of any sort. At least, not as far as trading, or entertainment was concerned. Oh well, she was sure they would tell her later what they wanted her to do.

Anything, legal, she had said, to them, which received a puzzled look from Lyra, who had stared at her, and said.

"What, their laws, or, ours?"

Rhian had laughed, and just smiled at her.

Curiosity rose within her, and she strolled, with a backward glance or two, straight for the town gates. It did not take long, just a few minutes walking and she was there, and through. The gates were unguarded, and let onto a long cobbled street, quite wide, more like an avenue.

The gates she noticed, may not be manned, but they were new, but a year or two old, and in fine repair, great bands of steel reinforced the thick oaken beams, which one upon another formed the panels of the doors, they were further laced with huge steel rivets.

It was a serious set of doors, for troubled times.

The town beyond the gates, was a different matter entirely, unchanged it was a glimpse, a snapshot of the world, before Dragonstrikes, before anarchy and brigandage, and before the threat of annihilation over shadowed all.

It was Nirnadel thought, quite wonderful. It was clean too, very little debris, or waste upon the streets, drains, not new, quite old, possibly as old as the town itself, were very much in evidence. It was, in every way superior to the little she had ever seen of Carseport.

She slowly strolled along the cobbled avenue, the buildings, white washed, wood and stone, three or four stories, over hanging the alleys, sometimes the streets. There were many of these, leading off from the main thoroughfare.

She expected the stink of the city, but the first thing she smelt was bread, nearby there must be a Bakers. She paused and looked, and yes, there was, the Bakers, just on a corner, mostly in fact in the alley, just a corner of the terraced building on the main avenue.

Mmm, she made a mental note, to call in there at some point, and see what wonders might exist within. Bread certainly, buns most likely, and, what pies might follow?

She smiled, since leaving her fathers Palace, she'd made every endeavour to become a connoisseur of food, and pie was not actually down as a major food group, as far as the People of the Wagons, were concerned, they lived off the land, vegetables and stews, being popular, hunted game, quite frequently, when it was possible, no pastries, and risen bread, not really their speciality.

They did make unleavened breads, and creations in dried wheat paste, and these were good.

Her attention, snapped back to the road, a cart had, rather quickly come up, and she had to step fast to get out of the way. It was a small one horse farmers cart, making a delivery, and she stared after it, and a handful of great metal milk urns, were quite visible, secured on the back.

Empties she guessed, being taken back to the cowsheds, some miles distant, she supposed.

A few more people were around and about, they generally seemed to be shop folk, tradesmen, and others whose errands took them abroad in the early morning.

There were many shops along this avenue, she realised mostly food related. Butchers, Fishmongers, Grocers, and then as she stepped out into the town square, Jewellers, Tailors, Cobblers, Cabinet Makers, Ironmongers, even a bespoke armourer.

She stared. Paper, there was a Paper and Ink Maker, right next to a Scribe, and just across from a Solicitors office, and what could be a Moneylender, yes, she thought it was.

Paper, of a proper good quality, and some decent ink, was high on her wish list. She was impressed. She took a breath, she had brought no money with her, so she could really buy nothing now, and she contented herself to window shopping.

Further around there was quite a splendid looking building, older still than the town, an old semi fortified coach house, it still had its original defensive walls, though they had clearly not been maintained at all, for some time.

The actual Inn itself, however, was another story. It looked as though no expense had been spared in making it a top quality establishment, finely glazed windows, new paintwork, fresh beams, new thatch.

She paused, thatch was a surprise, she noted the rest of the buildings used slate for their roofs, another expense.

"Hello!" A mans voice greeted her.

She had spent so much time staring at the buildings she actually hadn't noticed the man approach.

He was a young man, muscled, wearing a thick green felt hat, of a design she hadn't seen before, thick khaki jacket, khaki trews, woollen, quite heavy duty, and solid looking boots.

He smiled, and idly flicked a strand of blonde hair, away from his eyes.

"You look lost! Are you new here?"

"Yes, but not lost, just looking around!"

She smiled nervously, taking a step back.

"Oh, it's alright, I'm a visitor here, myself, but, I've been here a few times, it's quiet something."

He continued, still smiling.

"Aren't you over dressed?" She replied.

"Yes, yes, but I've come straight from the mountains!"

He pointed away, south and a little east, or west.

Yes, he pointed south west.

"Oh, what brings you down from the mountains?"

"Well, I can't really say, a bit hush hush, scouting, you know." He continued.

His expression went from slight boyish embarrassment, to self conscious amusement.

"Well, I'm thinking of getting some breakfast in the Inn, will you join, Miss?"

"Oh, I'm Nirnadel!" She said, failing to think of a false name, or much other than his deep brown eyes.

"I'm Erik Hauengris, well, come on!" He said, half turning towards the fancy Inn.

"Oh! I have no money!" She exclaimed, and now she felt embarrassed.

"I have money at home, but not on me!" She quickly followed up.

"That's alright! I'll get it, naturally..." He continued.

Feeling slightly astonished, hesitant, and a bit nervous, she followed him in the Inn.

They had breakfast..........

Chapter Twenty: Fog, Fog Everywhere.

Berythus Naechos sat miserably in the dark. It had been hours since his lantern had gone out. His travelling companion just sat there, marked by the occasional bright glow from the end of the tube of paper, and 'herbs' that he appeared to be sucking on.

While the light had lasted, he'd watched him roll it up, mixing tobacco from one pouch, with greenish brown stuff, from another packet. These all ended up in what on curious enquiry, he had called a 'cigarette paper.'

He then lit it with a match, and sat contentedly smoking it.

The smell reminded Berythus of certain temples, and certain rites. He had sighed. This would be a long night.

Jaeson sat and smoked. For a dream, it was all amazingly realistic, so realistic, he coughed, that he actually felt every detail of the hard cold rock he was sitting on.

Why, he thought, can't I dream of somewhere nice to be? All quarries, slimy caves, and nasty alleyways. Even, my office is better than this, he pondered, leaning back, and letting his mind wander, the herbs playfully tweaking his neurons, and massaging his nerve endings.

His mind drifted. He knew he shouldn't but he started falling asleep.

Hah! Who dreams of falling asleep?

Apparently, I do, he thought. Minutes passed, the lantern had gone out, and he awoke, falling off his leather chair.

It was dark. A soft luminescence came through the windows.

"Oh, you're awake."

The little priest said from the darkness.

Light flooded the darkness, exposing a smallish, tatty office.

"Oh!"

Exclaimed the priest, as, recognising where they were, Jaeson had switched on the electric table lamp.

"Well, well."

He had got up, and now steadying himself, on his very own writing desk, he gazed around.

"Home, sweet home." He continued.

It certainly looked like his office, at least superficially. It must be his office. He turned, pulled a curtain aside, it was cheap, drab, chocolate brown, and he looked out, into the street beyond.

It sure looked like Boston, but, in the fog, foggy and dim, so very dim streetlights.

Somehow, I'm back, but, so is the priest. So, this must still be some kind of dream.

He checked his gun, not fully loaded. He took a box of shells the detail was perfect, from his bottom desk drawer, and reloaded.

For good luck, he put handfuls of shells in his jacket pockets. Who knew when he would have the chance again?

He stopped. Why was he worrying, this was just a dream. Wasn't it?

Berythus, was just staring at him.

He resembled a scolded dog, looking at reproachfully at a mean master.

"Well, I'm 'home,' if home this turns out to be, too bad you're still stuck here."

He observed, showing no emotion.

"Yes, I need to get back. I have to get to the conclave of High Priests. They need the information I have."

He offered staring bleakly at a tall dark varnished wooden filing cabinet.

"It really is of the utmost urgency." He added.

"Why not just go to sleep, and wake up home?"

As Jaeson spoke he allowed himself a smile. He realised, he had cigarette ash down his front, and took a few moments to brush it away, with his hands.

"That's what I did." He added.

"Yes. You know, I thought this was about me. But you know, I think you could be the key to this, somehow. Yes, somehow, you are a focus for a break, or a bridge, some kind of link between worlds."

Berythus was taking a breath, to continue, but a sudden knock sounded at the door.

"Wow. Customers, at this hour."

Jaeson wondered just what hour it was, his watch seemed to think it was ten passed three. It was possible.

"Come in." He tried.

Someone tried the door, but it was locked. Of course it was. He stepped over to the door, its top glass frame emblazoned with his name, and found the keys in his pocket.

He opened the door. Beyond was a scruffy young man, flat cap wedged firmly, his ears protruding sideways like cup handles.

"Oh Willy. What brings you here at this hour?" He asked.

"I've been trying your office all day, how'd you get in here without me seeing? Anyway, you told me to look out for that posh fella, and I've seen him, down, by the docks. Near one of them fancy boats."

"What, a yacht?"

"Maybe. That could be it. Lots of odd sorts with him too. Swear they gave me the creeps, and they smelt too."

"What was the boat, ahem, yacht, called? Did you see?"

"Yeah, Emerald, just that I think, unless the rest, was covered, or somethin'"

"Emerald, great, here's the usual for your troubles."

He'd been fishing in his wallet, and he pulled forth, a twenty dollar bill. He felt generous.

"Ah, thanks!" Said the youth.

He nodded to both of them, and headed back out the door.

"You pay, for informers, for spies?" Berythus seemed surprised.

"Yes, it's my job." Jaeson smiled.

"Oh. Should have asked him to keep his eyes open for anything unusual." Added Berythus.

"What in Boston? Ha! I'm not made of money. Come on, let's go see the harbour."

The Harbour, was just where he'd left it. Every so often, he would go down there, as a part of a case, or just for information. It was a crossroads, a junction, a nexus, not always, but often, useful things could be found out there.

He liked boats too.

In the dark, they had walked, and it had been a little way, every moment half expecting, to find themselves somewhere else altogether, carried away by the mists.

The fog had been their constant companion, its clammy folds enveloping everyone and everything.

Still they had got there. They had arrived, and cautiously, carefully, watching their footing on the wet paving, they had crept along the harbour side.

It was unspoken, it was not discussed, but it was a given. They did not want to be seen, or heard, by anyone.

One boat seemed to have lights, and activity. As they approached, details became clearer. It was a sailing yacht, of good size, and its deck was busy, boxes being loaded, people talking. They went closer.

"Look, wait here, whilst I get a better look."

If it was the man he was searching for, what was he up to? Smuggling? That didn't seem to make sense. Doing a moonlight flit, maybe, but that didn't seem to fit either.

Chapter Twenty One - Flying Blind.

Albaer Frederics sat at the Science computer. He had been running scans and performing data analysis on the approaching anomaly for about a day now. Nothing seemed to add up.

They were still that bit too far away to launch a remote sensing package, usually used to orbit objects of interest, unusual planets, asteroids, stars, or even moons.

He was working with their long range scans, and if he didn't know better, he would believe some damage had befallen the instruments.

He ran countless, thorough, diagnostic, tests. Everything checked out. He scratched his head. Unlike the others, he maintained a short crew cut hair style. Like the others, he didn't bother with clothing, it wasn't needed. He bent over the monitors, set out in an array before him, comparing, contrasting, and assessing, their displayed data.

It was illogical, it defied accepted astrophysics, and celestial chemistry. The figures, on the one hand indicated a stellar mass, a star. On the other, they indicated at best a debris cloud, of small particulates, in yet another way, the data resembled a planet, with gyrating moons.

So many moons. How they gyrated, it was like a dance. They sped up, they slowed down, they swapped places, they looped around each other, sometimes, sometimes they eclipsed each other, almost seemed to touch each other, and then they would spin away again.

The moons, they should just be round, or ovoid, but, even at this range they, were odd. Odd lumpy shapes, not like asteroids are lumpy, almost crystalline, almost organic, shapes, with, even at this range, a discernible plasticity of form, a variability, and irregularity of disportment that shouldn't be, in any orbiting moon.

He wondered if they could be artificial, or even alien artefacts of some sort. Rumours and tales used to tell of huge superstructures, built by ancient races, stellar constructs to harness power, or provide city space, or transport.

None had ever been found. Perhaps he thought, this might be the remains of some such construct.

Yet the data, so much of the data did not gell, did not add up. It was almost as though it was a light show, a hologram projected into space. A light show alone, nothing real behind it.

Matter had a signature, and this signature was largely absent. Light and gravity, certain radiations, were there, but if the instruments were to be believed, no actual matter was present.

He sighed. This was probably the break through of the century, may be the millennium. Maybe it would be ranked as one of the greatest ever scientific discoveries.

He couldn't understand what he was seeing.

Idly, he looked at the monitor. The radiowaves were in quite an interesting pattern, sort of recurring, but variable. He carefully, played back a section through the audio speakers.

The hairs on the back of his neck stood up. It was music! Not just accidental white noise variations, but beautiful, very beautiful pipe music. He sat entranced, and indeed, began to hum along.

A smile spread across his face, his imagination soared, and he saw the birth and death of stars, of matter, of energy, all gone, all begun, all exploding, and imploding, in a dizzying fantastical pavane, a dance in eternity, on eternity, outside of eternity, after, and before eternity.

Its beauty was so breath taking he forgot to breathe. His mind flew off, whirling and swirling, in and out, far and near, and joined forever the beautiful dance, as he sang in time with the music.

The Medical Officer found him, sat before his equipment, a beatific smile upon his face, a joy beyond all words, a love beyond human comprehension. He was at peace, or at chaos, either way, he was gone.

Karen Straker carefully assessed the body. No physical trauma, no biological contaminants, no trace, nor apparent reason for death. She sighed. She carefully got him into a body bag, and with John, the Navigator, carefully carried him to the zero gravity access well. John going first, they carried, pushed, and pulled, his wrapped form, down and then into the modest cargo hold.

Once therein, they found a small storage frame, unfolded its black mesh work, placed the body within it, strapped it down, and locked it onto a spare space on the bulk head.

John said a small prayer. Prayers were still fashionable, on many planets, and surprisingly, a large number of starship crewmen perhaps due to the inherent danger of their jobs, followed one or more traditions.

There were so many traditions.

Pilot Captain Therese Jameson looked at John, he was clearly disturbed.

"How did he die?" She asked.

"Causes unknown, not a mark, not a sign or clue, just a smile. Such a weird smile, like he'd just won a jackpot, you know? Completely happy. So happy. Gives me the creeps."

John look down at the avionics console.

"Well, the sensors, are still running, and they are recording data, but we have lost our specialist. Can we continue the mission?"

She looked down, at the display, still some distance from the anomaly, and picking up a little gravitic turbulence, but not too much.

"Well, you are the Captain." John said.

"Yes, I am, but this should go to a vote. Too many unknowns. We could probably justify taking our current datasets back for further analysis, before, anyone goes any closer."

She rubbed her eyes.

"We won't get our bonus, and we face a penalty for the loss of a crewmate." John looked grim.

"Yeah, we'll lose on this mission, if we go back without having completed our mission objectives."

Sometimes she hated the Empire.

Everything was run to the beat of the Credit drum. How was the Empire ever built? She was sure Accounting Androids did not build Empires. Still there it was, the Imperial Reconnaissance Service, was run by the numbers.

They would gather in the Galley, and vote.

Chapter Twenty Two – One Mans Mountain.

Adan stared down into the Middle land. Whatever, whoever, had been spying on him, had shut the door on him. He thought he knew where, but when he tried to look, nothing, not a trace.

Whoever, or whatever, was well hidden. He had felt, yes, he had felt like a Mage, he wasn't sure though, it was strange.

He looked around.

"Are you alright?"

Kershaggulumphie, the Lord of Oceans, fishy tailed master of the sea, top god in the world, at the moment, at any rate, looked at him closely, his cobalt blue eyes, narrowed.

Adan turned.

"Why?" He asked quietly.

"You're sparking!"

The Lord of Oceans leant back as a small blue spark shot passed him.

"I am. Oh! I am!"

Adan, surprised, realised, that, yes, he was running a charge, his fingers crackled. The Hammer, was still, purring.

"Is this normal?" He asked, trying to stay calm.

"Well, we're all different! So, for you, probably. Also, you are probably annoyed, by whatever, you sensed going on below."

The Lord of Oceans, smiled, and leaned forward. He continued.

"You know, you need a USP. I think, yes, I think I know what it should be."

"I need a what now?"

Adan sat back down. He needed to get back to the world, well, the other world, the middle world, where, he would test this new strength against the enemy, against the Devourer.

"I will be instructing my Priests, to spread the word, about you. You need worshippers now, not many perhaps, but some, and my people, will see you established. We're partners now."

The Lord of Oceans seemed pleased, happy even.

"Okay, but what is a USP?"

Adan wondered if his feelings were showing, perhaps, a thundercloud?

Reality seemed to follow thought.

"Oh don't worry! Don't sit under a cloud! USP, unique selling point, who you are, as a god, what you stand for, what you don't stand for, you know, your identity. You see."

The Lord of Oceans smiled.

"Leave it to me, I'll sort it out with my High Priests, and I'll let you know. Something weather based, I should think."

Adan looked at him.

"You know I just want to kill that creature, after that, well, I have no plans."

"Don't worry about that either! Trust me if you can get rid of that creature, that Devourer, no one will be more pleased than I, and afterwards, it's you and me. This world will be ours, and we can make of it whatever we want."

Kershaggulumphie held out his hand, and a mermaid brought up a conch shell, frothing with some kind of beverage.

"You know this can be a good life, and once you're done, with the Middle land, you'll have your own Palace, whatever you want, and well, take it from me, it can be quite cushy."

The Lord of Oceans drank deeply.

"You should try the beer, it's good."

"Thank you, no. I must get back. I must see things through, sooner rather than later. Later we can catch up."

With those words, Adan stood, looking for the way back to his mountain roost, he realised, the way back was wherever he chose. The portal, opening out onto his mountain ledge, appeared before him, and he stepped through, closing the portal behind him.

That, he thought, was easy.

A couple of Dragons, Lamluca, Eristyx, and Hookooli were perched, or wrapped, in various positions, awaiting his return.

Lamluca greeted him.

"It hasn't stirred. The beast remains in hiding. Even though, you have left it be, it has stayed with its head down."

Lamluca's thoughts entered Adan's brain, well, his philosophical brain, for now he was a god, he had forsaken the flesh of man, for a form of energy. It seemed in many respects the same, except it wasn't. He hadn't had all the details explained to him, nor would he truly have cared, if they had been, he was determined.

He gazed across from the mountains, across the miles, the vast wildernesses that had replaced the lands of man, overrun by the servants of the shadowy Devourer, to the citadel and the ziggurat.

Except, there was a movement, something out of place, something unusual. The river, the great wide estuary, winding it's way through the continent, western seaboard, deep into the interior, gradually shrinking, until it and its tributaries, were just little intermittent streams and springs.

It was a ship. A fine ship, a ship with a Triton flag, three decks, fore castle, and aft castle, hundreds of men, ready for a fight. He could feel their excitement, their adrenalin, these were serious men, and there it was, a familiar mind.

After all, these years! His comrade, in study, in misadventure, in bar enterprise, aboard a ship, heading into the worst country imaginable.

He smiled, of course Garim would be around, somewhere. He would have to keep an eye on him, and yet, what in the worlds was he doing? He must know he was heading into danger?

Adan scanned the route ahead of the ship, actually, it was clear of anything significant. Well, as far as he could see, and he felt most uncertain about that now, his mind going back, such a short time before, when that strange Mage, had spied upon them.

He needed to plan. Long range mental wrestling matches, may have helped in the past, or they may not have, he could not decide. He wondered if he had been played, had he fallen into a trap? Had he been snookered, his own brute force turned against him? Or had he helped restrain, what would otherwise have been a steamroller, crushing all before it, flattening all mortal resistance.

Certainly the creature had retreated, fortified, driven back by the Dragons, and his will.

The Hammer purred contentedly, its runes glowing, far more than they had ever glowed before.

Somehow it was happy. It seemed to know what was coming and it was pleased. It wanted battle, or was it battle it wanted? He could feel it wanted something, and something more than just to be at the side of a god, it had a purpose.

He could feel it. It had a purpose, a goal, and so far, he was progressing its plans.

He hoped they were good plans.

As he sat thinking he realised, he didn't know what to do. He needed advice. He had hoped that the Lord of Oceans might have had some ideas, but it seemed contrary wise. The Lord of Oceans had looked at him, as though he had the key, the solution.

He looked down at the Hammer. The key. The key to what?

All those years ago, Heilynn had told him the Hammer was a tool, he hadn't said what sort of tool. Adan as he sat there, put his chin upon his fist. He needed to find out. He needed to find out before he did anything else.

Chapter Twenty Three - In Flagrante Libraria.

Lyrinsos, sat on the floor, the cold, stone floor, his head in his hands. It was all too much. There were too many books, and, quite likely, the ones he needed were missing. He rocked gently.

He didn't regard himself as being weak willed, or particularly soppy, or even particularly prone to bouts of sentimentality. However, the thought of returning, flanked by his attack alligators, a great honour, apparently, empty handed, gave him the willies.

He just didn't know what to do. Behind, and safely beyond the alligators, lurked, waited or sagged, the librarian Mary Lin, her cardigan now firmly buttoned up.

She had given in to the inevitable, clearly Lyrinsos was vulnerable, but in his weakened state, the slightest, least hint of horror, or anything unspeakable, might throw him over the edge.

She hadn't risked removing the cardigan, also, it was cold. Not the cold of stone floors, or winter drafts, more the soul sucking cold, of a meat locker in an abattoir.

A condemned meat locker, full of brains hungry zombies, who have only dined out in {censored} for the past year. A desperate place indeed.

She looked around. Well, the forbidden section did not look that bad to her. He was acting all weird, fancy going to pieces after reading barely a page of one of the minor works? What was wrong with the man?

She thought about that last word carefully. That would be the answer there. She looked at the stacks of books, shelf after shelf, bookcase after bookcase. She was undaunted!

"Look." She began.

"I can help you search, what are you looking for? If you tell me, I can try and find, something useful, or at least make a start."

She looked down, she wasn't sure if he had even heard her.

He sat and rocked. Sometimes he let out a low moan.

She shook her head, what had he been looking at? Oh yes, anything banana stained, or near the trail of the banana devotee.

She'd seen bananas before, and idly, wondered what they might actually taste like. They weren't a fruit that actually appealed to her, although, come to think of it, she'd never seen one in a green grocers, in the Middleland.

She wondered if the erstwhile banana eater was from some other world. They had had this problem before, people would wander in, completely lost, and you would find they were from some other place altogether, and hopelessly lost.

Before the troubles below (note, not the Below, but the Middle Land, she thought of every where not above as below), Libraria's temple had maintained a small colony of the lost and found, people who had wandered in, and needed to be filed somewhere.

It was on a nice sunny island, if she remembered correctly.

She looked down again, then across. She got closer, and carefully tried to prise the damaged piece of fly leaf, from his clammy blue scaled hands. He just sobbed louder, and rolled to one side, she fell on him.

It was not a fatal blow, luckily, but the shock did bring him a little to his senses. He found himself buried, beneath a lavender, and sweat smelling landslide, his natural survivor instincts cut in and he swam, well, wriggled for safety (and air).

Something, was happening above him, the pressure varied, and the landslide shifted, found its feet, and making unmentionable noises, and unladylike swearing, was rising from him.

Suddenly, he could breath again, but more, a light, a bright white light, was before him.

Someone said:

"Hello."

It was a deep man's voice, and it emanated from a glowing white form. His eyes adjusted. They were white enruned and besigiled robes. Jewels that glowed with their own light, littered the garment. It was a bit much really.

"Who?" he managed.

"Welcome, to the restricted, I should say forbidden section, and who are you, and what do you think you are doing in my library?"

Mary Lin, spoke as forcefully, and with all the assurance she possessed, which right at that moment in time, was not much.

The white haired, white bearded man, elderly, and yet young in countenance, was clearly not someone to trifle with, and as he had stepped from thin air, in a blaze of light, not moments before, she didn't want to push her luck.

"I am Alurici, Archaeus Magnus, of the order of Mages, and well, I'm here to return one of your books, very useful it was too."

He waved a medium sized folio, of old yellowed pages, at her, a little self consciously.

"Well, you shouldn't take things without permission. This IS a reference section!"

She placed great emphasis on that last point.

He smiled.

"Ordinarily, dear lady."

He smiled, and she melted.

"I would always ask permission, before availing myself of the contents of another's library."

This was of course, a lie. Many times in the past, the old Arch Mage, had ransacked, looted, pillaged, even burnt and destroyed, often with the owner in occupation, the libraries, laboratories and studies, of his rivals.

She didn't need to know that.

"Oh...." She said smiling. For an older, probably extremely old Magi, he was quite charming, and handsome in an 'I only have cats for company' way.

He knew the effect he was having, and felt, not a little scared. Must turn down the charm he thought.

"Well, I'll just be putting this book back....."

"Oh, its no trouble."

She caught the book, and his fingers in his hand.

He thought quickly, yes, there it was, 'Power Rune Kill', just on the tip of his tongue.

He smiled, like a hungry tiger, and continued.

"Dear lady, I really must get on, you know I'm trying to save the Metacosmos?"

She gazed at him blankly, she was his willing slave, if he made the right sacrifices.

Some sacrifices of course were too much to ask of any man.

"That sounds so exciting! This gentleman here was trying to do the same thing, but he seems to have gone to pieces, you aren't going to pieces any time soon are you?"

"We should get better acquainted, I can get you a special Library Card you know, good anywhere! Oh what am I saying! My name is Mary Lin, I'm Libraria's deputy, I'm in charge, whilst she's, absent. You know I suppose that makes me practically a Demigod!"

Alurici looked at her. No, no she wasn't. She was a mortal woman, who had been in the Upper World a considerable length of time, possibly hundreds of years.

He risked some flattery.

"Well, I can see how you could be mistaken for Libraria, her very self!"

She glowed. That was the right, and right obvious button to press. He glanced down at the distressed blue, merman, flanked by his nonchalant, now rather bored, alligators.

"Who's he?" He asked.

"Oh, he's Lyrinsos, an emissary from the Lord of the Oceans. Very important, but a little, ah, indisposed."

She tried to be kind, she felt like being nice. She'd heard of it, and now was a good time to try it out.

"Ah, the secret is in the Bananas."

He lent down, looking into Lyrinsos's eyes.

"Yes, one good bunch of ripe Bananas, guaranteed protection against tome induced insanity, and general malaise."

"Oh the yellow fruit! How clever of you! How did you find out? And where did you get such a wondrous thing?"

She asked, genuinely interested.

"Oh well, it was an accident you know, I was wandering your library, and well, I found a small stash of them. Well, I helped myself to them, and found I didn't need the special glasses against horror inducement. I was surprised, such a simple thing."

"Will they help him?"

She asked, not really caring, but thinking she should, at least for the show of things, and he did have that pair of alligators.

"Well, I haven't any left, so I've been returning the books. I've cribbed what I needed anyway. But, well, for that poor fellow, well, looks like the damage is done."

He lied again. He smiled. He was shamefully good at it. He still had some left, and, he was looking at ways for their cultivation, in the laboratory of course. Who knew what effects the plant itself would have on hapless passers by?

Imagine, an extra middle land plant that protected against the madness of the Great Big Ones ! What a wonderful thing!

"Is there any chance of a cup of tea?"

He asked. Wishing to change the subject, and well, there was one last book he wished to see. The Grand Artefactory, the Compilation of Objects Diverse, Divine, and Deviled.This book he wanted to see. Technically it wasn't forbidden, and wouldn't be in the 'Forbidden Section'.

"Yes! Yes, of course!" She said enthusiastically.

This was turning into a good day.

"I may even have some cake."

She smiled mischievously. I bet you do! Thought the old Arch Magus, allowing a twinkle to his eye, but just a little one, no sense in over doing it.

Lyrinsos watched them walk away. Something important had just happened, and he had missed it.Now, it had passed, and it was very, very dark.

Very dark. Very cold. He shivered. The two alligators watched his recumbent form, speculatively.

Chapter Twenty Four – Lordy Lordy!

Archeus Magnus Alurici, was without doubt the best surviving all round generalist Mage, in the whole of the world of Graeffenland. No one in the North, or West, or the Isles came close to his knowledge and understanding.

Well, except Xagigg. King Xagigg, Necromancer, Master Mage, Lich, spirit of an ancient Mage who had, possessed the unlucky Sir Wallmer all those years ago.

Xagigg, had like Alurici, existed for thousands of years, in one form or another. Unlike Alurici, Xagigg had been dormant, trapped in a magic ring, for a good thousand or so of those years.

Alurici, also possessed one of the best libraries in the world, several of the best laboratories, and herbariums in the world. In one of his laboratories, the crystalline, bejewelled matrix sat, glowing and humming.

Nearby, in mid air, quietly parked, and still recording, whirred his view of one tiny part of the Metacosmoverse.

Looking within, one would see, the erstwhile PAM, nameless and anonymous, to all but his closest friends, and known by pseudonym, to nearly everyone else.

However, we can just call him PAM.

He had found time to change, his new body, was slightly tubbier than the old thin one, but nearly as tall. Luckily, long practice, and an apparent love of theatrical costumes, had supplied him with an abundance of possible clothing options.

Somehow, he found another black dinner suit. This he wore, with a nice multi coloured bow tie, which really looked as though it could spit water, at a moments notice, or spin in a beguiling and amusing fashion, at another moment, maybe, both at once.

His face, lined with care, concern, and possibly a chisel, was a mask of concentration. He loved a challenge, and saving the Metacosmoverse, was just his cup of tea.

He had found a packet of three hundred year old stale jelly babies. He munched them. He munched them determinably, they had little flavour, but chewing helped him think.

"If." He spoke out loud.

To himself. No one else was there at that present moment in time. His Blue Cabinet of glowing, pulsing, heaving and braying, magick, was empty, except for him.

"No, no that won't work."

"Wait."

He held one hand up, as though someone, some unheard voice, except to him, had spoken, and was distracting his chain of thoughts.

"If, the very fabric of reality, is becoming undone, there must be a seam. A beginning, an ending, and ..."

He held his chin.

"And, like a zipper, if it can be undone, it can be done up again!"

He stopped himself. His smile of triumph, fading.

"Well, no, what if it has buttons? How do you re-button reality?"

"I suppose one could staple it together....."

He scratched his dark black locks, his hair and its style magickally changed, when he did.

Oh yes, this was still the Mage of the Blue Cabinet, as Graeffenlanders would have called him, but physically, outwardly he was so different.

His face showed no trace of the gunshot wound that had triggered his most recent 'change,' fortunately.

He still felt cross about it.

He was only trying to help! Normally, people would be grateful for his help, maybe not straight away, but at some point. That fellow, he thought, who'd sounded American, had been most hostile. A thoroughly unpleasant chap.

This was getting him nowhere. Dimensional, metaphysical anomalies, and what had those two strangers, one trigger happy, got to do with it?

Unless, one of them, was the Zipper! One of them, was opening the tear in reality, and perhaps, could, close it again.

But how?

"How? How do you reseal, a breach in the very fabric of the Metacosmoverse? And, and why, would it happen now?"

He pondered.

"What, what if it's part of a natural process? What if this was just the normal descent of reality into entropy?"

He strode back and forth.

"But if it's natural, like night following day, how can it be stopped."

He stopped.

"Oh dear. What if it was stopped, once before, and now, it's given way, whatever was postponing the inevitable, has gone, and the natural process, is in full swing."

He looked sad. Well, sadder.

"Oh dear."

"Well, I suppose, the best place to start, is at the beginning. Yes, if I go there, perhaps, I can get some more ideas."

He turned to the great panel of dials, knobs, and switches. Turning this, adjusting that, the Blue Cabinet, hurtled through the Metacosmoverse.

"What will I find?" He said out loud, his great bushy eyebrows almost meeting, in a great frown.

Chapter Twenty Five - Laying in the Gutter, but Staring at the Stars.

Lord Drool opened his eyes. The glass roof, its panes clean, well cut, well set, brassy, though hard to tell that now.

No other light, except the cold silvery light of the stars.

He felt, numb, he couldn't move his head, but his mouth worked. He worked his lips. He tried swearing, profusely, profanely, and with little effect.

A wheezy noise accompanied all his attempts at speech.

He stared at the stars. He wondered what they were called. He'd never been particularly interested in the stars before, now, he just wanted to curse them, roundly condemn them for looking on, impartially at his fate.

How had it come to this? He sniffed, his reptilian, black nose wrinkling.

Barely a week ago, the firmament had been absolutely the last thing on his mind. Ah, he missed the uncomfortable cold, hard, stone throne.

What a throne that had been! His slaves had spent months, and much blood, carving it from the heart rock of the mountains.

They then detailed it in rubies, emeralds, and gold. Traditionally, it should have been washed in blood, in usual goblin fashion.

Who had time for tradition these days? No, barely was it done, than there was another crises.

The latest in a series of crises. Memories arose, taunting, teasing, unwilling and unbidden. Lord Drool had a long, a very long memory.

He had been alive, if a goblin can be alive, he thought they probably were, as they could, eventually, and usually with considerable force, be deprived of animation. I move therefore I am, he thought, ruefully, and tried to laugh.

A breathy wheeze escaped him.

He used to be able to manage a diabolical laugh, once.

He remembered the first time he'd laughed that laugh. Only twenty years or so ago.

The high point of his career, he could see it now, the day he brought Adan, and the Relic that had slain the accursed Edric, enemy of all goblinkind, to the great cavern of the High Chief.

How fantastic, beyond all his wildest dreams, and when the High Chief himself had offered him a quaff from the great Cup itself, and explained their cunning plan to slay Adan, how he had laughed with pleasure!

Of course, Adan, whatever he had been, had sat down to feast, as though it were a great honour, and indeed, he was guest of 'honour.' They had all watched with mounting horror, as he survived every course, finally even taking a drink from the great cup, the great goblin brew of power, and instead of exploding in fiery, fungal destruction, as humans do, he had merely belched phosphorescent fumes, hiccupped, and called drunkenly, for more 'nectar'.

The Goblin Chiefs plan had fallen surprisingly flat, and that night they re-gathered in conclave. The Chiefs put their heads together, and, finally, they decided. They would pull out the worst enchantments of their treasure vaults, the most accursed items, and the deadliest too.

They also gathered a hand picked, 'honour guard,' a regiment of goblin warriors, to send back to Graeffenland, with Adan. They would take a small castle for him, and, if the accursed enchanted devices did not slay him, they would try.

They could not leave something as powerful as Adan alive. Not if they could help it.

He remembered, he would stay at Adan's side, as a general factotum, until the strange being, was appropriately disposed of.

Of course, the Adan creature played into their hands, accepting the various noxious accoutrements, with blindingly foolish naivety, and, they didn't seem to slow him down, hardly at all.

Even, the nightmarish demon steed, that should have borne him screaming away into a darkling nether abyss, fell into line, accepting a name from him without comment, barely a spark of disagreement, and served as any intelligent horse would.

This did not really surprise him. He could feel his initial elation fading. Life, long experience had taught him, rarely was this good.

There was always a catch. He tried to curse again. Again just a hollow wheeze. He should have known things could not be that good. How many times was the silver lining, the glint of a daggers blade? How many times was the light at the end of the tunnel, merely the glow of a magma pocket about to burst?

He'd fled. He'd put two and two together, and he'd run. Maybe, that was he mistake. No, he didn't think it was the main mistake. That girl. He'd done so much. He'd fought, claw and fang, killing rivals at every turn, beating mobs into gangs, gangs into his very own tribe. He'd grown, taller and stronger as his prestige, and supply of slaves increased. He had become a Chief. He'd styled himself a Lord, in name, but was a tyrant in nature.

He'd built a realm of his own, in the dark places of the world, and then it happened. The Devourer. He'd fought its minions, had a few victories in the caves and tunnels. Finally, he'd made peace with it, had come to terms, even tentatively made alliance with it, through its general of course, the Fist, as he was called.

Lord Drool croaked, his vocal chords straining to find moisture. That was really odd, he thought. Still, his chain of thought returned, petulantly, dreaming of horrors and torments he could inflict on that girl, should they ever meet again.

He'd captured the girl. Not just another meal, or slave for his warriors, no, she was a Royal Princess!

Not just any Princess, there were few enough of those around as it was, these days, but THE Royal Princess! Nirnadel, daughter of the great foe, of goblin kind and the Devourer himself.

Such fortune, such providence, such an opportunity, and, she'd talked him into letting her go. She'd convinced him, the Devourer was the death of all, and could not be reasoned with. He'd seen it her way. Had she used some spell, some special enchantment that could penetrate their antimagick amulets?

They'd invested a lot of time, and wealth in those amulets, knowing Xagigg, and his minions, were powerful in the magick of command and domination.

All, for nothing. She had convinced him, and he had ordered her release. Set her free, his lieutenants staring mutely on, his deputies, and warriors all wondering what was next.

Civil war, was next. His tribe, split into factions and it was all he could do to hold it together. Many joined a band that left, heading South, going to join the Devourers armies, underground.

He'd harried them, as best he could, even, he curled his lip, he, had supplied information to the gnomes, his enemies, who fearing trick or ambush, had been slow to act, but decisive when they did. He did not know just how many actually reached Arshan, but some would have. Weakened, discredited, no one likes a loser, the days became one long round of assassination attempts, political intrigues, and careful retrenchment, careful rebuilding He'd moved north and east, dug out new caverns, new roads, new halls, hopefully secret from the enemy, (all of them).

New magick, he'd heard the rumours, an army of magicians, who could kill at a distance, drilling like common pikemen in the city square. This he could not ignore, a new source of power, a new threat, a new opportunity, and so he'd travelled, with a handful of guards, discreetly, to make contact, and strike a deal, with a certain human noble.

This had been his biggest mistake of all.

Chapter Twenty Six – Gnomes of the Desert.

The warm dusty air blew in through the narrow slit in the wall. It looked out, from the discreet low mound of the secret dug out, the forward observer post of the long range desert gnomes.

A headscarf wrapped the observer on duty, his brass rimmed goggles, coating with dust with every other gust of wind.

The rest of his face was obscured, but as Bish Sterosch wiped his goggles, again, adjusting his red helmet, below the dust coated scarf, he knew it was going to be a different day. His nose, mouth and regulation length beard, neatly trimmed, were also tightly wrapped under the dust caked scarf.

Watch Gnome was the worst duty imaginable. The dust, despite all precautions, got every where. No one was ever dust free, and, what was worse, in the distance, his personal responsibility, swayed fruit trees, alongside the great river. The great cool, wet, fish laden river.

He watched the wading birds, landing, flying off, free. Oh, he envied them, what he would give to be free, to safely sit, paddle, and fish quietly in those beautiful waters. Apparently, gnomes had, in times past, done just that. He sighed. He was a volunteer, they all were, the gnomes were very democratic, really democratic, despite being ruled by a technically absolute monarch.

The Alt Konig, the king of the gnomes, above and below, was an inherited position, but also a job. He worked, and he ruled, but always took advice.

The result of all this, plus the long lives of the gnomes, would have resulted in an utopian society, except for everyone else.

Bish Sterosch gazed through his viewing scope, bringing the distance closer. He ceased his musings on what the world would be like, if there were only gnomes, in it, probably a paradise, was his first thought, and gazed speculatively at the human ship, a big one, slowly cruising east on the great river.

It was, a bit of a shock. He'd not seen a ship, let alone a large one, here at all. In fact, he didn't think he'd ever actually seen a ship. Well, a human one at any rate.

But, there it was. An old southern warship, well, maintained, three, no four decks, towers, fore and aft. He looked carefully, scanning the length of the ship.

Humans, lots of heavily armed humans, many in armour, too. They looked liked islanders, mostly, he tried to estimate their numbers. He stopped at fifty, and they, came and went. He suspected there were very many more on board.

He turned his gaze to the flags and pennants. Just flags, a red banner flew, below it, a blue with slanted trident, indifferently fluttered. He heard of this, they all had. Really, it wasn't his field of speciality. He was, after all, in a land reconnaissance unit, monitoring enemy troop movements, and the enemy used no ships. Well, used no ships, so far.

This was currently a dull and fruitless task. He remembered this flag though. It belonged to Captain Fortunes flagship, a notorious pirate and looter, who had spawned a fleet of ruffian ships, profiteering from the abandoned wealth of the ruined nations of the south. He was frowned upon by the people of Gnomoria, and deeply distrusted.

It was, he thought, no surprise. Someone was bound to go into the ruined cities to recover, what could be salvaged. Perhaps, the gnomes envied him his opportunism, others certainly did, but had to settle for trading with him, for the choicest items, and cargoes.

Gnome society was, highly structured and orderly, and profiteering was deeply despised.

Here he was though, sailing slowly up river, heading presumably to Eghior, the great port city, not that far away. They were in fact, sailing deep into enemy territory, with no fear, and presumably, what they believed to be a significant force.

He sat back, lowering the scope. Old Eghior was a snake pit, Arshans forces seemed to have turned the city into one great encampment, dedicated to war.

Somebody, probably ought to let them know. Probably, he stood and moved quickly, deeper into the small outpost. Down a few steps he went, the architecture, primitive though it was, was sturdy and efficient, the height of gnomish field engineering, of course no one would expect any less of the units commander, Major Tincture, old hand at engineering, fierce warrior, and fish aficionado of note.

The outpost was, almost as close to the city as they could get. Portalling, the magickal transport method become so popular amongst the gnomes, in recent years, could not safely get any closer. Those who tried, tended to vanish, gone. Or reappear, elsewhere, in pieces, somehow, torn apart by incomprehensible forces.

Major Tincture, his ruddy, desert baked, battle scarred, slightly pickled, yet friendly visage, looked up, lamplight casting shadows, against the walls, his beard braided with military precision.

Spread before him on his service issue folding, map, lunch, and at a pinch, emergency shield, table, was the latest cartographic masterpiece.

Daily updates, minute by minute, recorded by the keenest reconognomes, transcribed in triplicate, appeared before him. Two copies, with his mark, would then be portalled out by messengers, to the Head Quarters Below. It was an efficient operation, swift and accurate, but they still made little progress.

He looked up, and the gnome of the watch, stood before him, mumbling incoherently.

"Take the scarf off! For the sake of the Sacred Rods of Mij Troutbreaker!"

The hasty messenger quickly realised his mistake, scrabbling with both hands, unwrapped and drew down, the dust caked scarf from his face.

"Sir!" He said, saluting promptly.

His helmet, tilted at a rakish angle.

"Please....." Indicated the Major, eyebrows rising, indicating a small stool nearby.

"No Sir! A ship! Human, sir, armed to the teeth, progressing easterly up the estuary. Right now, sir!"

Bish Sterosch grinned. Some action at last!

"Really?!"

The Major exclaimed. Genuine surprise sounding in his gruff old voice. He stood up.

The watch gnome carefully did not stare. The grizzled old gnome before him had really been in the wars. He'd lost both legs, in a terrible, heroic battle in the tunnels of Sar Nerfen.

He did however, have nice, shiny new legs. He had some fine prosthetics made, by the philosophical alchemical mechanicians, of the advanced gnomic war laboratories. They resembled, brass, articulated girders. They were articulated, in exactly the same places, ordinary legs were articulated, great brass joints, cogs, pulleys, and gears ran through them, visible, through the large cross bar meshes.

They ended, in rubber coated splayed 'toes', a little duck like, if the duck was made of polished brass, and of course, black rubber.

As he stood up, the great brass pistons gently hissed. The cogs, well oiled, and visible within the scaffold legs, spun, transferring motive power from the small, steaming alchemical engines attached to each hip.

He had, had many problems in the early days, especially in no smoking zones, such as restaurants and carriages, until the proprietors realised, not only was he a war hero, not only was it only steam, but he also had a powerful kick and knew where to plant it.

He'd even tried scenting the steam, but he'd had so many strange looks, he abandoned that idea, rather quickly.

Clothes, were another issue, military, or civilian. At first he'd tried getting trews to fit, but the brass always split the seams, so, these days, he sported desert issue shorts, and presented quite a startling image.

Long practice, had made him extremely dextrous, and in short order he had traversed the extent of the tunnels. Picking up the viewing scope, and dusting it off, he held it up to his eye, and gazing through the slit he scanned the horizon. There it was.

He paused. A warship, quite a large one, bristling with troops.

"Signal!" He yelled.

Scrabbling and running sounded behind him, as the duty signals gnome raced from his small niche, and hurried to his side, notepad and quill, at the ready.

The Major dictated quickly, sharp and crisp.

"Field Operations, Major Tincture, to forward Scout Team GF1. Take skiffs proceed all speed. Make contact with ship. Stop at all costs. End."

He lowered the scope.

The signal gnome saluted, quill still in hand, turned and rushed away.

Chapter Twenty Seven – A PAM in Time. Saves....

The Archeus Magnus Alurici had returned to his great tower. He was tired. He was over caked, so caked his first stop was to pour himself some of Blugars Detoxifying Potion, and Foot Liniment.

The tea was, however, quite satisfying. The access all stacks library card, was also, most useful, and though a boring grey, with large capitals, pronouncing Chosen of Libraria, the no return date, had an appeal all its own.

He had also found the book he wanted.

"The Grand Artefactory, the Compilation of Objects Diverse, Divine, and Deviled."

He read out the title. He was tired, so he sat on one of his easy chairs, a lovely yeti fur lounge seat. He sank back into the fur, sipping his potion, and turning to the first page.

Hammers, he thought, something about enchanted hammers, but first, lets just have a bit of a read. There may be something useful, here.

In another chamber, his beautiful crystalline matrix, glowed and shimmered, still tracking and following, a certain PAM. PAM of course, as earlier mentioned, was a newish term, used most frequently in the gnomish lands, and applied quite specifically to a branch of magick, incorporating, the philosophical, the alchemical, and the mechanical, in a blend of Art, and dare it be said, some new kind of knowledge, a sort of Philo-sense, or even Psi-sense.

This particular PAM, was busy, checking this, noting that, adjusting the other, spinning dials, and moving levers. He was busy using a very sophicticated Philosophical Engine, to find out, where his zipper was stuck.

"Yes, yes. I think that's it. Who would have thought, it could be there? In fact who would imagine anything could be there?"

He smiled grimly.

"So, I need to capture, or coerce our errant zipper, and see what happens if I take him to point zero."

He stroked his chin, and then pressed a button. The glowing central column, lights flashing, and sound braying, gyrated. The miraculous blue cabinet, hurtled through the dimensions.

Soon after, it appeared, flashing into existence on a fog shrouded sidewalk. Its door opened, and the dapper, dinner suited PAM, stepped out. In the distance, a glow, and the sound of voices.

He headed that way, cautiously.

There was a yacht, one or two people, moving about, and two people, crouched by some crates.

"That's the fellow who shot me....." He muttered under his breath.

"Well, let's just put him out of the picture."

He stepped lightly forwarded, a small flute, of shiny silver metal, coming to his hand. It was a sacrifice, but guiltily, he thought, worth it.

One blow, and the rough, fedora be hatted man, who had previously shot him slumped senseless to the cobbles.

The other man, dressed in shabby robes, stared in shock and fear, up at him.

"You really should come with me, old chap, and we'll sort this mess out."

Berythus Naechos stood up carefully, and stepped hesitantly, towards the mage of the blue cabinet.

"Come on, come on, there is no time to lose!"

The thin little priest moved a bit quicker, scuffing on the cobbles.

"Look, carefully now, there's a good fellow, here through this door."

The priest looked aghast at the huge room, within the small cabinet, he seemed overwhelmed.

"Yes, yes, I know it's a bit overawing, but you'll get used to it. Anyway, I'll soon have you home."

"Ye-es." Stammered the priest.

"I have important information I need to get back, to the High Priests Conclave, it could end the war."

"Yes, yes, I'm sure it will be a great help."

PAM closed the door, and began dialling, tugging, pushing and rotating, coordinates into his great Philosophical Engine.

"Now, to see if we can pull up this zipper."

Back in the real world, the Archeus Magnus, had reached the section on Relics, concerning Hammers, specifically, one old Hammer in particular, the Hammer of the Gods.

He read. Being an old cynic, his first thoughts were, which Gods? Old, ancient ones, forgotten ones, best forgotten ones? Who knew, most of the texts, were relatively modern, written in the last three thousand years. The Hammer, was older than that, forged long ago, with strange runes and glyphs, carved or moulded into its unknown alloy.

He paused. An unknown, an alloy from, where? From another world? How would it get here? He checked the entry, forged before the dawn of time, by the ancient gods, of unearthly metal, with a power from beyond.

From beyond? From outside the known metaverse, or from some place within it? The Elder Horror, the Great Big

One, the Devourer itself, that was from beyond, but beyond where?

He paused, where were they from? All this talk of beyond, was foolish, they must be from somewhere, after all, if it was imprisoned it was imprisoned somewhere, not nowhere. Imprisoned. Yes, he thought, originally they had been imprisoned, but they weren't imprisoned before. They had been elsewhere, they had been 'Beyond.'

Yes, he thought the creatures had turned up, from elsewhere, because the time was right, as Spring followed Winter, as Autumn followed Summer, they had arrived, and through skill, or artifice, cunning or luck, the shamen, and the early Mages, had imprisoned them, not sent them back, but halted their process.

Were they part of a process? A natural process, an inevitable process, that humans had blocked, paused, frozen for a space of time, only delaying what ever was meant to be?

A chill went through him, maybe humans were unnatural? Maybe, they were the interlopers, against the nature of reality, transgressing, against the true destiny of existence?

Quickly, he reached over to a bowl, and took a banana. He peeled it unsteadily, and carefully nibbled the fruit whilst clearing his mind. Too many connected dots, too many insights, and he was tired.

What if, what if, he allowed himself to think, what if the Hammer, was theirs? A tool, or a symbol? After all, it only looks like a Hammer, to us. To them it might be a symbol, an embodiment of some key principle or philosophy. A key?

Quickly, he reached for another banana. Of course it wasn't, it must belong to some ancient warrior god. He carefully ate the banana, savouring its sanity restoring taste. An ancient sacrificial warrior god, who did not make it, but was doomed to die with it, to usher in a new world.

A new world, a key, and a lock. He put down the banana skin. If it was, then things were worse than he anticipated. Their chief ally, a pawn, unwittingly completing the Great Big Ones plans, again?

Again, this had happened before, again this insight came to him. What if, the 'Hammer' symbol, was all that was left of the old world, of many old worlds, time and again?

He closed the book. They don't have a plan it just happens. Every so many tens of thousand of years, they appear, and the world is 'recycled.'

Books, he thought books on Shamen. How did they stop the process, how did they end the cycle. He put down the tome, on a low mahogany table, just beside him, stood up and walked, slowly towards the stairs down. He would see what books he had, his personal collection was quite extensive, he would refresh his memory.

Down he went, his low boots tapping on the stone flags. Ah, he thought, the warm golden light of his library lamps was welcoming like an old friend, beckoning him in.

He paused. He had not left any lights on. Cautiously he approached the open doorway, more of an archway as, in fact, no door was present.

He stepped within, four or five deadly spells ready in his mind, ready for anything he might find.

A familiar face turned to him. A fine white beard, adorned a balding head, whose eyes looked over the rims of a rather fancy pair of tortoise shell effect reading glasses. The portly gentleman, in classical dark brown stars and moons, Mages robe, had turned to watch him enter, and with no embarrassment said.

"Hello, Archeus Magnus...."

"Hunbogi, well, Master Hunbogi. One of the last, too."

Alurici gazed levelly at him. Unannounced visits by Mages, upon other Mages, especially their libraries and laboratories, was rarely a good thing.

Normally, it was followed by melodramatic speeches, recriminations, unlikely and implausible, or simply unacceptable offers or demands, subtle back stabbing, or an outright fire fight.

Alurici was prepared, by long experience for any of these.

"We must talk, the world is about to unravel, and we need to try to stop it." Hunbogi sounded genuine.

Almost on principle Alurici felt he had to disagree, but instead of a long drawn out debate about why they should do so, he just said.

"Yes."

"The Shamen you know, they had the key."

Hunbogi continued, indicating an old volume on anthropology gripped loosely in his right hand.

"Did they actually have The Key, though?"

Alurici enquired, thoughtfully.

"No, I mean they had the secret, they knew how to re-imprison the creatures."

Hunbogi, looked around and moved towards a rather nice paisley upholstered seat. He sat down, and flicked the book back open.

"Yes, but they weren't set free to start with, they weren't originally imprisoned."

Hunbogi started, nervously.

"Oh, that's different. This book talks of keys and gates, dream quests, and visions. Do you think it's reliable?"

Hunbogi closed the book again.

"Well, it can be relied upon completely to convey the opinion of the author...." Alurici mused.

Yes, he thought what good was any tome, it was all conjecture, it was all theory, it was all so much mythology.

"You know we need to do more analysis. It may be possible to replicate, what the old Shamen did."

"Well, you know it was just one Shaman, some fellow called Alowetawulfa, from a northern tribe, according to the legends."

"No hammer involved then?"

"No, not at all, Mages of a sort, some kind of primitive hedge wizards, and other Shamen, but mainly they lay it at his door."

"So, we have to imagine ourselves Shamen, and try to figure out, what he knew." Alurici drew up another chair and sat down, steepling his fingers and closing his eyes.

"I'll get the herbs." Said Hunbogi getting up.

"Yes, it has to be authentic."

Chapter Twenty Eight - Bubbles.

Nirnadel, her blonde hair falling behind her, adjusted her colourful skirts, and sat down. Erik, had bought breakfast, fresh bread, smoked meats, cheeses, and tea. Simple fare, but very tasty.

He had booked himself a room, and ordered hot water for a bath, a large bath, apparently. She'd over heard him.

The Inn was very well maintained. Carpets, polished woodwork, horse brasses, paintings hanging on the walls, a fine selection of beers and wines, only in Gnomoria had she seen the like, and actually, this was better.

She sipped the small beer he'd bought her. It was cosy in the Inn, the hearth crackled in the back ground, the few other guests came and went wrapped in their own little worlds. It was quite a large Inn, extending far back beyond the square, easily accommodating forty or even fifty diners, and countless revelers.

During Market day, it would surely be full. Erik had the right idea to get his bath, now. He hadn't seemed that dirty, but he had assured her he was. Life amongst the Wagons had perhaps dulled her senses a bit, she did bathe regularly, every stream or pool, and waterfall, were seen as obligatory bathing opportunities, at least in warm weather.

She remembered her pool back at the Palace. She did miss it, but you know, you only got so dirty, and then, well, you got no dirtier. It was healthy Lyra had said. Rhian had commented that they used to have soap. Different times, Lyra had retorted. Soap wasn't everything, she'd continued.

There in an upstairs room, a large bath was being readied. With soap, and hot water.

Erik nursed his beer, he smiled. She smiled back.

"You know. You could do me a favour." He began.

"Oh, what would that be?"

"I think I've pulled a muscle in my arm." He indicated grimacing.

"Oh, we have herbs and all sorts, back at the camp! We can knock you up something in no time!" She replied.

"My main problem, I'm going to have trouble getting my jacket and shirt off." He looked embarrassed.

"Oh, is that all. I'll help you." She moved to stand up.

"Not now, when I have my bath. I can't get my clothes wet."

He smiled sheepishly.

She was reminded for a minute of Fudge, just something about the laughter lines by his eyes.

"Oh, don't worry. I'll come up with you and help. It's no trouble. You did buy me breakfast after all."

"Ah, that's really good of you! I'll be going up in a minute."

She sat back and finished drinking her beer.

A serving girl came up, looked at them and smiled.

"Your bath is ready, sir." She smiled again, and walked away.

"Thank you, well, we'd better go up! I know the room number."

He led the way, wending between the tables to the oaken stairs, leading up. She hesitated, and then followed. She wondered if these Inns would be better than the ones in Gnomgart, which she realised, had been her yardstick of quality for sometime now.

At the top of the landing, several intersecting corridors joined, they went straight ahead, away from the square.

She looked the other way.

"Oh, all the rooms with a view of the square are quite expensive here. Few of the rooms really get much of a view." He offered.

"You been here a few times?"

"Oh yes. This is the main town, hereabouts, apart from Heidelheimberg, which to be honest, is bigger, but just not as nice."

"Here we are." He continued.

The door wasn't locked, and opened inwards on a beautifully appointed large room, with no windows.

It did have a sumptuous large bed, with beautiful sheets, and a rather large bath tub.

"Oh, this is good!"

"I hoped you'd like it." He said.

The bath tub was steaming and bubbly.

Bubbles, I haven't seen bubbles for years, she thought. Back at the Palace, bubble bath was not unknown, just, generally unavailable. Apparently, since the collapse of trade, many products simply did not get traded, and if they weren't made locally, they were hard to find.

Graeffenlands domestic soap industry, had been up North. It had been flattened by marauding goblins, burnt to a crisp during the Dragonstrikes that followed, and then forgotten about by the survivors. Soap had been a low priority. The gnomes of Gnomoria, and the city of Gnomgart, made their own Soap, from fish oil, which though effective in some respects, kind of defeated the object in other respects. The gnomes found a fishy odour, attractive.

She was mesmerised by the Bath. It was a large tub, two maybe three people, could actually sit in it at once, and there were fluffy towels. Her lip trembled. Warm fluffy towels.

Erik smiled.

"Help me with this, please?"

He'd started unbuttoning his jacket.

Tearing her gaze from the fabulous bath, she crossed to him, and began unbuttoning his jacket. He turned and she gently pulled the jacket down and off his arms. He gasped slightly.

"Sorry!" She whispered.

More gently she eased his shirt down and off his arms. She examined his arms.

"I can't see any swelling." She said.

"Ah, you're probably not looking in the right place." He offered.

He slipped off his boots, thick socks, trews, and then his underthings. He really was quite fit and well muscled. She closed her mouth. She wasn't embarrassed, the folk of the Wagons were often nude, especially when bathing, being body conscious was not an issue. She was just surprised.

"It's a big bath, there's lots of room." He continued. He smiled, and then looked nonchalently away.

Bubbles, fluffy towels, hot water, and a well built young man. He had bought breakfast, and beer. No one could say he was too rough, or, in fact unattractive.

She smiled. A hot bath, whats the harm? She disrobed, skirt, blouse, shoes, underthings, in one heap. She looked at them, must be laundry day soon, she thought.

He was looking at her, with a clear and growing enthusiasm, despite the bubbles. She paused, then stepped carefully into the bath. It was hot, and she carefully lowered herself in, submerging beneath the bubbles, slowly, trying not to make too much contact, with her host. He just smiled, and gently guided her legs either side of him within the bath.

It was a big bath, the heat and the beer made her feel quite languorous. She felt cleaner already.

"You don't shave your legs? That's a bit rustic." He had found the soap, and unbidden, had been liberally applying it to her feet, which by turns he was lifting from the water.

"No, hey! Now, why would I?"

"I'm not criticising." He said.

"Not my place, but there is a razor here, and I have a steady hand."

Nirnadel burst out laughing.

"Go on then." She smirked, and sunk a little lower in the bath.

He lent over the rim of bath, and located, a gleaming steel blade. A slight moment of panic hit her. What if he were an assassin? She was almost completely at his mercy.

Except for her wealth of necromantic knowledge, the great Word of Command, for one thing, and he had no Amulet, and, as much exposed soft anatomy, as she did.

She caught her breath and waited. Neither of his arms seemed to trouble him at all. I've been lured here on a ruse, she thought. This fellow planned shennanigans, from, the, ahhhh, start.

He had gently lifted her leg, softly smoothing creamy soap, from ankle to knee, with alternating caresses, squeezing the muscles in her calf, ever so gently. This was new. The blade, swift and barely felt, swept away the creamy soap, and a bit of grime too.

Dreamily, she almost felt embarrassed at the grime, but didn't really care. He finished her lower leg, gently stroking her knee, as he lowered it back in the water, and moved to the next leg.

She felt quite warm, a rising, falling warmth that seemed to permeate all corners, well alright, one or two corners and niches in particular.

Again, he caressed, he smoothed, and soaped, finally gently sweeping soap, hair and grim away, with skillful strokes of his silvery blade.

"You okay?" He asked.

"Gaak" She replied, trying to avoid a mouth full of bubbles.

"This is your first shared bath?" His smile had dropped, concern flashed across his face.

"Yes." She managed, her cheeks flushed, reason and intellect, firmly on the back seat.

"Oh." He looked a bit uncomfortable.

"It's fine, whats next?" She asked, huskily.

Her instincts seemed to have an idea, and following their prompting she drew her legs, against his buttocks, and pulled herself closer.

"I can live with this custom." She added, drawing closer.

He looked most perplexed. He was thinking.

She drew closer still, almost wrapping her legs about him, nearly sitting in his lap. He brought his arms forward, and caught her gently under the arms, and then held her back.

"Oh, oh, you misunderstand! It is just our custom to share hot water, with our friends! You know, baths are such a luxury!"

The words took a moment to sink in. He wasn't planning shenanigans, or at least, not the shenanigans she had anticipated.

Disappointment washed over her, as she sat back.

He smiled.

"I'm flattered." He added.

"Maybe later." He continued.

"You know, you're good with that whole leg shaving thing." She observed.

"Much practice." He said. Indicating his own legs.

The fluffy towels seemed remarkably friendly.

"It's for mountain climbing." He added.

"How?" She asked.

"Ah, it reduces air pockets, in the leggings, you know, climbing trews, otherwise you get hair frost. Very nasty, causes rashes, sometimes makes people fall off the slopes. Yes, can be very bad." He spoke hastily.

Her eyes narrowed.

"Do you prefer men?" She wasn't subtle.

"What for bathing, well, it is more usual to share a bath with a male friend."

"It is?" She was baffled, and the water, amongst other things was cooling fast.

She idly scrubbed a few bits, wondering how long it would be, before she wrinkled.

"Bathing is enjoyable." He said sulkily.

"So are other things!" She had retreated back to her end of the bath, and had drawn her knees, that now seemed rather pale, up to her chin.

He climbed out of the bath, and found a towel. She watched, his rather handsome form, vigorously toweling off.

"Throw me a towel too!" She asked.

This he did.

More self consciously, she got out of the bath, both covering and drying herself with the towel, somewhat awkwardly, at the same time. She'd better get back. Inn's were fun, but at some point, her folks would miss her, and presumably come looking.

What they would think would be any ones guess. She stopped herself, actually, they probably would just laugh, and not be troubled at all. Their society, their customs, her customs, were actually fairly free and easy. She relaxed a bit. Why was she getting uptight?

So, she just shared a nice bath with a complete stranger with some kind of hair fetish. Big deal.

"Are you really going to sleep in that big bed all alone?" She enquired, feeling quite mischievous.

"Yes, I expect so. I like a big bed." He replied, a bit less grumpily.

"Well, it's still morning, just, and I've got things to do." She stated, pulling on her clothes, which now, shouted their need for laundering, from every colourful crease and rumple.

"Well, I may see you around." He smiled, relaxed again.

"You may." She found the door, opened it and left.

Mark all that down to experience, she thought, still it's got to be on of the most interesting......

She stopped that thought right there.

She had reached the head of the stairs, and below in the public bar and restaurant, sat a hooded man. He wore robes, scruffy robes, like a monk or a priest (of a poor temple, which these days was actually most temples).

He had one most remarkable feature, which sent a chill through her, and brought a lump to her throat.

He wore a band around his eyes, a wide band with an eye emblem, that completely covered his upper face, and about half his nose. He was dressed, just like the mystic who had attempted to kidnap her on board that ship, a year before, and who had pursued her in Vondrbeorg, with a giant mutated horror, for a hound.

She backed away. She hadn't been seen, not yet, but that might not matter. He may have already seen her earlier, he may know she is here, and just be waiting for the right moment to spring his trap. She shuddered. Her breathing had stopped, and her lungs were clamouring for a breath. She breathed slowly, and turned. A back stairs, she looked around. There could be one at the end of the corridor she'd just come down.

She headed that way, trying to step as quietly as possible. There was a stairs, but, it led up. Remembering her fun escapade on the roof tops of Vondrbeorg, she turned back to Eriks room. She wasn't playng mountian goat again. Besides she'd put on a little weight.

She opened the door, and locked it.

"Hello? Oh, it's you again, what did you forget?" Erik gazed around the room, curiously.

"Look, I'm in trouble." She said.

"Well, it wasn't me, but honestly, I'm not surprised." Eriks face looked serious.

"Haven't you got family you can talk to?" He continued.

"What? I don't understand half of what you're saying. Yes, I have family, quiet a decent one, camped out in their wagons at the Fairground just outside of own, that's not the problem." She sighed, she was getting agitated.

"So, just what is he problem?" He now sounded tired.

"Look, downstairs, is a man, he's after me."

"Oh come on! I'm not getting involved with jealous lovers or angry husbands!" Now Erik sounded cross.

"What? No, nothing like that. This guy, he's pretending to be blind, wears the band over his eyes, with the eye insignia emblazoned upon it." She whispered now.

"Yes, I've seen him. He came in on the coach I was on. What of it? How on earth do you know him, or he you, he's only just got in town." He was curious.

"I said, it was in Vondrbeorg, he wants to capture, maybe just kill me. He's a servant of Arshan, and the Devourer!"

"How can that be? None of them get past Kenovass, or the mountains! You girl, are crazy."

He laughed, and sat down on the edge of the bed.

"How do they get here ?! They don't fly, that's for sure! I've seen the Dragons, nothing gets past them! Ha!" He grinned.

Nirnadel looked at him askance. He had a point, except, she knew he was wrong. Some agents had managed to get past the defences. How they had accomplished it she couldn't imagine, except, under the mountains. Lord Drool, oh yes, he'd been all for an alliance with Arshan, how many others of goblinkind, had gone over to the enemy? There was no love lost between the goblin folk and, everyone else. The goblins hated everyone, even, each other.

She sat on the bed, next to him.

"Please help me get passed that bizarre man, just take my word for it he's dangerous, and don't worry about the why, I'll..."

There was a scratching at the door.

They both looked at it. Eriks smile vanished.

"It may be too late. Are you armed?" She spoke quietly.

"Only my climbing pick." He replied in a whisper.

"What sort of thing did you say he sent after you?" He continued, soberly.

He carefully reached round, finding his pack, and opening it, he drew out a small hand pick, sharp and pointed one end, hammer head on the other. It was small, but it was better than nothing.

The scratching resumed.

"You know that sounds like a dog" He said.

"You're right it does a bit, I'll look."

She stepped over to the door. There was no peep hole, there was a key hole. She looked through it carefully.

She could hear snuffling, and then she saw a black and orange striped tail. It wagged.

She straightened up, and opened the door.

Fudge padded in, eyeing Erik with deep suspicion.

Erik climbed on the bed. He looked worried. He stared at Nirnadel.

"You know that, thing?" He said, in shock.

That thing, fixed its glowing yellow eye, and slightly later, its glowing orange eye, on Erik. He quailed.

"You'll hurt his feelings. He's friendly. He's a faerie dog, he's come looking for me. I think I'll probably be safe enough now, at least by day. I've got to get back and warn the others. Honestly, if that fake mystic, has brought his many armed pet with him, everyone is in danger."

She looked down the corridor, waved, and quietly advanced to the head of the stairs. The mystic had gone. Fudge panted behind her, and followed her down the stairs.

She observed the bar room, looking all round. No sign. Just the staff, and a couple of drinkers at the bar, in fairly smart, townsmen's garb. They had nice hats, she thought.

Home, that's where I need to be, she continued, wondering if they had sent Fudge to find her, or if bored of sitting guard, he'd come of his own volition, to see where she had got to.

Chapter Twenty Nine - Coming Round.

Pain. Sharp pain, flashing lights, weird donkey noises, braying, cobbles coming up to meet him, hand slipping off the crate, the crate before him, beside him, above him, cobbles cold upon his face. He lay, darkness filling his vision, filling his mind, shivering, uncomfortable, light returning, dreaming, dreaming……..

Boston grey and grimy, a slight salt tang on the air. Rattle, crash, bang, of the street car making its way along the street.
    No asprin in the drawer. The dark wood drawer, stained and pitted, old brass fittings coolly comforting his fingers as he slowly slid it back.
    There it was now. The letter, unfolded, spread out, still crinkled, on his green leather desk top.
    Some broads last fling, smoothed out, its folds, two horizontal, arching it when his hand lifted away.
    His fingers, tough, rough, but not crude, not a musicians hands, though they'd played a tune or two in their time.
    Yeah, he'd had it rough, New York PD, beat cop, then detective.

Hell! Good times, bad times, when he was young, and the world was shiny and new, like a fresh struck penny, or the first slug from the box.

Why was it the first bullet always gleamed that special way?

Hah! Guns!

His was before him, in bits. Cleaned, oiled, and polished, like the jigsaw in his mind.

Idly, slowly, he put it together. Piece by piece, his .32 revolver came together.

Who was this broad? This Isabella?

She'd been alive this morning, now dead, her blood still dampening the tatty carpet, outside his rundown service office.

Damn, it had needed some colour, but not the burgundy hue of spilt dreams.

She'd been coming to see him. This was a guess, but probable, hell, he was the only renter in the building, apart, from the shop on the ground floor.

Run down shop, run down offices, run down city. Except it wasn't. Boston was doing good, but not everyone shared in that.

Somebody, had stopped her, stopped her hard, and cold, and had fled.

One shot, one flash, one crack of thunder waking him from the sports pages, scattering his thoughts with the newsprint fluttering to the floor.

His gun, out like lightning, into his hand, now covering the door, half glass, half light board, and paint. Shadowy corridor beyond.

He waited, his gun waited, eager, hopeful, like a shiny puppy, wanting to add its bark to the clamour.

Just quiet, no noise, not a footstep, not a whisper, and then shouts in the street. Someone running.

He'd crossed the floor, smoothly opening the half glass door, thin, so thin against the stale gloom of the corridor.

The smell acrid, blood and gunpowder, oh he knew that smell so well.

The body, slim, blonde, dishevelled, dead. Patterns on the wall like ruby constellations, and splodges on the carpet, like lakes on an old map.

She was dead, that was very clear, her bag, a nice looking black leather one, thrown up before her, its contents scattered away from the stairs.

The stairs wide enough for two to pass, were behind her, she hadn't seen her shooter, she lay, face down, her dark fur coat around her like a shroud, one eye wide, stared in surprise, her rouged lips parted.

He'd heard no cry. Death had been sudden, and there was the envelope, only document visible.

Carefully, he'd retrieved it, and with a cautious gun barrel, he'd nudged the bag open further.

No, that was all, nothing more, no driving licence, cheque book, library card, nothing.

The letter went in his pocket, and he'd returned, the seven paces to his desk chair.

Boston's finest had appeared, taken the body, taken his name, taken their time, his brief statement, and gone.

Had he known her? No, not yet.

That had earned him a stare, cop to ex-cop. They had seen his sign over the door, Jaeson Smith Private Detective.

They smiled, and laughed. Another wife or girlfriend, just another murder, vengeful husband or crossed lover, they didn't care. They did their paperwork, and they left.

He'd seen no rings, so, maybe not married, not engaged, not committed. Her skin was smooth, hair a strong yellow blonde, not old then.

Twenties? He pondered, maybe a little older, but not much.

Money, but no money. No cash, that he could see. He thought, he paused, he reviewed what he had seen. She wore decent clothes, the shoes seemed new, their soles fresh, the leather shiny. The coat was fur, the handbag new, not cheap, not bought on a market stall.

There was just the letter, it had a fine Boston address, with but one name.

Isobella.

She'd been coming to him. She'd been in trouble, and in a hurry.

The letter, he read it again. It said nothing bad, nothing to be afraid of, in fact, things to look forward to.

The rough handwritten words were as follows:

"Isobella, my heart, you and I shall be together, not here, not yet, but soon.

I shall set things straight, and then we'll leave.

Somewhere new and fresh.

Perhaps, San Francisco, things are better there.

You'll see, it'll be fantastico!"

It was signed, 'Giovanni' with crosses, that was all, informal, but personal. Someone liked her. Who gets shot down when someone likes them?

He sat back, he'd visit her address, and ask.

He stirred, in his sleep on the cobbles, moaning slightly.

Chapter Thirty – A Long Drawn Out Dinner Party.

Nirnadel stared into the square, Fudge leant against her leg. Before her, a coach, a nice one, black, green and gold trim, a leopard rampant upon a mountain, encircled by a crown.

The door open, a coachman standing beside it.

"Please, your majesty, your carriage awaits." The coachman, a tall blue liveried man, of middle years, with a nice blue pork pie hat, with feathers, held the door open.

"Oh, I'm not majestic at all!" She offered, by way of stalling for time.

"Please, your mother said you would be here, and bids you join her, and my noble master the Count, for dinner."

He stood there, looking a bit uncomfortable, as though he really just wanted to be gone.

"Fudge comes with me." She said, indicating the faerie dog, who looked up, and shrugged, doggily.

"As your majesty wishes." Said the coachman, bowing, and looking up.

"Hey! Don't I get a coach too?" Erik spoke, laughing from the doorway.

"The Count will send for you, later, Sir." The coachman rose from his bow, still holding the door.

"Thank you. I'm sure I'll be delighted to join my lord Count." Nirnadel spoke.

"So, you're a Princess!" Erik, laughed, earning a frosty glance, from the coachman.

"Yes, but I gave it up. It didn't suit me."

Nirnadel climbed in, up the small steps, and into the cabin. She was met by plush silk curtains, beautifully upholstered seats in purple leather, Fudge jumped up, and in. Finding a spot on the seat beside her, and gazing out the window.

The coachman closed the door. A minute or two passed, and then, the coach lurched, clattering away towards the castle.

Minutes passed, she gazed out the window, the town, its fine buildings standing proudly in the morning sun, soon the noon day sun, passed by her window. The east gates came, and slowing a little the carriage passed through them, and then past fields, woods, rocky slopes, winding up the slopes, on what must be a fine smooth road, another sign of the prosperity of the land, up and up.

She looked out, the town and the land rolled out to her left, and then her right as the road switchback and climbed, higher and higher. The air chilled, as the coach climbed.

She looked at Fudge, he looked back.

"Is my mother really there?" She asked Fudge, wishing she'd asked earlier.

He looked at her, his yellow, and orange glowing eyes, fixed on hers, and he nodded. Good enough, she thought.

They were there, a great rumbling, as they crossed perhaps a drawbridge, she supposed it might be, then a clang, as something, a portcullis, she suspected, fell into place.

The coach stopped in a large courtyard.

The door opened, the coachman, bowing as he held it open.

Fudge, then Nirnadel, stepped down.

"Well, we're here, isn't it gloomy!" She exclaimed.

It was a large courtyard, two of the ball games so popular on other worlds could have been played in it, with spectators, and little interference between them. The huge walls soared into the air, casting shadow over the whole courtyard.

Towers plunged into the dizzying heights, piercing the clouds, and a likewise heaven defying keep, sat astride the very peak of the mountain itself.

"Gosh." Nirnadel offered, no one in particular.

Fudge looked at her, sat down and scratched, back leg and paw, seeking the hard to reach places, just behind his right ear.

Another footman appeared.

"Your majesty!" He bowed low, his blue livery, a match for the coachman, but without such a heavy outdoor coat.

"Please come this way! A suite of rooms is prepared for your majesty."

Again, she was waved to follow, this she did, in through two great double doors, the chill of the courtyard mountain air following her in. Fudge dutifully padded behind her.

"Oh dear! How many stairs will I have to climb?" She asked, camping up the Princess routine. Fudge stared at her, he'd heard her tale of climbing roof tops and wonder what she was up to.

"Your majesty, need not be alarmed, we have the latest artifices from Gnomoria. Behold! A chamber that moves! Up or down! Fear not I shall operate it for you. It is perfectly safe."

He paused.

"But if your majesty prefers, I can arrange a palanquin, to carry you to your accommodations."

"No, the moving chamber will be fine." She smiled.

Her fathers palace had one too. This was getting eerily familiar. Her father, was he behind all this? He was powerful, he could have made these arrangements, to bring her back into the fold.

The footman indicated a great brass cage, surrounding a small room, he pulled the mesh like brass cage doors open.

He bowed and indicated the chamber within.

She stepped within, Fudge and the Footman followed. He touch a small jewel on the wall, it depressed, and glowed. The room shuddered, and moved up. She noticed, the brass mesh formed a tower, through one side of the mesh framework tower, she saw the floors, great stone slabs roll by. She noted, unlike King Xagiggs moving chambers, this involved chains, and great cog wheels, oiled and fine of quality, gnomish work for sure. The finest quality work too, without a doubt, the power source a mystery to her.

Ruefully, she realised she did not even know what magick Xagigg had used, not for the first or last time she wished she had studied more than just Necromancy. Her father, had been a Master Mage as well, as a Master Necromancer, and now of course, a Lich.

Where did this leave her? Technically she was a Royal Princess of Graeffenland, but in reality, King Xagigg, would never 'die' he would exist in his undead state until, he was violently deprived of it.

She needed her diplomatic head on. She focused. First she would say 'hello' to his lordship the Count, whatever his name was. No one had said. She'd never studied this part of the world at all.

The moving room, stopped moving. Smooth, no lurch, no jolt, it was good!

The mesh brass doors, drawn aside by the footman, who made himself small, flattening himself against the wall of the cage.

Fudge not interested in precedent or courtly manners, trotted out, Nirnadel smirking slightly followed. It really was an impressive castle. Great woven rugs covered the flagstones, beautiful tapestries depicting wild fabulous animals, hunting scenes, fables of old, covered the walls. The window at the end of the corridor, they were now in, high arched, and glazed in colourful glass, a scene in a forest depicted, she couldn't quite make out what.

The light, from the window, enhanced by jewels that glowed set in the ceiling, and running the length of the corridor. She was deeply impressed. She was sure she was meant to.

"This way, your majesty. The Royal Suite has been assigned for your use, for the duration of your stay. Please."

He indicated, a short distance down the corridor, a beautifully ornate double door, in the wall opposite the moving chamber.

She stepped carefully and slowly. Her mother was here somewhere was she? She felt any minute the other shoe was going to drop. This was all wrong. How did this Count know she was here? Why in the world would he want to fete her like this, and the honorifics were all wrong. She should be addressed ma'am or royal highness, not majesty. Xagigg wasn't dead, surely?

Well, technically King Xagigg, was dead, and had been so for many years. He hadn't stopped functioning, one of the advantages of lichdom.

This could be awkward. Of course if the King, her father, had in fact, kicked the final bucket, somehow, then that would mean she would be Queen. That would be bad. The Bone Legion would collapse, unless Ten Grief could maintain the enchantments, and she suspected he could not.

Fear clamped round her heart. Arshan would win, if the legion failed.

The beautiful doors were flung gracefully wide, within a great vaulted chamber, sumptuously furnished, many doors leading off, again, on the opposite wall to the entrance doors. A line of servants, two maids, two more footmen, and a slightly taller man, in more ornate dress. They all bowed or curtsied.

The slightly taller man then stepped forward. He was greying, at least around the edges, were hair remained, mostly, he was balding, slim and birdlike in his manner, his hands fluttered a little as he spoke.

"Majesty, I have the very great honour to serve as your Butler on your fortuitous visit to my lord the Count's demesne. I am called Karles, if its pleases your majesty to address me by name. I and my staff will meet your every desire."

He bowed again.

So, no Count. Not yet, and not according to protocol. Good, she thought, things are already creaking under the weight of inevitable inexorable reality. She liked that.

"Where is my lord, the Count?" She asked with a little smile.

"Majesty, he is deeply involved in terribly important matters of State, that demanded his complete attention, it was entirely unintended, and no offence was meant. Please let us attend you."

He's going to turn out to be some mad sorcerer, and he's stuck in his laboratory, because his current pet project has over run, and he's forgotten the time. Nirnadel grinned.

Fudge coughed, and nodded when she glanced at him. Mind reader, she thought.

"Well, attend me, then." She smiled. Finally, after all these years of being a princess, someone was really going to treat her like one!

Chapter Thirty One - Checking Out

For Lyrinsos, life was all about the cold stone floor, the bumping steps, the pains in his arms. He opened his eyes.

Books, stacks of books, above, beside, ahead, everywhere!

"Gaaaaaaaaaaahhhhhh!" He yelled.

His arms, pulled out straight, were released.

"Aaaaaaaarrrrrrrrrgggggghhhhh!" He expanded upon his earlier dissertation.

He was, head downwards, on a cheesegrater, made of stone. Except, as he drew his arms to him, he slide further down, the cheesegrater, and he realised, it was actually a stone stair, a rather long one. He was now at the bottom.

He looked at his forearms, lacerated by many teeth, and yet, not that seriously.

"Ehuh." He completed his ruminations.

His whole body ached, he was bruised, from head to foot, and rolling over, found at least his front wasn't bruised.

He wriggled painfully forward, and clear of the stairs, he struggled painfully to his knees.

His loyal attack alligators gazed at him. They had clearly dragged him clear of the Forbidden Section, and were trying to get him somewhere safe. Probably. Looking at them, he thought they might have been keeping their options open, as to exactly how safe, their destination was going to be, at least for their unconscious passenger.

He staggered up. There was a bulge in his bag. He looked, yellow fruit. Someone, had helpfully filled his bag. Fruit really wasn't his diet of choice, but he tried one anyway. It was okay, and the strange headache subsided a bit.

He looked around. Yes, he believed he knew where he was, they were on the path back to the main desk, where upon he had first encountered Mary Lin.

He vaguely remembered, a figure dressed in great white robes, talking, friendly, at least to the librarian, books, a book about artefacts, something about artefacts.

He walked slowly, determinedly, his alligators falling behind. He would find out, whatever he could from the librarian, and then he would report back.

The Lord of Oceans needed to know, if an artefact was needed, if an artefact was the solution.

Hours passed, and finally, he reached Mary Lin's desk. She was absent, the library was dark, the lights were going out, fading?

"We've got to go!" He said aloud.

"As fast as you can boys!" He addressed this to his alligators.

They raced, (well as fast as alligators can race) he limped, and staggered, fuelled by yellow fruit, they might just make it.

The stacks themselves were shimmering, losing their meta reality, losing their substance. The great Hall of Libraria was vanishing.

She must be dead! The thought rocked him, even Libraria was gone.

They passed the bodies of dead cats, many dead cats, struck down in poses of running, jumping, dodging. Magick! Someone has killed the cats!

Why would that end Libraria. A horrible idea struck him, what if Libraria had devolved somehow into, Cats?

Was it possible? Had she become one with the moggies?

With the death of the Cats, wait, what if the Cats were her main worshippers!? By the gods.

The doors themselves lay ahead, sprawled over the threshold, a female figure, he recognised.

The Librarian, Mary Lin, quite dead, crispy dead, in fact.

Who would do such a thing? Why would they do it?

The building was becoming misty.

Nothing to do but flee, and this he did, getting onto the pathways between the palaces, he looked around. Only Kershaggulumphies place was left, and, a small clear patch, shiny new.

Worry about that later, he shook his head. It's going to be too late. We've lost already. The Devourer has already won. A cold dark despair rose within him, a tear rolled down his cheek.

Slowly he finished the journey back to the Lord of the Oceans Palace, where things were still business as usual. He looked around, stared at chairs, ornaments, people, pools, fish, other people, and was guided, his face horror struck and ashen,(well, a more silvery hue of blue), gently to the Lord of Oceans presence.

"How did you do?" He asked gently.

Lyrinsos stared up at the last god in the world.

"You're the last." He gasped out.

"Not quite. We have a Lord of the Skies, a Thunder god." The Lord of Oceans stared intently at Lyrinsos.

"Oh, that'll be the new patch that's formed." Lyrinsos slumped down, as he spoke.

"Yes, the new chap has some stuff to sort out before he joins us, up here." The Lord of Oceans, smiled. He still felt confident.

"There's a Mage, searching for an artefact, or at least, looking into artefacts, and.... Someone killed Libraria!" Lyrinsos shouted this last titbit of information.

"Yes, I saw the Mage, and I think I know who he is. I'm watching out for him, and when he appears in the world, well, we'll see. He's, shielded at the moment, some magical defence."

"You saw him? Couldn't you stop him?" Lyrinsos stared in disbelief.

"No, I was just watching. One minute he's having tea and cake, next minute, it's all power rune this, death spell that, it all happened fast, and dangerous Mages are out of my league." Kershaggulumphie looked, disinterested.

"You're a god! Why didn't you stop him! Libraria is one of us, one of you at any rate! What is wrong with you?" Lyrinsos felt dizzy, he'd never felt so angry.

"Don't worry! When I know where he is, I will be making arrangements. You need to rest, go, have the rest of the week off. " He smiled. A cold hard gleam, had reached his eyes.

Chapter Thirty Two – Taxi!

He'd hailed a cab. This he did but rarely. He preferred the street car, he liked to walk, to disappear in the crowds. Cabbies talked. Sometimes. Sometimes they talked to him if he asked the right questions.

Today's cab, was driven by an old ex soldier, battle scarred, gash above one eye, healed into a mean scar.

He asked about a young blonde, the driver of course, had never heard of any Isobella.

"Look fella, I can ask around, see if anyone did any pick ups when, this morning?"

"Yeah, early, first thing this morning." Jaeson smiled. Sometimes they talked.

"Hey wait for me, just here. I'll be back. I won't be long, but I'll be just up the street here." He added.

"Hah, you're wasting your time! All these big shots have their own chauffeurs, there own sets of wheels! Ah, good luck to you anyways!" The cabbie called after him.

Good luck, there was nothing about luck in this case at all, it was all bad, dirty, rotten to the core, luck, good fortune, nowhere to be seen for that poor young woman. What was her story? Why didn't she rate the chauffeur and the limousine?

He felt sure she had left in a hurry, and without wanting to be seen. No luggage, few possessions. Why so few, if she was running away, what if she was thinking of running away? Why come to him?

Nothing added up.

He walked up the avenue, occasional trees dotted the pavement, or sidewalk, as the walls loomed over all. These were some wonderful places. You couldn't see it from the roadside, not unless you were lucky and caught a glimpse through one of the gates.

Sheesh. He'd seen the insides of one once, all manicured lawns, flower beds, huge rooms, big bedrooms, petty, petty people.

The bigger their pocket books, the smaller minded some people got. Damn, he was glad he was poor. Poor but honest. Some money would be good.

It wouldn't ruin him no sir, and he'd be nice to his servants, if he had any. Perhaps he'd just sail away around the world, forget America, forget the scummy, city streets, with their vice, their thieving and their betrayal.

Yeah, he'd buy a boat if he had money, buy a boat and sail the world. He was there. This was it. The address on the envelope. He triple checked. Yes, no question.

He pressed the bell, set into the wood work, on the side of two great double gates, built in black shiny painted wood.

Under stated, or stating everything? He wouldn't be sure until he saw the owner, if he got that far.

Some Major Domo would head him off, unless, he was really interesting.

Minutes passed, then a few more. He heard the crunching of feet walking down the gravel drive. Good someone' in, and going to at least say 'hello.'

He set his jaw grimly. Maybe they already knew, maybe not. Would he break it to them, that their Isobella was dead. No, he'd see how the ground lay first, that was the hardest job anyway. He'd learnt that on homicide. He never forgot the looks on the faces of those he'd had to tell, had to let them know their dreams were burned to the ground, and soon to be six foot deep in it.

A side door opened.

Damn it, I'm losing my touch. I should have seen that door, should have covered it. Who's going to throw open the main gates to talk to a stranger?

"Good Morning, Sir. How can we be of assistance?"

Coolly civil, this man did not really want to be of service to any washed up salesman calling at the door, did they know? He wasn't sure.

"Good Morning, I'm looking to speak to Isobella, please." He said quite casually, watching the tall middle aged man, his thin face impassive.

"I'm sorry Sir, there's no one of that name here." The flunkey replied. He didn't bat an eyelid. Not a twitch. This guy was cool under fire, or, there really was no Isobella here.

"Thank you. Must be my mistake." He turned and walked back to the cab. Not there. He gone to the right address, the one on the letter, the letter she had had in her bag, so she had received the letter from here, somehow.

But how? Who was there but not there, none of this made sense. He waved at the driver of the cab, who drove up and met him half way.

"No luck then?" The cabbie offered, grinning in a I told you so manner.

"No, and... yes." He smiled grimly.

Something was wrong, it all smelled wrong, he would check the morgue, see if they had found something he hadn't.

"Take me downtown, Police headquarters." He said.

"Whoa! You turning blue bottle now?" The cabbie gasped out in mock surprise and indignation.

"No, I just need to get reacquainted with a new friend."

"A new friend? Hah, well, it's your funeral."

A few minutes later he was there, settling up with the Cabbie, who turned out to be called Padraig, who'd promised to ask around, about blonde broads, and let him know.

A minute later than that and he was climbing the steps, gazing at the fancy stonework. Why did these places have to look like they belonged in a museum, or as a museum? He'd never cared when he was on the force. Why would he care now? Strange that he did.

Up the steps through the doors, a nod at John, another at Richie, past the desk sergeant. These guys all knew him, knew he was one of them, once, all half hoping they didn't need him, or become him, themselves.

"George!" He called out. A thin faced, slim Lieutenant, he'd done a favour for a few months back started and looked up at him, from across the open sea of desks. Ha! He may not make much some weeks but at least he had his own office.

His name across his rickety old door, it was some consolation.

The lieutenant got up and crossed the office to him.

"What can I do for you, this fine day?" He said smiling. The smile never reached his eyes. No one really liked

Private Eyes. Everyone thought they had it better, everyman's grass was always greener than someone else's.

"Hey! I won't stop you punching your clock for long George! I just need to take a look in your morgue."

George stared at him, then smiled, a bit more real this time. The morgue tour, once in awhile it came up, some people hated it, some people didn't. The lieutenant, was one of those guys with no fear of cool boxes, and the morgue was just another day in happyville, like anywhere else.

"Sure! I'll remember to put in some overtime to make up! I'll put you down, as assisting a distressed relative."

He grinned some more, as he led Jaeson towards one of the back stairs.

"So, whose the lucky stiff?" He asked.

"Some blonde named Isobella, you guys will have received her this morning."

The lieutenant paused, all friendliness gone and wariness settling in. Jaeson was surprised.

"You sure it was a blonde?" George asked, looking away.

"Yeah, may be out of a bottle, but blonde alright."

"Okay, look, we check with Bill."

They walked into the cooler room, cold steel autopsy table decorated the middle of the room. It was empty.

"Not started in yet. Well, I think I can tell you how she died. A bullet in the back. That's how. Anyway, did you guys ID the corpse."

Bill stared at him, he wiped his grey hair away from his eyes, and brushed his hands on his shirt. Holy father, thought Jaeson, just how many tells has this man got?

"Nope. No blondes this morning." He stated flatly.

Jaeson stared at him. How could that be possible.

"You're jerking my chain right? Dead by gunshot wounds right? There's no where else a body would go, this is the place! Unless, was she not dead?"

No, he thought. He answered that question for himself straight away. She was dead. Dead as his career, dead, as Bills eyes, she was gone, barring some kind of divine intervention. So where was she?

"Tours over children." Said George.

"Let's go." He added when Jaeson didn't move.

"Okay." Jaeson spoke quietly, his mind racing, and he turned and followed George, back out.

This was all wrong. He supposed Giovanni might know, that was his last lead.

Chapter Thirty Three – Afternoon Delights.

The suite of rooms really were fit for a King, or indeed a Queen. Nirnadel, just went with the flow. Her dirty trail worn blouse and skirt, was whisked away, to be replaced by several layers of fresh underthings, and after a little negotiation, and seam adjusting, a rather beautiful emerald dress.

The adjustments took under an hour apparently the Count had a large staff, including a fine tailor. This was unexpected. Her hair was expertly washed, brushed, cut and styled, again, by staff, who whizzed in when needed, then just as swiftly departed.

Just how many people did the Count employ? Oh, if her fathers palace had had as man staff, she'd have stayed. Well, perhaps only a bit longer, she felt sure the wander lust would have surfaced at some point any way.

Nothing was too much trouble, in fact some things were almost insisted upon. She relaxed. There was a sumptuous bathroom, with apparently, 'running water,' she wondered, if she ever became Queen, could she hire this Counts architect?

She suspected that, by the time she did, most people alive would be dead and gone, if she wasn't also.

Fudge submitted to a bit of grooming, and a bath. None of which improved his appearance in the slightest, but seemed to amuse him greatly. He knew the first mud hole he found would rectify any mild attempts at cleanliness inflicted now.

Something dogged at her mind, apart from Fudge. The coachman had said her mother was here.

"Excuse me...." She began, attracting the Butler's attention.

"Your majesty?" He moved with speed and precision, and was by her side, smiling obsequiously down.

"Look, I understand some of my friends are here, in particular my mother, who in actual point of fact, really is a Queen, albeit an absconded one, but all the same more deserving of the title of 'majesty' than I." She spoke carefully, and not too loud.

The Butler had leant forward, as she spoke, and now he lent back.

"Your majesty, is technically correct, but I have firm instructions from my master the Count to afford you full honours of State." He replied carefully, no hint of smile or frown.

"I would really like to see her, please." She added.

"Well, your mother and grandmother are getting ready, or relaxing before tonight's dinner party, but I'll send a messenger and see if they can wait upon your majesty's pleasure now, if you wish?"

"It's okay, I can go to them." Nirnadel, felt a little out of her depth. She was in charge except she wasn't in charge.

"Oh, your majesty, I'm sorry, protocol forbids you to call upon other guests in that way, they must wait upon you, in your private salon." He indicated another door, just across the room.

She'd had a peek earlier and it was a very nice drawing room or study, except there were no books. Just plush armchairs, loungers, and some very nice paintings. Also, it had no windows, being on the inside of the Keep.

Well, she thought, there it was, the catch. The gilding on the cage, she was a prisoner again, a very well kept one, but there it was. You are our top customer, our number one priority, so long as you do as we say, when we say it.

Fudge looked at her, he'd caught the vibe too, and was watching everything, and everyone, more intently.

"So, when can I see them. My grandmother is here too?" This was news.

"Oh yes, she is the special guest of the Count, and, indirectly, the reason for the dinner party, your majesty."

"Oh, thank you. If they can come see me before dinner I would be pleased." She said, quietly, realising, the odds that they would appear, were rather low.

She looked at Fudge. He stood up and discreetly, slinked towards the door.

Good boy, she thought. Fudge had got the message, he would see if he could find Rhian and Lyra, and find out what the score was. Or he would find the kitchens, which, going by the standards of the rest of the establishment, were likely to be very good indeed. Fudge grinned. Nirnadel narrowed her eyes.

Come on Fudge! There's a good boy! He slipped out after another servant, it was a busy room. It had been perfect, but apparently, it wasn't, bits of the room seemed to be changed hourly, clearly some standard, or test was applied that was failed by some part of the anatomy of the room, almost randomly.

She needed some quiet.

"I would like to rest for a bit." She said.

No sooner had she said that, than she was guided almost forcefully into the large stately bedroom, and helped to change into a rather ostentatious nightgown, and then helped into the gigantic bed.

She lay on the bed. This is ridiculous, she thought, there are still two maids sitting in the room. They were watching her, what for, she didn't like to guess. Despite herself, she fell asleep.

She awoke with a start.

Ding-a-ling! A bell rang.

"Oh Plank, I'm up!" She said.

Except, this wasn't Graeffenland, and Plank, her zombie Butler, was not present. Karles was present, a slight surprise upon his face. This was possibly the most emotion she had seen so far.

"Oh what is it?" She asked.

"Your majesty needs to get up and ready, for this evening, pre dinner drinks are served in half an hour."

She stood up, and was accosted almost immediately by her maids, in minutes, she was stripped and re dressed, this time in a low cut ruby dress she did not remember agreeing to. The day was going from bad to worse.

More embarrassment was to follow, she was not that embarrassed normally by little things, but when she needed to attend her toilet, she was still the centre of attention. She almost couldn't go.

Who she thought, trains these people?

Finally ready, feeling like a prize pig, about to be walked out in front of a panel of farmers. She was called.

"Drinks will be served now, your majesty." Said the Butler.

"Oh good. Do I get a choice?" She asked, as she was guided, by her footmen, and the Butler, back to the lift.

This is it she thought, it's going to be human sacrifice. The old Count isn't just going to be a mad old sorcerer, but he's going to have some strange rite or ritual, that requires a virgin princess.

Well, it probably won't work then, she thought smiling. She'd just sorted out that hurdle, the other week, with Dorestan, a rather nice man of the Wagons, who'd been handy during an exceptionally long revelry. Someone's birthday. She couldn't remember whose. A long party though.

The lift went up. Almost to the top, and the brass mesh doors opened, by the Butler, on another massively vast room. Hall, being the more correct terminology she realised. It was quiet something. The twilight still came in through various, great arched, leaded stained glass, windows, in fact some sunlight glanced in still from the west side, glancing off the leather seats, the wooden chairs, the tables, the waiters, the other guests.

She walked into the room, and the Butlers voice boomed out:

"Presenting her Royal Highness Princess Nirnadel of Graeffenland!"

"Hello." She said and waved at the five people, sitting around the small table. Two she knew straight away, and then there was Erik. He was there, in a smart blue suit. Another suited individual was there with a band over his eyes. A chill went through her.

She approached slowly, Rhian and Lyra, were both there, coifed, dressed elegantly, Lyra in a beautiful yellow evening gown, and Rhian in a similarly beautiful blue gown.

She sat beside them.

"This is nice." She said, alarm written all over her face.

Rhian grinned.

"It is, very." Lyra stated, smiling.

"Count Bruno has always been a spectacular host." She said encouragingly.

"You've been here before?" She asked.

"Oh yes, a few years ago. He's very accommodating, and rich." Lyra winked, and smiled more broadly.

"Oh no!" Nirnadel spoke, a bit more loudly than she intended.

"Hello, again! Turns out we're at the same do!" Erik offered jovially. She glared at him.

"And who's the mystic?" She emphasised the last word, whilst staring straight in Rhian's eye.

"I am Laudacros, a simple medium, and clairvoyant, humble guest of the Count this night." He smiled, bowing his head slightly.

"And I am Count Bruno Orvull. Welcome to my home, one and all." A deep voice proclaimed.

The voice belonged to a medium tall man, not fat, but not thin, his hair dark brown, in quite a young fashion. His trousers deep vermilion, his jacket a slightly darker hue, his shirt, fancily embroidered, his shoes, slippers of a traditional old southern style, their long toes curling. For some reason, he sported a scarlet tasselled hat, no brim, it just sat, stove pipe like, upon his head.

Nirnadel gazed at him in surprise, he looked middle aged, and yet, he couldn't be more than forty?

The Count smiled at her, gazing warmly into her eyes another chill gripped her. This was how a fly must feel, caught in a web.

He walked quickly over, and she rose, pushing back her chair, before a footman could move it for her.

"Your majesty!" Said the Count, bowing low, taking her hand and kissing it.

Nirnadel turned to Rhian, who was grinning, and then Lyra, who winked. Oh come on! What is this? Nirnadels thoughts ran wildly. Did they expect her to fall in with this Count, had they lost their senses?

"Are we expecting anyone else, or is this it?" She asked, dropping all formality. She was tired of playing this game. Cat and Mouse, was not for her. She wondered where Fudge had got to. She didn't like to ask Rhian, if they'd seen him. If he was roaming loose, they might need him, later.

"No, your majesty, we few will have a nice discreet dinner....." The Count did not get to finish.

A whoosh of air, and a figure stood in the room. He was dressed in fine charcoal robes, their runes, standing out, in beautiful arcane patterns. His forehead, with its third eye in a triangle tattoo, and his shaven head, under a purple skull cap, his brown eyes ranged around the room.

"I am Ten Grief. I understand there is a dinner party? Forgive my intrusion, but I need to speak to the Princess, at some point, and now, seems a good opportunity."

His voice was confident, his manner certain, his face smiled, but his eyes were hard.

The Count stepped back, away from Nirnadel, whose attention was now all on Ten Grief. He'd changed, no longer the gawky young apprentice, he'd filled out into the Mage and Necromancer he now was.

"Please join us for dinner! It would be my great honour to have one of the hero's defending us from shadow of chaos in the south." He indicated one of the chairs.

Nirnadel sat back down, pulling in her own chair, again. These footmen really were inattentive.

Rhian sipped her wine.

Why do I not have a drink? They said there would be drinks. Nirnadel beckoned a Footman. He came over. Bowing low.

"Less bowing, more wine, please." She said.

"Yes, your majesty!" he hurried away.

"May I sit beside you?" Ten Grief asked Nirnadel.

"Of course! What no, 'your majesty'?" She replied, as he sat down.

"Do you like that?" He asked quietly.

"No, please keep it informal!" She whispered.

Wine appeared, with extra glasses. Ten Grief just stared at his glass. The wine was red, Nirnadel tasted it, and it wasn't too bad.

Rhian nudged her.

"You're in demand. Money or Power, which do you prefer?" Rhian smiled, as she whispered in Nirnadel's ear.

"Are you trying to get me married off?" She asked in return.

"No, but enjoy it while you can!"

She smiled. There was something amusing, and exciting about the attention. Except of course, tomorrow she wanted to be back with the Wagons, and her people. That worried her, what if, she wasn't 'allowed' to go back? Could she escape, could they all escape, if she escaped? Would they want to go on the run with her? Was she being selfish? If she married one of these suitors, perhaps the Count, that could give security and privileges, to her people.

She looked down at the old stained wood of the table. A voice by her ear spoke.

"It is customary, for the guest of honour to sit at the head of the table, majesty." This was the Butler Karles, discreetly whispering in her ear.

An idea struck her, and she stood up. Her chair flew back, and she banged, not to hard, her hand on the table.

"Wonderful, lovely people!" She lied loudly.

"Please, let us all be as equals at this table for tonight! Let us dine as friends and allies, and let no rank, or formality be observed, beyond that necessary to having a good time."

Lyra spluttered, wine spraying out in front of her, and laughed.

Ten Grief smiled.

The Count nodded.

"Let it be as you say, a little more informal. I, will sit at the head of the table, as host."

He smiled, a footman drew forth the chair, a fine, red velvet upholstered affair, and he sat down. He waved for more wine.

No sooner had he sat, than an ominous glow started in the corner of the great chamber, all eyes locked upon it, and a small figure stepped through.

She, for it was indeed a she, was dressed in fine leather, light yellow brown in hue, short swords or knives were strapped to her legs, and she wore a warm padded leather jacket. She, was a gnome, and quite unusual, not just in that she understood the art of portalling, which, in itself was a rare talent still amongst gnomekind, but in that, as a lady gnome, she was defying convention by being a field agent, a spy for the Alt Konig.

The Count stood up.

"What can we do for you, good lady?" He didn't seem pleased.

"I am here to represent the interests of the Alt Konig of Gnomoria, and the Gnomeland Below." She declared.

"Any servant of the Alt Konig, is of course welcome here, but we're about to sit down to dinner, can it not wait?" The Count sounded peevish.

"As I said. I am here to see whatever is discussed, is formally relayed to the Alt Konig, and that, his opinions on matters of great import, are considered." Either by accident or on purpose, she let her hand slip to her knife hilt.

"I see, well, in that regard, would you care to join us, for dinner? 'Lady'?" He sounded strained.

"I'm no 'Lady', you may call me Elbie." She pulled back her goggles, brass with colourful glass lenses, leaving them on the brim of her leather cap.

There was a sound of scraping, and a 'high' chair, was brought up, and placed to the left of the blind mystic.

Elbie, slowly walked around the table nodding at various people, and staring at Nirnadel. Finally, she reached her seat, looking at it disdainfully, and then resignedly climbing into it. She was only twenty inches tall, if she was a foot and a half.

"Friends! I have a beautiful, and resourceful kitchen, I have suggested soup, a simple broccoli and cheese soup, as a first course, but ask for your hearts desire! Time is not an issue, and you can have any thing you wish." The Count beamed, this was the part of the evening he most enjoyed.

He looked around.

"And now for a little music!" He clapped his hands, and moved back to his seat.

A curtain, neatly fitted, drew to one side, within, a great alcove, and musicians, who struck up a mainly string classical refrain.

Nirnadel drank more wine.

"You know, your father is concerned for you." Ten Grief whispered.

"He's observed your adventures, watched your travels. He didn't like to interfere though. You should say 'hello,' or visit. Do you teleport?" He asked.

"No. I seemed to have missed that art off my list. If you have a handy 'how to' guide, I'll gladly take it. Anytime." She replied.

Ten Grief grinned, and gazed around the assembled dinner guests. What a motley crew, he thought. The mystic held his attention, the warning prickle at the nap of his neck, killed his smile dead on his lips, it slid away, to hide.

"Yes, you are correct." Nirnadel whispered in his ear.

"Why is he here?" Ten Grief asked.

"Oh I have dealings with everyone, and this gentleman is a great spiritualist, and medium." The Count spoke from the head of the table.

"Thank you." Laudacros, inclined his head towards the Count.

Wind rattled a window.

A servant hurried across the hall, presumably to check, and close it.

The music played away, rising and falling, the guests, looked around the hall, a sudden feeling of embarrassment, or indeed just discomfort, filling them. No one seemed to want to make conversation.

"Shall we order our first course?" Enquired the Count, attempting a smile. He looked around his guests. This wasn't going as he had planned. New arrivals, including new rivals, seemed to be set on diverting his planned schedule of events.

Still Nirnadel, seemed impressed, maybe. He wasn't sure. She didn't seem to like formality, and she had lets slip a few, odd things. The night as they say, was still young. She would come around to his way of thinking.

A sudden awareness filled him, the band was still playing but the guests were all staring at him.

"Yes, dear, we all said yes." This was the grandmother, Lyra. He'd drifted away. He'd need to watch that.

Smiling, he turned to the chief steward, Anton.

"Please com...." His words caught in his throat.

Another great whoosh, a double whoosh, in fact, and two figures stood, just by the musicians, who muddled their chords, one falling over in surprise. They stopped playing.

"We're here on a matter of great urgency!" Said the fellow in great white, bejewelled (glowing jewels at that) robes.

He was clearly a mage.

The second fellows robes were brown, and also magey.

"Yes!" Proclaimed the second, more bald, but also white bearded, Mage. He had spectacles. They were tortoise shell. He was also smoking. He passed the rollup to the first mage, who drew deep.

"I'm sorry, I really must insist you come back another time! I am entertaining guests! We are about to have dinner!" The Count almost shouted, frustration welling up in his voice.

"Food?" A strange light shone in the eyes of the white robed Mage.

"Yes!" Cried the Count.

"May, we join you?" Inquired the brown robed fellow.

"Oh very well, look who are you anyway?" The Count asked, more quietly.

"I am the Archeus Magnus, Alurici." Declared the white robed Arch Mage.

"And I am Master Mage Hunbogi, the Wise and All Knowing!" Declared Hunbogi, a bit unsteadily.

He was drawing again on the roll up.

They both grinned at the Count.

"Do please, take places at my table. There is always room for more distinguished guests. Master Hunbogi, I did part of your course you know? The mail order magick, you remember? Are you still in operation."

Hunbogi's smile faded, an ex student. These he avoided. Some asked for refunds.

"Oh yes, this IS Castle Navorny Uis, and you must be Count Bruno Orvull."

"You know this man?" Asked Alurici, looking askance at Hunbogi.

"Only from a distance, you understand." Replied Hunbogi.

They took seats.

Ten Grief looked at the Archeus Magnus, and smiled.

Alurici just stared at him.

"Who's guarding the border?" He asked.

"Oh, General Rutger Tostwic, is most capable." He replied.

"He's one of your damned zombies!" Alurici offered, aggressively.

Ten Grief raised his eyebrows.

"How good are your herbs?" He asked.

"Tell me, can you let me know how to teleport? That would be really useful just right now." Nirnadel had leant forward, and was staring straight at the Archeus Magnus.

A mellow smile crossed Alurici's face.

"My dear young lady! I could teach you many things!" He smiled.

Ten Grief looked at the arch of the ceiling. It was really well executed, just like this Archeus Magnus should be.

"Would you like some?" Hunbogi's voice piped up.

"I have plenty, happy to share." His smiling glasses, looked around the table.

"Now, please let my Stewards take your orders!" Said the Count in his best everything is under control voice.

"Look, can we have some wine here?" Said Alurici.

"Yes, of course! More wine!" The Count nodded to the Stewards.

They came round, three young, blue liveried men, two with wine bottles, one with a stylus and notepad.

"More wine?" Some said.

"What would you like for a starter?" Followed by honorific of choice or indeed best guess.

Hunbogi snorted when he was addressed as your magocratship.

The stewards finally withdrew, and a roll up, smoking gently, was being passed around.

"Oh no, not for me! Where did you get those goggles?" Nirnadel, passed on the herbs roll up, and inquired of the lady gnome, whom, hadn't taken off her goggles or leather cap, and had pointedly asked for fish, as a starter.

"Top secret." She replied.

"Hah! There specially treated glass, to reduce the insanity blasting effects of certain blasphemous tomes, and, or, creatures of horror." This was the Archeus Magnus, his pupils just that bit more dilated than they should be. He'd taken a deep draw, on the new roll up.

She stared at him.

"What's with the herbs?" She asked.

"We are getting in the vibe of the ancient shamen. We are learning their arts from first principles and we are making great discoveries."

Bread rolls, fresh and warm had appeared. Without waiting, he and Hunbogi, had buttered their rolls, and were steadily tearing into them. They looked hungry.

"Oh, you know I had a dream about a shaman, a few days ago." Nirnadel mentioned.

They ignored her.

Except for the 'medium'.

"I know." He said, and smiled.

"It won't help you." He whispered.

Nirnadel looked right and left. No one else seemed to have noticed.

Thunder echoed above the music, which had resumed, after a brief hiatus.

A great flare of light blazed in the corner.

"Oh what now?" Exclaimed the Count.

A great figure, nine feet tall, in furs, great bushy brown and silver beard shrouding his youngish looking face. He gazed around the great hall, and fixed his eyes on Alurici.

Count Bruno Orvull, had never seen the like. He'd read all about giants of course, but they were just in books, and they didn't go around rending the dimensions to travel, as a general rule.

This one glowed with his own light, and seemed a little transparent. He stepped towards Alurici.

"Hey, whatever your name is..." The Count tailed off, he hadn't had enough wine to deal with this, perhaps he needed herbs.

The giant turned towards him. His eyes were like sledgehammers, he felt transfixed.

"We're just sitting down to dinner, won't you join us?" The Count managed. A cold sweat starting down his back.

The gaze relaxed, and his limbs felt free again.

"Please, find a place, and we'll bring up, uh, something for you to sit on." The Count continued.

"Thank you. I am Adan, I have a 'USP' apparently, but I forget at the moment, something to do with weather. Yes, I will eat first, then I'll want answers from one of your guests." As he spoke, he seemed to solidify, to become more real, if that was possible.

Adan paused, a slight delay wouldn't matter, and he could see what full manifestation was like.

The awestruck stewards, found a long lounger, which reinforced by stools, seemed to do. He sat at the far end of the table.

The bravest steward, enquired tremulously, what he would like for a starter.

"Oh, thank you. Just some fruit, would be fine." He replied.

He gazed at the Archeus Magnus, it certainly looked like the Mage who'd visited Libraria's halls.

"Maybe, some bananas." He added, watching the white robed Mage.

Alurici, weighed up the giant apparition. He could get off a teleport spell, in under a second, how fast was this new godling? Still if he was clever it wouldn't come to that.

"Does that count as power?" Nirnadel asked Rhian, in a whisper.

"I wouldn't get involved there dear, unless, he knows a shrinking spell!" Rhian laughed.

Lyra grinned.

"Leave that one for us!" Lyra added, and then looked thoughtful.

"We've met him before, remember?" She nudged Rhian.

"Friend of your ginger crush." She continued.

Rhian stared.

"He's changed!" She exclaimed.

"Maybe, he'll put in a bid later." Lyra whispered.

Nirnadel, looked at them both perplexed.

"Actually, I'm looking into the possibilities of growing bananas, purely in the laboratory, for their health benefits, you know." Alurici drew on the roll up, and then offered it in Adan's direction. He slowly shook his head.

"Nothings what it seems, that's what the shamen have taught me, traps everywhere." Alurici continued, blowing smoke out through his nose.

The lady gnome coughed, and then sneezed.

Adan waved, and the smoke, lifted on a small zephyr, swirled to the arch of the vaulted ceiling.

"What's the trap in a library then?" He asked.

"Yes, it is! Quite so!" Said Hunbogi, taking the roll up.

"What?" Said Adan.

"Precisely! The question is the trap, the answer is the spring!" Hunbogi continued enthusiastically.

"No, the question is the spring, the answer is the trap." Said Alurici.

"Or vice versa, either or, it doesn't matter, as soon as you open that book, they have you!" Hunbogi continued, enthusiasm undimmed.

"Like your Hammer." Said Alurici, grinning.

Adan looked down, a bucket of fruit had just been placed before him. It wasn't what he'd had in mind. Carefully he fished out an apple, with two fingers and inspected it.

He had brought his Hammer, it was on a long thong slung over one shoulder. It seemed to be sulking.

The starters appeared. Everyone ate. Even the medium, who if he wasn't clearly blind, could have been said to be staring at Adan.

The Count nibbled his duck pate, on toast, with salad.

It was all going wrong. Sure it was going to be the most memorable party ever, but by the gods, including present, company it seemed, it was not going how he'd wished.

His latest guest had been asked if he had any preference in music, and he'd said no, just nothing nautical.

Chapter Thirty Four – Finding the Source.

"Well, you know my dear fellow, I thought you'd get used to this all this." PAM addressed Berythus.

Berythus Naechos was cowering against one of the strange egg carton walls, it was solid, smooth, and cool. To his mind unmistakeably real.

It helped if he shut his eyes. This he had done. It helped more if he clapped his hands over his ears. Better still if he performed a meditative trance chant. This he did, constantly, for hours.

"Lalalalalalalalalalalalalala" Chanted Berythus.

PAM gazed at him. Clearly the poor chap had lost his mind. Oh well, it didn't matter. He'd scanned his dimensional reflux vibration, and had fed it into his great philosophical engine. He was tracing the line of the crack in reality, forward and back, using the poor priests reality signature.

"We'll soon be there, I know you can't hear, old chap, but we're nearing the origin point of the problem, yes, reality is unstable, oh dear me, most unstable indeed. Yes, I shall have to re-enter the Metacosmos a bit earlier, get a few more readings, hmm, perhaps here? Yes, I'll try here."

He manipulated a couple of dials, and twisted a knob. The central alchemical column groaned and wheezed to a halt, the magical coloured vapours and lights dimming down.

"Yes, looks like we're on some kind of starship, do you know what a starship is? No, well, nevermind."

"Lalalalalalalalalalalalalalalalalalalala!" Continued Berythus, enthusiastically.

"It's amazing! I do believe he can keep that up all day!" PAM put the child lock on the controls just in case.

"Better safe than sorry!" He muttered, under his breath.

He turned a dial, and the doors opened inwards. They had appeared in some kind of hold, a cargo hold.

With a little smile, and a light whistled tune he stepped out and immediately lost his footing!

"Oh dear! There's no gravity! It must be a really primitive starship, to have no gravity!"

He waved his arms and slowly floated towards one wall.

"It's just not civilized. Every starship should have gravity!"

He caught, what very much resembled, the rung of a ladder, running he could see, all the way up to a sphincter style hatch.

"Upwards, or is it downwards, and onwards!" He smiled.

He climbed easily, hand over hand, reaching the hatch in but a few moments. Looking at the glowing jewelled pad beside it, pressed a few. They beeped as he pressed them.

Whoosh! The hatch opened, sliding back into the neighbouring walls, in angular segments.

Beyond, a tunnel, in bright white, hatches on either side, and the same style inset metal ladder, running its whole length.

"Oh dear, still no gravity, hey ho, glad I didn't have any breakfast, still, there it is. Tally ho!" He commented, unnecessarily.

A light started flashing red.

"Oh dear! Whenever I go anywhere, there's always trouble."

A hatch at the far end of the tunnel opened. A figure, nude, hairless, slim, toned, youthful and athletic. The face a vision of horror!

"John, quick, do an atmospheric analysis, check for any foreign compounds, as well as oxygen levels." She wiped her eyes, and looked again.

"Oh, there's nothing wrong with the air on board this ship, but where's the gravity? Oh, I see! Just in the crew compartments! That's a bit cheapskate you know, but understandable."

PAM smiled, as innocently, and harmlessly as possible. If anything, she seemed more frightened.

"Who are you, how did you get on board, our sensors picked up no ship approaching. You, must be a hallucination."

"My name, is entirely academic. Just trust me, momentous things are afoot, terrible things, the entire future of reality is at stake!" He offered, as earnestly as the script would allow.

"Are you reading from that notebook?" She asked, confusedly.

"No, no of course not. I'm just checking some figures I noted down earlier." PAM quickly stowed his crib sheet, the rest was plain sailing.

"Odd, you know, I don't remember having any thing like that before." He mused, rubbing his chin in thought.

"So, Mister Aka Demik, what are you doing on my ship, and how did you get here?"

A male voice spoke up.

"Air checks out, normal, except some artificial fibres, and, you won't believe it, some cheap twentieth century cologne."

"My ship travels the dimensions of the Metacosmos, and, well, it's parked in your cargo hold. That's not important now, you're all in great danger!" PAM said, theatrically.

"We know." She narrowed her eyes.

"Can you, you know puts some clothes on?" PAM asked.

"No, why? Does it matter?" She replied.

"No, of course not!" PAM exclaimed, huffily.

"You still haven't told me why you're here?" She asked.

"I'm here to save the Metacosmos!" He stated, a bit loudly.

"Yeah, sorry. Where I come from that isn't even a word. Why should I believe you? Look we're stuck in the gravity well of a stellar anomaly, I don't have time for hallucinations, Mister Demik."

"Yes, I think I can get you out of here, just let me see your instruments." PAM asked, with a calming smile, really he most wanted to get somewhere with gravity again.

"Do you mean the avionics systems?" She asked.

"Yes, probably, they would do." He said.

She withdrew back into the cabin, and shut the hatch.

"John, you are Captain now, do not open that hatch on any account." She stated, quickly jabbing a hypodermic into her thigh.

"I'm going to sleep for a bit now." She strapped herself in as the drug warmly numbed first her legs then her torso and then rolled over her, wrapping her in a comfortable blanket of darkness.

"Right, well, that didn't go very well." PAM said to no one in particular. He looked back down the tunnel. There was, he'd noted, a science laboratory.

He climbed back down the tunnel, floating, pulling himself hand over hand, and there it was. He pressed the keypad stud. The hatch whooshed open.

He pulled himself in, swinging his legs round as the artificial gravity took hold.

"Oh that's so much better! Feet on terra firma, and all that! Oh yes! Here it is, their observations, and data sets. I'll just scan them into my hand held all purpose doohicky...."

He pulled forth a slim, knobbly metal wand, clicked it and it glowed, whirred, and hummed. Another twist and it projected a blue beam, conical in shape, and played it across the computer banks. The humming stopped.

"There it is, all absorbed, I'll just take these back to my ship, and run my own analysis..."

The ship lurched.

"Oh, looks like I'll have to go now. A pity. I don't think I'll write this up in diary."

Quickly he swung back out of the cabin, and, as fast as he could, he headed back down to the cargo hold. His cabinet, doors still open awaited him.

"Yes, time to go old girl!" He whispered. Swinging down, and pulling in.

Back inside, feet back on firmer ground, he plugged his knobbly blue wand into the philosophical engine, and threw a switch.

He watched a display, which, though not obvious before, had somehow always been there. His mouth fell open, quickly he pressed a button. Amazing how new buttons always appeared at need. A part of the magick of the philosophical engine.

A multicoloured filter sprung up between him and the display.

"Ah, that's better, some information is quite, ah, dangerous to look at, in the raw." He muttered.

"I know, the answer." Said a quiet little voice from the corner.

"I wrote it all down on this scroll, it's all here. If I can get it back to the High Priests council, I can stop all this."

"Don't worry old chap! I may not be able to save the crew of this starship, but I can get you somewhere safe, where you can be properly looked after. Don't you worry!" Said PAM, smiling warmly, down at the sad looking priest.

"But, I have the answer!" He whispered quietly, hopelessly.

"Yes, yes, quiet now, I need to think....." PAM steepled his fingers, and then pulled a lever.

The magickal blue cabinet vanished from the hold of the doomed Starship, whizzing off through the interlacing folds of the Metacosmos.

Chapter Thirty Five – Close Encounter of the Gnome Kind.

They stalked through the reeds, a team of six, each pair holding one end of a flatish, wide skiff. Paddles, of light wood, lay within. The reeds, like young trees, hide the gnomish party from all but the keenest and most attentive viewers. This means they were spotted almost immediately, by Captain Fortunes lookouts, who, were both plentiful, on guard, and very keen indeed.

The gnomes, however, did not yet know they had been spotted.

They waded on, finally, at a wave, from the lead gnome, the grizzled, grim faced Commander Jolly, whose scarified visage, alone, was enough to send goblins running, in all directions, but his, they carefully, climbed on board, their subtle vessels.

Drawing specially designed broad cloaks around them, coloured to hide them from sight, scented to put alligators to flight, they paddled, slowly but surely towards the great galleon.

The fit, battle hardened, toughened gnomes, made short work of the distance, their paddles rising and falling soundlessly into the deep blue waters of the great river. Soon, they were barely a skiffs length away, and at another predetermined signal, they drew forth long reels of rope, with specially designed padded grapples.

They drew up, threw up, the grapples that is, and proceeded, up the ropes hand over hand, each skiff tethered, to one rope end, so drifting, but not too far.

Up they climbed, silently, skilfully, passed windows and hatches, sounds of the ship reaching their ears. Looking up, no one to be seen at the rails, they raced up the last six or so feet, reaching the rails and hopping over.

"Hello, boys! What can we do for you today?"

Before them, thirty or forty, pirates, crossbows levelled, at them. The gnomes stopped in their tracks. Commander Jolly, pulling his face scarf down, on his desert white combat dress, stared up at the dusky skinned islander.

"Captain! We have guests!" Yelled the second Mate. This was Yarick, an islander from the south, his orange, and yellow head scarf, setting off, his smiling round face.

He liked the gnomes, they had a good reputation, but why they were on his Captains ship he had no idea.

He brushed his hands on his red damask frock coat, lightly resting his hand on his cutlass hilt. He felt nervous, the gnomes were watching him like a hawk.

"I am Commander Jolly, I'm here to talk to your Captain on a matter of some urgency."

The Commanders voice, was surprisingly deep, and very authoritative. Second Mate Yarick, gazed around, waved to one man, and spoke.

"Go see where the Captain is, quickly now!" He spoke.

"Do I need the crossbows?" He asked Commander Jolly.

"Maybe." Said the Commander, a deeply serious look on his face.

"Now, that's not very friendly. Come on, tell your men to set down their arms, and when the Captain gets here we can all talk, civilized, like." Suggested the second Mate.

"Stand easy, men!" Spoke the Captain.

Garim, the erstwhile, most successful 'Pirate,' well, goods salvager, and antiquities recoverer, in the world, stood, cream coloured shirt hanging vaguely open, dark baggy trews, bagging, and knee high boots, lurking, just below the knee.

He stroked the reddish down on his chin, and gazed down at the gnomes, and their startling fierce looking Commander.

"I'm the Captain! This is my ship! What do you want?" He asked, quickly. He counted six gnomes. Gnomes were dangerous, these were clearly a crack team, perhaps with alchemical weapons, in addition to their more obvious mini swords.

"You, must turn this ship around." The Commander spoke, his deep voice growled.

"Furl sails! Drop anchor!" Garim yelled, over his shoulder. Crewmen, their feet slapping on the decks, ran to obey.

"You, must go back." Insisted the Commander, looking decidedly unjolly if such were possible, and in his case, it was.

"Come on, why? What did you say your name was?"

"I am Commander Jolly of the Long Range Desert Gnomes, and you are sailing into trouble." Commander Jolly explained, slowly.

"Alright, we aren't sailing any more. What trouble are you saying we are heading into? The Horde? Is Arshan over there?" He pointed, vaguely up river.

Commander Jolly, deep lines of seriousness, creasing his forehead, sighed.

"Yes, yes he is. If you're headed to the city, Eghior, as was, that's just where Arshan's forces are, and you won't return."

The Commander continued just loud enough to be overheard by everyone on deck.

"We fear no one, not man, not possessed, nor demon monsters, we are warriors of the sea!" Declared the second

Mate loudly, to grunts, and muttered sounds of approval, from the crew.

Garim, Captain Fortune, smiled, esprit de corps was on a high, it always was, but they hadn't really fought any battles of note, not yet.

"Good, but how many are you?" Said the grizzled gnomish Commander.

"Two hundred, fierce and strong! What do you say to that, little man?" Said the second mate, a bit angrily.

"Ten thousand possessed, at least, thousands of weird mutants, hundreds of strange legged beasts that defy sense or reason, goblins too. That's just what our advance scouts have seen." The gnomish Commander offered firmly.

"It seems, you have stopped us from walking into, a disaster. You know, when first you spoke, I did wonder about launching a raid, just into the harbour, and out. You're saying the city is strongly defended?" Garim spoke slowly, still rubbing his chin.

A strange look passed over the gnomes face.

"No, it's an encampment, it's not even got patrols, there are just huge numbers of the enemy, based there." The gnome stated.

"Ah, so it's undefended? An army is based there, but it is not expecting action? Or attack?" Garim, smiled.

"No, they won't be expecting you, unless, they have already seen your ship." The gnome stared him in the eye.

Garim's smile faded.

"The city is a mess, the chances of you, or your crew, finding anything of value, is slim. It is a nightmare, and somewhere within, to the north east, is the old citadel, rebuilt larger, cruder, and the dwelling of the Devourer itself. This is where you are thinking of taking your men."

Commander Jolly, allowed himself a smile. It was thin, self conscious, and knew it was out of place even before it got started. It did not get near his nose, let alone, his eyes.

"Alright, you've given me much to think about. I need to consider all this information and then in council with my men, decide what to do." Garim continued, nodding towards his men, when he mentioned the council.

"What's to decide, life or death? What choice, just go back the way you came." Commander Jolly exclaimed.

"It still needs to be thought through and discussed, we are a democracy!" Garim declared.

Cries of 'yeah', 'sure' and much laughter, rose from the crew.

"Now, now, lads, we've got rules!" Garim, had turned towards the crew.

Commander Jolly looked at his feet. Humans, he thought, were idiots. He contemplated how much alchemical 'bang' powder, would be required, to sink the ship, looking at the size of it, and the depth of the river, it wouldn't actually sink, more wallow. It just didn't seem a very satisfactory idea.

"It won't take long, just an hour or two, and then, assuming the crew agrees, we'll head back down river to the sea. It'll take us a couple of hours to turn her carefully, anyway." Garim spoke quietly.

"We do not want to run aground." He added.

"We will give you time, but reach the right decision." Said Commander Jolly, flatly.

Chapter Thirty Six - Man of Mystery.

The cobbles were hard, shiny, wet, and cold. Jaeson Smith, his head, bleeding a little, blood slowly coagulating, matting his scalp. He groaned, his dream jumped a little.

He looked out at the street. People walked, hurried, drove or dawdled. Just a normal Boston day, he walked down the steps. No body, there should be a body, but no body.

Giovanni, Italian name, Italian word, 'fantastic.' Yesterday, life had been 'fantastico.' Now it was a dead broad, and crushed dreams, and where would Giovanni be?

He was well off, but not old money, wrong side of the tracks, that's why they were leaving town. Wrong side of the tracks, well off, and Italian. With money to buy furs, perhaps, if the lady did not have money for furs.

He turned his feet towards main street. Somewhere nice, somewhere that sold nice furs, and somewhere Italian too, that might offer a discount to a brother from the old country. He'd start there.

Meandering, what was the rush? The lady was already dead, and dead lost to the system, whatever had gone wrong there, who knew? Someone must know. No one's body just vanishes.

Unless, it was the Mob. Italian beau, needs to smooth out some ruffled feathers, from the wrong side of the tracks, and the body goes missing, sounds like the Mob.

Bent coppers, the worst. Someone must have been paid off, to remove the body, or not even deliver the body. Hah, must be sensitive, if they care where the body ends up!

The Mob didn't usually care about that. Maybe, the family? Maybe they were hushing it up?

Odd, that, wrong side of the tracks, mob connections, not wanted, but that's not worth killing someone over, or hiding the evidence. None of this made any sense.

Ah, another tailors, this one was a bit posh, very smart, a Mister Luigi Genetto, proprietor. It had fur, too.

"Excuse me." He began.

"Why certainly, you can be excused. Whata hava you done?" Smiled the friendly tailor. A medium sized, tubby gentleman, whose eyes twinkled as he spoke.

"An acquaintance of mine was in here, oh, just the other day, buying furs for his lady, you know, Isobella, and Giovanni?"

"Ah, si, si. A lovely young couple, so very much in love!" He beamed.

"Well, I wanted to send them something, a tie, maybe, a scarf too, something pretty for the bride." He smiled.

Finally, someone who had met Isobella, and would admit to it.

He paused, why on earth would that be a problem for anyone?

"Here we are, some most beautiful ties, and I'll bring the scarves..." He hurried away.

He had no clue about ties, and so picked out a nice blue one.

The tailor returned, with scarves, decorously draped over one arm.

"And, here we have the very finest scarves!" He set them down.

Jaeson picked one, a colourful one reds and greens, with a pretty butterfly motif.

"Ah, you have a very good eye! That is a very fine scarf, indeed!"

"Can you forward them for me? I had the address." He patted his pockets.

"But I seem to have left it in my diary, back at the office." He continued, looking sheepish.

"That is no problemo! I have the address right here, oh, I'ma sorry, it's just his business address." The tailor looked downcast.

Jaeson leant forward, 'Marvello Imports and Exports,' the rest obscured or too small to read, but docks, did stand out.

"Ah, it's okay, I'll take them back to the office." Said Jaeson, a smile breaking across his face.

It had cost him a few dollars, but there it was, an address. Mob to the bone, Giovanni, worked on the docks, doubtless some kind of smuggling. But Giovanni, was just a small cog, the tailor had said it all, young. Some young dude wants out the familia, going to go make a new life somewhere else with his young bride to be.

The tailor finished wrapping.

"That'll be $52 please." He smiled.

No wonder he was smiling.

"Ten, twenty, thirty, forty, fifty, uh, sixty dollars. I'll need the change please." Jaeson counted out bills from his wallet.

"But of course! And .... Here you go!" Smiled the tailor.

"If you ever want a suit, you know, I could fix you up real nice." The tailor eyed his old, battered outfit, thoughtfully.

"Oh, well, yeah, maybe, but, I'm always in and out the warehouse, on the factory floor, smoke and dust and dirt. You know, wouldn't be fair on the suit." Said Jaeson, as he tucked the change away, and then the packet under his arm.

"You need a piece for that." Smiled the tailor.

"Oh yes, big rats, always." Jaeson threw away, as he turned and walked out the door.

"Good luck." Grinned the tailor, the guy hadn't even haggled.

So, to the docks. No time like the present. He checked his gun, all in order there. He hoped he wouldn't need it.

Chapter Thirty Seven – Second Course.

Nirnadel, had enjoyed the soup, apparently a strong blue cheese subliminated into a hot broccoli liquefaction.

Alurici, the Archeus Magnus, and whatever else he may be, had stared with fascination at his, and then renamed it, while secreting a small amount into a stoppered test tube, for extended analysis at a later date.

He'd also cleared his bowl, mopping up the dregs with a fresh bread roll. Erik had stared at the giant all thro the first course.

Finally, Adan had looked up at him.

"Do I know you, man?" He'd asked.

Erik had almost jumped out of his skin.

"Yes, we met! At the top of your mountain. That's why I'm here! Ah, you glowed less then. Nice to see you're getting out, can't be good for you to sit at the top of a mountain all the time!" He wittered nervously, toying with his duck pate.

Adan bite into apple. It was okay.

The two Magi, smoked through dinner. Hunbogi didn't like his fish terrine. He didn't say why, just drank more wine, and drew more of his roll up. When one finished, he'd draw out a fresh paper, and then crushed herbs, poured from a pouch, which he would expertly roll in fractions of a second.

Nirnadel smiled. Whether it was the food, the warmth, the music, the strange herby smoke, she felt relaxed, so relaxed, and she was enjoying herself.

She smiled at Erik.

"We'll have to have another scrub sometime." She grinned thinking of the mornings, bubbly adventure.

Erik coughed, and looked, if anything more nervous.

The head Steward hurried up to the Count, a worried look on his face. He whispered briefly. The Counts face became a mixture of surprise, disbelief, consternation, and finally sad resignation.

He stood, tapping his glass.

"My dear guests." He paused.

Everyone looked, more or less in his direction.

"Ahem, it looks like there has been a small, trifling, ah, riot, in my kitchens. The panic is over now, but some wild beast has, helped itself to our provender. Except, the beef stew, which I understand is excellent. I hope that will be alright for everyone?"

Lyra, Rhian, and Nirnadel looked at each other. Nirnadel giggled.

Elbie stood on her seat.

"Fish or nothing!" She declared.

"Well, we'll see what can be done." The Count looked at the Steward, who shrugged and nodded. There must be fish left somewhere.

"While we wait, and ..... do you have to keep smoking at the table?" Enquired the Count of the two Magi.

"Oh no, we, er, don't have to do anything." Alurici smiled, and took a long drag on the roll up.

Hunbogi grinned.

"Life is just an illusion, all just a cosmic dance, dust motes in the sunshine, faeries floating on the waves of infinity, at the bottom of my glass...." Hunbogi crossed his eyes, and waggled his empty wine glass. It was duly topped up.

"You said it was all a trap? What was that all about?" Spoke the giant, otherwise known as Adan. He rested his hammer on the table, it whined.

"Oh, and if I'm having stew too, it better not turn up as half a cow." He stared meaningful at the bucket of fruit, largely untouched.

"You wasted my brother Mages, I was there I saw you do it." Hunbogi took back the roll up, and took a long drag.

"I didn't know what was going on, ask Rhian, yes, her there, she brought by ship all the way to your wretched island.

I didn't know there'd be Dragons." Adan scowled, a dark cloud, quite literally swirling into existence over his head.

"Oh, it was all Xagigg's idea, any way, Dragons shouldn't be cooped up in binding enchantments." Rhian retorted.

"But its okay for faeries to be enslaved that way." This was Elbie, gnomishly staring at Lyra, Rhian, and to a lesser extent Nirnadel.

"Oh yes, it's traditional." Said Lyra, nastily.

She reached down into a small bag, and drew forth a glowing blue bottle.

"Well, this is why I'm here at any rate." She said.

"Ooo!" A gasp escaped Eriks lips.

"Oh now that stuff, is nasty." Quoth Ten Grief, who had been bemusedly watching proceedings.

"What's so bad about it?" Asked Nirnadel.

"She doesn't know!" Alurici giggled, drawing deeply from a fresh roll up.

"She doesn't. What happened to her majesty this, and that?" Asked Nirnadel of no one in particular.

"Oh, that looks like the Woodfolks potion." Said Adan, leaning over.

"That is mine!" Shouted the Count, surprise and annoyance writ large across his features.

"Not yet." Said Lyra.

"We haven't agreed a price."

"What price is a Soul?" Asked Leudocros, smiling, his bandaged face turning from one to another.

"That's dark magick." Said Hunbogi.

"Will someone just tell me what it is?" Said Nirnadel.

The stew arrived. The Stewards duly placed bowls, more bread, and spoons before the guests.

Adan received a large bowl, and a ladle. At least it wasn't part of a cow, raw.

Fish, eventually arrived, for Elbie, who still stared, with barely concealed hatred at Lyra and Rhian.

The stew was very nice.

Nirnadel put her spoon down. Sipped her wine, and stared at the glowing blue bottle.

"I still want to know what it is." She looked pointedly at Lyra, who smiled and looked away.

"It's a power potion." Said Rhian.

"Used to power the great binding enchantments used on faeries, that, used to be used on faeries." She smiled at Elbie.

"While they worked." Said Lyra flatly.

Elbie stabbed at the remains of her fish.

"I've tried it or one very similar." Stated Adan, looking thoughtfully, at the blue glowing bottle.

"Will no one tell me what it is?" Exclaimed Nirnadel.

"It is power, the power for me to complete my researches!" declared the Count.

"What research are you doing?" Asked Alurici, genuine academic interest gleaming in his slightly blood shot eyes.

"Why is my Hammer a trap? Thank you, I will try that...." Adan carefully took the half expired roll up from Hunbogi, and positioning it carefully between his lips, gently sucked.

"You know, you killed my friends." Said Hunbogi. Staring at Adan.

"Hah! They weren't your friends! They were barely colleagues!" Alurici smiled, and drank more wine.

"My research, is a whole new field of Magick!" Declared the Count forcefully, and portentously.

"Nothing new under the Sun, old boy." Alurici observed dryly.

Ten Grief smiled, and shrugged, at Nirnadel.

Erik, coughed.

"Well, that was very nice." Lyra added.

"Why is it dark magick?" Asked Rhian.

"Will there be desert?" Enquired Hunbogi.

"It is inevitable." Said Leudocros, leering.

"Naturally, in a few minutes." Said the Count.

"Explain to me, what the problem is, with my Hammer?" Said Adan, staring forcefully at Alurici, who even as a mighty Archeus Magnus, or Arch Mage, felt the power behind the eyes.

"When is a Hammer, not a Hammer?" Said Hunbogi, giggling.

"Alright, when is a Hammer not a Hammer?" Asked Adan, a light drizzle wetting his neck.

"What would you like for desert, my lord?" Said a Steward.

Chapter Thirty Eight – Down Among The Dock Men.

Mists rolled, lapping, caressing, stroking the recumbent, dripping form, laying upon the cobbles, stirring and moaning uncomfortably.

Jaeson Smith walked from the tailors, parcels under arm, wrapped in thought. Marvello Imports and Exports, shouldn't be too hard to find. Sunshine filtered in through the clouds, he wove and wandered through the crowds, in the distance the sea, from time to time visible as the road curved and twisted.

Down he walked further and further, until the sounds of workmen, back from their lunch breaks assailed his ears, and there, the wharfside lay before him, rail way tracks to one side, sea and warehouses to the other. Old, decrepit, but busy, very busy. People from many lands touched the shores here, some for a while, some never left.

He was glad of his scruffy suit. Just enough to fit in, not too rough to stand out. He walked up to a rangy muscled stevedore.

"I'm trying to find Marvello's?" He asked.

"Huh." A grunt, and a hand pointed, arm extended, showing the way down the street.

"Thank you..." He nodded, and set off. Just a few minutes later, he was before the battered, rain and salt stained doors of their old warehouse.

"Marvello Imports and Exports." He said aloud.

He approached the doors. Silence, he pushed them, the door on the right swung inwards. Dim light filled the interior.

He stepped in.

"Hello?" He said, not too loudly.

No flashlight, he cursed himself for a fool. Never mind, he walked further in, to his left, piles of boxes, to his right, trucks covered in tarpaulin.

A bit quiet in here? He wondered, slowly walking towards the back of the warehouse.

A small room, lit from within, caught his eye. It, too, seemed empty. He walked over, maybe they have a staff list, clocking on cards, something. The door, wasn't locked, he opened it.

A low moan greeted him, and to his left, lying on the floor, yet tied quite firmly to a chair, a youngish man, dark haired, slim, beaten, face swollen, bruised, bloody, lips mashed, teeth bloody.

Moaning slightly, he turned his head, staring at his new visitor.

"Hey, what going on?" Said, Jaeson crouching down, and working the knots loose.

They were tied, tight and nasty. They took time to shift, finally giving way under his tough old fingers. The wrists beneath were bruised and scrazed. He untied the mans ankles, finally he stood looking down on the now recumbent figure, half curled into a fetal position.

"You can't stay here, this place clearly is no health farm."

"You're coming with me." He said.

Here he was, playing good samaritan for some stranger, well, why not? Who knew what would come of it?

He reached down, lifting the man by his arms.

He moved, half carrying, half dragging, the man with him.

"Ungh!" Said the man, as he lent, almost entirely, on Jaeson.

"Right....Come on we'll get you out of here." Jaeson offered.

"Where the hell do youse think your going?" a light, but menacing voice came out of the shadows.

Another door, now, open, three figures stepping through. One medium height, black leather gloves, glistening, hat, brim shadowing his eyes, mouth twisted.

The other two, more burly, or more fat, one of those, loomed behind, grinning, menacingly.

They spread out, loomed out, blocking the way to the door, covering the room, easily.

"You another one of his fag friends?" Asked the man in the menacing hat.

"Hey, let's keep this friendly. I just found this guy, thought I'd get him to a doctor....." Jaeson offered. This was bad, whatever this kid was mixed up in, they now had him pegged for it too.

"You set him down there..." Pointed the man in the hat.

"Yeah, what did he do?" Asked Jaeson, carefully weighing up his chances.

"What did he do? What did he do? You sonavabitch!" The man in the menacing hat, looked purple, veins bulged, in his temples.

The figure he was holding lurched, and swayed, falling against Jaeson.

"So, you killed the girl?" Jaeson asked, curiosity overcoming his sense of self preservation.

"You're going to the Morgue!" Shouted the purple faced threateningly behatted man.

The guys behind, laughed, they chuckled.

Distracted the guy with the hat turned.

"It's no laughing matter! My cousins a fag, and you're laughing? You watch your mouths!"

"She's dead?" Whispered a voice, in Jaeson ear.

"Yeah." He said, and found himself being shoved to one side.

Flashes, gunpowder, smoke, filled the air, screams and cries.

"You bast.....!" Began the man in hat, cut off by blood spraying from his smashed throat.

Jaeson's gun blazed, blazed in the hand of the beaten man, but didn't blaze alone. Another gun fired.

Deafening, flashes, indoor thunder roared, then stopped, slumping bodies, dripping blood, acrid smoke, silence.

Jaeson slowly got up. Hell, he loved dum dums, but they made a mess.

Four dead, or dying hoods. The beaten man, maybe he was Giovanni? Who knew? He used the scarf, to pick up his gun, and wipe down the blood, he holstered it. Time to go, no sense being part of this scene. He cast one last look back, and the dead and the dying.

Pieces falling together, no broads in the Morgue? Bastards could have told him, I bet they laughed when I left, he thought. He walked briskly out the warehouse, along the harbour side street, and circling around, back towards his office.

Isobella must have been one helluva girl, he sighed, time for coffee, and maybe, definitely, something stronger.

He felt it running down his neck already, oh, that wasn't right, he was wet, walking down main street in the sunshine? No, wait, he wasn't walking, he was lying, lying on the cold hard cobbles, water pooling around him.

"Hello, old chap. Sorry to waken you so rudely, but I rather think I still need your help."

A figure, in some antiquated dinner suit, leaned over him, holding a bucket.

"Come on then, get up, let's be having you!"

Strong hands, the priests and the strange mans, lifted him upwards, to his feet, and walked him, groggily through the mist towards a glowing doorway, in what resembled nothing less than a blue cabinet.

"We have a metacosmos to save dontcha know?" Continued the strange figure.

Chapter Thirty Nine – Starstruck.

Glowing mists, beeps, animal moans, where was she? This wasn't her sleep couch? Her body ached. Pilot Captain Therese Jameson, tried to focus, light swirled about her.

She turned, the moaning was beside her.

"John? What's happening?" She spoke, thickly. Her throat struggled to form the words.

Everything seemed, so strange. Could it be some atmosphere leak? A side effect of the drugs?

The ship lurched, and swung. How would she feel that, the artificial gravity should take care of any inertial disturbances.

She looked around. John was there, slumped, and groaning. He was wearing some strange suit, what was that, a survival suit? It looked very odd. The mists cleared a little, she looked away, and looked down at her hands, they were fine, she was fine, so far.

Poor John. What could do that? What was going on?

She moved. The floor moved beneath her, when she pressed her foot down, the floor distorted, quickly she lifted her foot. The floor tried to come up with it, and released, making a weird sucking sound.

What course are we on? She tried to make out the instruments, some seemed to be working, was it all in her mind, was the ship still there and solid, just her perceptions, being twisted out of joint?

Were they really that close to the anomaly? It might explain the distortions. She adjusted her position carefully, everything ached when she tried to move, as though, the molecules in her body all wanted to go, in different directions, or the same direction, at vastly different speeds.

Would she end up like John?

She fixed her eyes on the controls. They seemed to ripple, they seemed to waver, to wobble. Slowly, carefully, she reached out. Anything more than the slowest motion hurt, hurt beyond belief.

She concentrated. Autopilot. She found the button, she pressed it.

A screen just to her right flickered, different values, pictures, charts, warning signs, symbols, all flashed up.

At least the ship seemed to still be working, how long would it hold together? Maybe it was already too late? She brushed those thoughts away, she had to focus, she owed it to, well, whoever was left.

She stared fixedly at the screen. Click, click click. Different options scrolled by. Auto return. She selected 'yes'.

The ship began plotting, and adjusting to follow a return course based on its initial course of entry to the anomalies 'star' system. If 'star' system could be applied to such a chaotic location.

She'd done all she could. The Ship, if it could move, would do so. If it could. She tried not to think about it, trying to stay relaxed, when every jolt, even every breathe, was painful, was a trial enough.

The intercom, she could try and see if anyone else was left.

She looked for the intercom. There it was swimming in and out of view, as her vision, or the very world itself, rippled dramatically. Could she reach it? She tried, slowly, painfully, she reached for it, gradually millimeter by millimeter, her hand moved closer, closer, and then she threw the switch. Static, gurgling, whistling static. It was too much too hear, too much to bear, she flicked the switch off again.

She lowered her hand again, slowly painfully. Another ampule of sedative. There was one, somewhere if she could reach it. She couldn't do anything about the ship. She had to hope the computer could do the job, despite the hostile conditions outside.

She reached down beside her, with her right hand. The medi kit, there it was, still open from earlier. She reached into it, finding the distinctive ampule, with the symbol for sedative, a single raised star. She flicked off the plastic cover, and slowly raised her arm, jabbing the needle in her leg as soon as she could.

The sedative passed into her system and she slept.

The starship continued to tumble through the rainbow blaze of colours and radiations, a coruscating ring of forces, surrounding the very heart of chaos itself............

Chapter Forty – Dessert.

The stewards dutifully and promptly, took all the orders, for dessert. Other stewards, with long practice ran up, and cleared away the dinner things, wiping down the table, where crumbs, or enthusiastic spillage, had occurred.

One almost took away the glowing blue bottle, but was stopped, and apologised to Lyra, as she quickly took the bottle back.

The Count grinned.

"I'm sorry, Mistress Lyra, my staff are quite enthusiastic sometimes. Still, at some point we must talk business." He smiled, and relaxed. Things could be worse, and the dinner guests, were behaving themselves, albeit, two wouldn't stop smoking, and he rather suspected, the fumes were mellowing the crowd, himself included.

The stern looking giant had even managed a smile or two, the two Mages, had all but declared him their enemy, Rhian also, he had gathered, just about, had been involved in the destruction of the Council of Mages no less. He didn't care about that. He had heard, that they were very fussy about just who, they allowed to practice magick.

Much more interesting, the old Wise Woman, Lyra, had had the power to bind and control faeries no less! That would have been an Arte to know.

Nirnadel carefully watched the Count, he had done little but stare at Lyra, and the glowing bottle of power, all evening, except for the occasional glance at her and the other guests.

The food had been good, the wine better, but she was growing more uncomfortable by the moment. Ten Grief's silence, his knowing smiles and occasional narrowed eyes. He had barely touched his wine, and had seemed, well, quietly amused by all the proceedings.

Rhian, sat between the overly cheerful Lyra, and the pensively distracted Nirnadel, felt bored, also a little worried. That gnome, Elbie, had stared daggers at them all evening, and she was glad she had brought hers, she checked discreetly, and they were still strapped to her legs, ready, in case of need.

She was glad Adan hadn't seemed to have borne a grudge, especially, as he had seemed to have grown considerably in stature, physical and spiritual since last they had met. The Hammer though, that intrigued her. He hadn't had that back in the day, and now the Mages had declared, most mysteriously, that it wasn't what it seemed, and, in fact it was a 'trap,' or was that just books?

She had always suspected books were dangerous, and to have it confirmed as so, rather pleased her. Who needed books anyway? She didn't, more trouble than they were worth. Just a pair of good well balanced throwing knives, a nice wagon, good horses, and friends to share the journey, that's all anyone needed. Well, she could extend that list to include good liniment, her muscles did ache a bit these days, especially, when it was cold.

Ten Grief carefully maintained his posture, dignified, aloof, calm. He could barely contain his excitement. He hadn't realised just how much he adored Nirnadel, and there she was, sat beside him, making little conversation, and looking for all the world like a trapped bird, looking for an escape. It would be the work of seconds to teleport, both herself, and himself, to somewhere more amenable.

Things were even better than that. He was eating at the table of one of the wealthiest, most influential aristocrats in the remaining civilized world.

It got even better, the last of ancient Magi, somewhat high, by the look of them, were also at the selfsame table. The Mage, the Arch Mage of legend, Alurici, Archaeus Magnus, enemy of his Master, Xagigg the Great, sat at the very table he sat at. Unprotected.

What a coup! If he could bring the heads of the remaining Magi, to his Master, what could he ask as a reward? Practically anything. Possibly even a Princess's hand.

Attached to the rest of her body, preferably. Sometimes Necromancers could be so very literal.

He gazed at the gnome, who returned his gaze, with disinterest. No, the gnomes were of no consequence. He'd seen them fight, they were good at that, and their philosophical alchemical engines, far from the toys they were, were spectacular.

No, not of no consequence, for little people, they thought big.

This could be, his day, his great chance to shine, to become more than Xagigg's right hand man, to become his heir apparent. He let himself smile, once again, and glanced to his right, almost out of habit, as his empty plate was collected. Spiced ices? Or fruit pies?

"Spiced ices, with a little cream?" He asked the Steward, who duly noted his order.

He looked further to his right. Adan, giant or godling, now, sat, like a lord enthroned, on the makeshift bench, at the far end of the table. He caught his eye, beard creasing as he smiled.

A smile, no Adan, was unimportant, he would not come into this at all. Next to him, Alurici himself, sipping wine and smoking incessantly. He would have to be careful.

Alurici hadn't cared much for the stew, he'd eaten far better. He didn't let it show though, he was so relaxed! He'd never been this relaxed, ever! He sipped more wine, dragged a little more on his roll up, which he passed back to Hunbogi. Those Shamen had it right from the start. Everything was so clear now, the world and all its secrets lay at his feet, he giggled slightly, beneath his feet!

He would have to look out a good flying spell, or perhaps enchant something appropriate, a chair, a bed, no, no, a carpet! A big tasselled carpet! Oh that would be so cool! He would sit and chill, and fly anywhere, as the mood struck him!

There was something he needed to do first. Oh yeah, save the world! How wonderful would that be! Also, he thought, I need to kill that Necromancer, the Princess, and her relatives. Perhaps the Count too, he was clearly some kind of evil sorceror. All this talk of new magick! Must be dark arts, and his guest was clearly one of the Devourers minions, so he was in bed with the enemy too!

He sipped more wine, smiled at Ten Grief, and raised his glass, to the Count. The Count nodded, and smiled. Yes, bring the whole Castle down, heretic wizard and all. Alurici grinned, happily took back the roll up and puffed.

Hunbogi looked at Alurici. He'd seen that look before, this dinner party was going to end with a bang. Could he stop him? Should he stop him? By the gods, bye all the Magi, well, that was just them now, most of these people deserved to die, but there was the bigger picture to consider.

"So what is wrong with my Hammer?" Asked the deep voice beside him.

Hunbogi turned back to look at the giant Adan.

"Let me have a look at it now." He stared, a little surprised when Adan simply lifted the Hammer and placed it on the table beside him.

"Here it is, what do you make of it?" Adan said, a bit quieter.

The Hammer crouched, almost squirmed on the tabletop. The table did not over balance. He tried to lift it. He couldn't. Ah, some sort of discretional weight enchantment. Or some sort of geospatial inertia.

"Well, there are runes, but not runes of power, quite a few of them, twenty two, yes twenty two runes, yes running in a line. He sipped a little wine.

"Actually, that last, yes! That's an old symbol or rune for the world!" He peered closer, an electric charge sparked through the Hammer. It didn't like being stared at.

"You know, ha, ha, if you looked at the Hammer itself as a rune, it might mean cycle, you know, in the forbidden glyphs of the elder horrors......" Alurici chimed in.

"What twenty two runes, on a cycle rune?" Adan spoke bemusedly, thickly. He was quaffing wine, rather quickly, and the roll up, though it hadn't had much effect, had had some.

"Twenty two world runes, on a cycle rune....." Muttered Hunbogi. He stared at Alurici. Alurici smiled back. The smile of a hungry beast, who knew the kill was not far off.

"We need to talk, no action, not yet, but really talk. Twenty two." He emphasised the last two words, in a harsh whisper.

"What's so significant about twenty two? I don't follow?" Adan asked, as he watched the desserts being brought in.

Hunbogi looked at him, and took off his glasses. He wiped them and, leaning to one side so a nice bowl could be placed before him, replaced his glasses. Apple Pie, apparently, Hunbogi smiled.

"Well, twenty two?" Insisted a voice beside him.

"Twenty two times before, twenty two worlds, born and destroyed, twenty two cycles." Hunbogi muttered.

"How could that be?" Adan asked, and then remembered the land of Summer, where he had spent a brief interlude with Ulfheid, a life time ago. Perhaps it was possible.

"How can anything be? Isn't that the real question? Why should anything be? Wrap things up in theorems and philosophies, and it all comes back to the same question, why?" Hunbogi, began eating Pie.

Adan pondered, he had a point. Why, should anything be anything? Why should the sky be blue and not green? Maybe somewhere it was. Maybe some when it had been, or yet would be.

He looked at his spiced ice. He tasted it, it was nice, a bit sweet, and the yellow colour reminded him uncomfortably of a certain kind of snow, but otherwise, it was most enjoyable.

"But why is the Hammer dangerous?" He asked, between mouthfuls.

Hunbogi looked at him, up and down.

"Well, that's not too much of a problem!" Adan laughed.

Hunbogi looked startled, and looked back at him.

"I'm surprised to hear a young man say such a thing!" He replied, arching an eyebrow.

"Ah, but I'm in my forties! Not old but a good age!" Adan replied.

"Yes, and you've already grown that tall, wait 'til you've put a few hundred years behind you, as we have, and you may think differently." Hunbogi munched.

"Well, I'm only corporeal as a courtesy!" Adan muttered.

Alurici choked, coughed, and spluttered.

"I think you've missed the point!" Hunbogi quietly offered.

"And the boat!" Alurici laughed.

"Look, make more sense, why is this Hammer dangerous?" Adan asked.

Hunbogi handed him the slightly burned down fresh roll up.

"Look, stop thinking of it as a Hammer, start to think of it as a symbol, a marker, a designator." Hunbogi continued.

"Designing? Designing what?" Adan asked, drawing deep. The smoke of the burnt herbs was starting to have more appeal. It made the Mages arguments become a little clearer, but they were still like mud. Wet, runny mud, at the edge of a deep river. For some reason he thought of Garim.

"No, a designator, a pointer, an indicator. You see we think, Alurici and I, that the Hammer, the symbol, is a sacrificial talisman, to be worn by a willing victim, whom then gives themselves to the Great Big Ones, in order to end the world." Hunbogi managed, bits of Pie pastry going everywhere.

Adan just stared at them. This would be his life down to a tee. Any good break, was really bad. A mighty Artefact, gives him great power, but actually, is just fattening him up to be a sacrificial munchy for the elder horrors. Just typical, just a normal day in his weird life. He sighed.

He also wondered, if there might be cheese and biscuits.

Chapter Forty One – Desert.

Garim, otherwise known as Captain Fortune, stood on his bridge. Commander Jolly, standing legs braced, in a heroic gnomic pose, stood on the rail beside him. He wished he wouldn't do that. Was it bravado, was it the thrill? He didn't know, but it worried him.

He didn't want to watch an important gnome fall to his death, not on his ship, at any rate.

"How long will it take, your men to decide?" Commander Jolly had asked.

"As long as they need." He had replied, scratching his reddish fuzz.

He had, some limited understanding of gnomish military structures, he'd read a book on it. Basically, all the gnomish warriors, were volunteers. Hereditary volunteers, who upon attaining adulthood, automatically volunteered in one of the service branches. Likewise, they volunteered to serve wherever they were needed in times of crisis, like now, and otherwise, had other jobs and other lives. He thought it sounded like an inherited short straw. He wondered who had first come up with the idea, and who had been the first gnome daft enough to sign up to it.

Apparently, most other professions were inherited also, including a certain amount of wealth. Gnomes were quite practical about wealth, having plenty to go around, they knew the only real wealth, was time and the opportunity to spend it, how one chose.

The Commander had been a little surprised at how democratic he was in running his ship, but pleasantly surprised. At least, his crew couldn't blame him too much for whatever happened next, after all, they had voted for it, themselves.

He looked into the middle distance, sand, sand, and more sand. Who would want to live in a place like this?

Answer, people who did not want to live in a place like anywhere else, and those who knew no better.

He wondered, if perhaps, in some far flung age, the ancient ancestors of the former locals, all presumably dead, converted or fled from the Devourer now, had really, really, really, angered the gods?

Perhaps they had, and the deserts had rolled in to consume the farms, the vineyards, the forests of fruit trees, the pastures and the hunting grounds. However, the people had stayed. They hadn't died out, or fled. In fact they had developed really good ships, but instead of using them to leave and go somewhere nice. They'd used them for piracy, and then trade, when robbing people subtly had become more convenient than doing the same at swordpoint.

Time, as it usually does when people are waiting, dragged by slowly.

"Would you care for a drink, of anything?" Garim asked the Commander.

"Nope." He said, without turning his head.

Garim waved towards a rather tubby, red garbed seaman, whom jumped up and scuttled rapidly, to his side.

"Captain, sir?" Spoke the man.

"Cooky, bring me water, and maybe a ships biscuit."

"Aye Sir!" He hurried away.

Shortly after, he returned. A mug of tepid water, and a dry biscuit, in hand.

"We've some dates too." He offered.

"Yes, Yes thank you." Garim replied.

A paper bag, filled with stoned dates, duly appeared.

Garim selected one, and ate. Not his usual choice but beggars can't be choosers.

He laughed. He was no beggar, but he was living the life of a monk! Technically, he was one of the richest men in the world. He'd earned it. Well, no, he'd taken it, helping himself to unguarded, forgotten or abandoned property, wherever he and his crew could find it. Property, he thought is theft. He munched his biscuit. He should retire, enjoy his loot. Except, he enjoyed the quiet joys of pillage, and it would not last forever. Soon the easy money would be all gone, and his erstwhile comrades would be eyeing each other and him, up, as their next possible targets.

Yes, he would have to make provision for that.

"Captain! Captain Sir!" A scruffily dressed seaman ran up, leaping up the steps, across the deck, and likewise almost vaulting up the steps to the bridge.

Commendable enthusiasm, whoever he was.

Garim, was a successful Captain, admired and respected everywhere, he went, at least when he brought his men with him. However, he had a dreadful memory for names. He smiled, he remembered the mate he had promoted, and then promptly forgotten the name of, he spent two weeks desperately skirting the issue until, Cooky as it happened, realised his plight and quietly reminded him.

Cooky's original name had likewise gone with the knowledge of last weeks breakfast, into the memory filing cabinet of eternity, somewhere down the back of the drawer.

"Hello, yes?" He managed to the otherwise anonymous, but enthusiastic crewman.

"The Crew have decided Sir!" Said the crewman beaming. He was well aware of the Captains hopeless memory, but didn't care. It was generally considered a mark of ill fortune, below decks, if the Captain actually remembered ones name. It generally implied some form of punishment duty might be imposed, such as promotion.

"And what has the Crew decided?" Said Garim, feeling optimistic, that the Gnomish Commanders explicit description of the horror, madness, and overwhelming odds, to be faced by proceeding, had been well absorbed by all.

"We go on!" Grinned the crewman.

"Thank you. Okay, raise anchor, lower the sails, a bit , you know, slow ahead! Over there!"

He looked down and across at the Gnomish Commander.

Commander Jolly, really looked surprised.

"Are your men all idiots?" He asked.

"Can they not count? Do they not know the difference between ten thousand and two hundred?" He continued.

"Yes, judging by the share outs, I would say they all know at least some fundamental arithmetic, but they are very brave." Garim offered by way of explanation.

"They are very stupid." Said Commander Jolly.

"As, I said, they are very, very brave indeed." Garim smiled. Secretly, he hoped their escape plan, well, device, would do the job if needed. Perhaps, his crew believed it would. They had been suitably impressed when he had showed them, so perhaps that's why they thought it worth the risk.

The sail unfurled, a little, the anchor lifted, at a great effort. The ship hardly budged. Very little wind was present, they'd be hard pressed to go anywhere.

"Run out the sweeps" The second Mate yelled somewhere below. A good crew does what's needed, thought Garim, he turned to Commander Jolly.

"Are you leaving us, or joining us, on our little trip?" He smiled.

"You know actually, we'll stay onboard for awhile, and see what we see up river." The Commander, had been thinking about this. They weren't really responsible to what might happen to a crew of human pirates, and two hundred men, added to the Devourers Horde, really wouldn't make any difference. Possibly, they would subtract considerably from said horde before passing into posterity. Either way, it wasn't that important. The ship, he'd noted could easily be sunk if need be, especially when vulnerable in the shallow river.

"Yes, we'll see how your trip goes." He actually grinned at Garim, who adjusted his hat, and chewed another date, with vigour.

Chapter Forty Two – Off to See The Pyramid.

Jaeson Smith sat in the deck chair, its colourful fabric looking most out of place in the stark girdered interior of the 'blue mages' cabinet. Why the priest had chosen to call him the blue mage was anyone's guess, except perhaps that the cabinet was, actually blue, a dark blue, with incongruous posters or in fact graffiti painted on it sides. This included one rather good work by some man, presumably, these days he didn't know anything for sure, called CoOpsy.

He sighed. He was having a bad week. He had nothing to show for it, his one good lead, for a paying client, had in fact, sailed away. Now, he was clearly having some kind of episode, or he'd been drugged. He wouldn't mind it if it were drugs, hell, some of the herbs he'd used in various ways, probably counted, he just wished they'd asked first, an invite to party, not a reverse gate crash.

This guy, in his funny suit, with his weird mannerisms, he'd guessed he must be in Vaudeville, or British, or both.

Berythus was there too, sharing his mad dream. He looked if anything more hopeless. He leant over and had whispered:

"I know his name, I heard him say it earlier. He said it was Aka Demik." Berythus had stared then, as though he'd imparted a great secret.

"I guess he's Egyptian, some kind of Britisher Ex Pat." Jaeson had mused aloud.

"Ohhh." Berythus had said, quietly staring with renewed interest at the figure, still doing its weirdling dance about the cabinets central altar.

"When can we go home?" Jaeson asked, quite loudly this time.

"Oh soon, soon. Don't worry your little heads about that right now! Momentous things are a foot! Destiny is being forged right at this moment! The whole future of the metacosmos is at stake!" PAM had said, quite gleefully.

"Okay, why not just you know, drop us off, me preferably in Boston, or nearby, a walk would do me good, Berythus, wherever he pleases, and then you can go save the world." Jaeson offered by way of optimistic suggestion.

"No, no, no, that'll never do at all! You're needed! Somehow, you two have both become irreversibly entwined in the sub quantii base relativistic hyper field, in a metagorical algorithmic entanglement!" Said PAM, without batting an eyelid.

Berythus whimpered, and sunk lower in his deckchair. He had a matching one, except if anything, it had more green stripes.

Jaeson stared the blue mage.

"You just made that up!" He accused. In truth, he had no idea what the man had just said, but instinctively, he felt it was rubbish.

"Just you go and prove it!" Said PAM.

He smiled, adjusted a few more levers, twisted another knob, pressed a few more buttons. Yes, his coffee would be ready in just a few minutes. He'd offer his passengers some too, but they seemed most ungrateful.

Fancy complaining about a chance to save the metacosmos? Back in his home dimension, people would be chuffed to bits to get a chance at an adventure like this. He shook his head. No coffee for them, maybe tea though, later.

He turned and smiled, impishly.

"We're nearly there! The Great Pyramid!" PAM said.

"You are Egyptian!" Jaeson exclaimed.

"No, no I'm not, and I'm not talking about your Earth either."

"What?" Offered Jaeson.

"No, where." Said PAM.

"Okay, where?" Jaeson felt mystified. He could also smell coffee. It smelt good.

"Yes! Exactly!" PAM beamed.

"Is that coffee?" Jaeson asked, giving up sensible questions.

"Maybe." Grumbled PAM.

He looked under the altar, for some extra cups. It would have to go around. He found some.

"Milk, or cream?" He asked.

"Oh well, cream if you have it." Jaeson replied.

"I really have the answer, you know, it took me weeks. I have it on this scroll." Whimpered the crumpled priest.

"Oh, be a good fellow and be quiet. Would you like some coffee? It might help." Offered PAM.

Jaeson sipped the coffee. It was really nice.

"So, at this pyramid, what do we do?" Asked Jaeson. He did not feel drugged. In fact he felt normal, which was deeply worrying.

"Well, first we shall see what we shall see." PAM answered, sipping his coffee, and idly gazing into dial.

"What, what do you expect to see?" Asked Jaeson.

"I expect to see, the Secret Masters." Said PAM with great gravity, a frown on his face.

"If they are so Secret, how do you know about them?" Jaeson enquired, bolstered by coffee.

"Oh, they are Secret mostly, but they get sloppy you know, and everyone knows, everyone who is anyone, knows, just who they are. It's kind of their little joke." PAM sipped, and stared at Jaeson.

"You've met them haven't you?" PAM continued.

"What? Don't be ridiculous!" Jaeson responded, indignant.

"Oh, they're aren't all human, but they have lodges, temples on many worlds, where the boundaries are weak." PAM whispered.

"You've been in one, that's why you have their trace signature!" He looked hard at Jaeson, as though weighing him up.

Jaeson went cold, his memory going back all those years, to New York and the bizarre temple, he'd blundered into, all unawares.

"Yes, I see." Said PAM.

"It all becomes clear now." PAM looked away.

"What do they want? Money? Power? Why would they threaten the metacosmos?" Jaeson asked, he'd finished his coffee, and was rapidly losing the will to live.

"Oh they have money, power, or its equivalent on their homeworlds, what they have is ambition! When you have everything what is left? Service? To the public? To the gods? To an ideal? They have chosen ambition. Their ambition is to remake the metacosmos. They're bored, nothing is left to them that matters, so they want to create something new, something fresh, and to do that, they need to sweep away the old world. Destroy the old world." PAM, found some fresh ground coffee, and began refilling the machine.

"Okay. I don't see how I can help with that." Jaeson said.

"I can." Berythus muttered.

"Dear chap! Do be quiet, I need to think, to plan out what I'm going to do." PAM sat on a convenient stool, that Jaeson could have sworn was not there just minutes before.

Chapter Forty Three – Coffee.

There was no cheese and biscuits. Adan was a little disappointed. He also, had begun to feel uncomfortable. There was a definite air to the dinner, a tension, just below the surface. He was tired, the Hammer, or the symbol, whatever it really was, now looked at him sheepishly. It looked as though it had been caught out.

Coffee, however, had been served. His was in a large tankard, he sipped it. It was good. Most of the guests were drinking it.

Nirnadel stood up, banged her hand upon the table.

"Thank you, my lord Count, for a lovely meal, but since we're all here, shouldn't we see if we can find some way, some way to end the menace of the Devourer?"

All eyes fell upon her. This was a good idea. They all looked at each other. Too bad they thought, this isn't going to work.

"I had a dream. I dreamt of the Devourer, and a book, a metal plate silvery coloured, and enruned. I drew it, here." She pulled out a piece of brown paper, on which she had scrawled some runes.

"The word Codex, was said by this Shaman, in my dream, as he held the book, the metal page, anyway, before the Devourer."

Alurici stared at her, he put his coffee down.

"May I see that?" He asked.

She passed the scrap of paper down.

Alurici stared at it, a strange light in his eyes.

"You know, this coffee is rather good." Hunbogi declared to the room.

A murmur of agreement ran around the room.

"Yes, it's very special coffee. Apparently, they only take the beans that have been eaten, well, swallowed, and passed by a particular rodent, or small mammal. These they roast, and I for one get the coffee." The Count smiled.

The guests around the table went quiet, cups were lowered.

Elbie piped up:

"You mean, my coffee, has been through a rats arse?" She sounded cross.

Hunbogi started laughing, and lolled a bit.

"I see you don't drink it?" Lyra mentioned.

"No, well, I have had a special batch made up, just for you all. A little insurance policy." The Count laughed.

Hunbogi slumped over the table. Rhian likewise slide down under the table. Lyra stood, dizzily, and then sat back down, she was seeing more than one Count. This was not good.

Alurici, teleported out, and then collapsed, still clutching the scrap of paper.

"What is insurance?" Ten Grief asked. He was quite unaffected, his amulet against poisons, was working just fine thank you very much. The crossbow being levelled at him from the shadows was a slight worry, however, and bringing the complex patterns and runes of the teleport spell to mind, he left.

"This is disappointing. Are you leaving us too?" The Count, smiling, addressed Adan.

Adan, gazed quietly at the Count. Oddly, he felt fine, and then he didn't, as he passed out, he also faded out. As he faded, he felt better, discorporation had its advantages, he also rose, drifting quickly up, through the tower roof, up amidst the clouds, and then, through the rainbow itself, into the Upper World, to of all places, the bare patch ascribed, plotted out, and assigned, to him.

He'd left the Hammer behind, in the mad Count's tower. He looked around, it would be nicer with at least some chairs, and then there were. Ah, he thought. If I can imagine it, it's here, fine. He sat down, and thought.

Chapter Forty Four – Zonthas.

Firelight flickered. Shadows raced, around the great hall, as the fire roared, then subsided. Before the great hearth, central to the chamber, the great sandstone chamber, the huge, and echoey hall, decorated with painted murals, sat a man.

He sat crosslegged. He was nude, except for a loincloth, his nut brown body, covered in blue whorl tattoos. His eyes, rolled up in his head, showed only the whites. He hummed, or murmured, a low tune, or litany, his hands, on his knees, formed strange finger gestures, on after another after another.

His forehead, bore one tattoo, a small triangle, the symbol of his duty, of his commitment, of his faith. Occasionally a crease would appear on his forehead, flexing the tattoo. Deep in his head, in his mind, he was troubled.

Things, were not progressing as they should. Plans were going awry. Already the great symbol, had been cast aside, not fully charged, not yet ready. Things were off track, but all was not lost.

Zonthas's mind raced, with the flickering shadows. He had to find a way to get things back on track, and he would.

Oh yes, this was Zonthas. Zonthas, an ancient shaman, for thousands of years, many thousands of years he had sat, sat in meditation on the nature of the world, of existence.

Five foot high, thin wiry, shaven headed, tattooed from head to foot. He had been there, when the last great conjunction, when the planets, the stars, the dimensions, and other celestial objects had all fallen into line. He had been there, amongst those who, with great skill and cunning, had woven the great magick that had thrown the proverbial monkey wrench into the gears of reality, gears that would be straining, grinding one on another, for the rest of eternity.

The Great Big Ones wide awake, striding across the landscape, doing what they did best, tearing down reality, ready for something new, were thrust into imprisonment, in their very own special pocket dimension. The natural urges of creatures frustrated, their destiny defeated, their instincts invalidated, their urges unfulfilled, reality continued unabated, unrenewed.

The Shamen, the Mages, the Tribal Chiefs, all celebrated, their world was saved, their people would live, live and thrive.

Zonthas was there, he remembered. It all seemed good at the time. The tribes flourished, built great civilizations, great cities, and then began to decay. Corruption, evil, greed, war and strife, grew, and grew. He'd watch the Necromancers fight their wars, for fun and profit. He'd seen the Mages rise, more wars, more horror. The pointless cycle continued.

Zonthas found the truth. The Metacosmos was imperfect, but it was perfecting, every turn of the wheel, brought it closer, to perfection. Real balanced perfection, not some frozen in time imitation of the dream.

He had sinned, he and his allies, all those thousands of years before, had stood in the way of natural progress. The wheel turns, except they had stopped it turning. He knew a part of the magick, he knew how it could be unraveled, the spring, so tautly wound, needed to be released.

Here, in his private dimension, his personal heaven, where he had known peace for so long, from here he could reach out with his mind, nudge this, push that, until things fell into place.

People of his old order, which he re-established across the metacosmos, came to him, learned or guessed, his will, and left. They celebrated his cause. The rebirth, the turning of the wheel, the recreation to a better state, one of many, many more to come, on their way to the ultimate, the final form, the final blend of perfect order, and chaos, matter screamingly transmuting in an endless ecstasy of perfect harmony. He might be wrong, perhaps the cycle would continue forever, slowly reaching the perfect state, but never arriving.

The natural order must be restored, the spell must be broken, the world destroyed and reborn again, anew. He would guide them, break the spell, and from the safety of his hall, guide the future world, to more tremendous evolutions of change, and advancement.

A sound broke through the silence. A whirring braying, groaning noise, like a dying coffee machine, too long in service, too little maintenance, an image floated in and out, resolving and fading, solidifying and then turning transparent again. Something, some transdimensional object, was trying, against all probability and expectation, to penetrate his great, ancient sanctum.

A smile, the first for millennia, crossed the shaman's face. He was master of all things here. His will focussed, momentarily, and the strange multidimensional magickal cabinet, was flicked across the metacosmos, like an errant fly.

Zonthas's will would not be defied, reality was his, his plaything, his project, his whole desire, life and joy.

He turned his mind back to the great chessboard, the world of which Graeffenland was but a small part. The pieces were scattered. Anger flickered across his mind. It had taken him years, years of hard work and planning, to get them all in one spot, and now, scattered again. The sacrificial pawn, too, was gone, how, to bring that back into the game?

He felt Xagigg, again. That dark mind, so easily manipulated, so easily gulled, was also like a rock, resisting change. Xagigg, through brute will alone, was slowing down the whole process. A process far from complete, yet nearing completion, but for the key, and the sacrifice to activate the final lock.

He gazed. Even now the Bone Legion, abandoning its guard upon the lands of Kenovass, marched, like an unstoppable wave, it's zombie soldiers resolute, and rather hard to 'kill,' towards Navorny, towards Count Bruno Orvull, and his captive, princess Nirnadel.

Even now, Arshan's forces, moving through secret tunnels, under empty lands, closed in upon their enemies. It was not quite right, but it might be right enough. He steadied his mind, and focussed his will, upon the world.

Chapter Forty Four – Deserted.

The galleon, cruised, slowly up the great river. The sweeps, and been withdrawn, back within the ship, and the sweep ports closed.

Garim sat below. Night had drawn in, he should stop, but they still had some way to go. He stared at the map before him, it gave little inspiration. There should be a harbour. Eghior had been a great trading city, in its day, what was left in the ruins, was anyone's guess.

His men hoped for loot, a hold full of cargo, perhaps a salvageable ship. He knew his Mates hungered for that opportunity.

Commander Jolly sat on the table next to him, his gnomes, with their long range scopes, were up on deck, scouring the horizon, for, anything. Anything at all. It was quiet out there.

Garim looked at the gnome Commander. He had said it was a great encampment. Someone should have seen something by now.

"If, the enemy is not there, if they are on the move, what will you do?" He asked.

Garim's cabin, was the best on the ship, large, well decorated, in reds and golds, beautiful lattice windows, fine furniture, fit for an admiral, indeed, in its day, before the ship was salvaged, it may well, have had such top brass on board.

A chandelier, golden, with two dozen candles, now lit, shone down on his chart table.

"If the enemy has moved, that is what my report will tell." Commander Jolly replied. With every negative report, he seemed more relieved, more relaxed, he gazed boredly out the window.

"For a soldier, you don't seem that keen on action." Garim spoke quietly.

Commander Jolly's head snapped round.

"You wouldn't say that if you had seen war."

"You know, I once fought as a spearman, in an army that employed no archers, because of the risk, of killing one of the enemy officers, who, just happened to be a cousin. Two brother Dukes, fighting it out between them, as gentlemen, so only peasants should die for that. That was their, philosophy." Garim quietly said.

Garim, thought back sadly. What a mixed up twisted world he lived in, and now, horrors and hardships, had catapulted him up, from monk, to vagabond, spearman to barman, barman to ships captain.

Now, he was sitting in council with a gnome commando. Why didn't he stay on the farm, stay illustrating books, hoeing fields of vegetables, and trying to learn magick. He woke up sure there was more to life, certain he had to leave, and he and Adan had left, shortly after, falling into one incredible, implausible adventure after another.

"War is hell." Said the gnome.

A knock, at the cabin door.

"Enter!" Garim called out.

Rogerios, poked his head around the door.

"We're here, boss." He smiled.

"All's quiet, not a light, not a sound, nothing, not a bird, night owl, bat or rat astir."

Rogerios continued.

"Okay, ready the men. Time waits for no one, we will send scouting parties in, and find out what's happening." Garim smiled back.

Rogerios turned, and closed the door.

"Well, you going monster hunting?" Garim addressed Commander Jolly.

"We'll see." The gnome spoke.

Garim stood up, buckling on his cutlass, he threw on his red damask frock coat. It wasn't armour, but it was his uniform, his men expected him to look the part. He selected a rather nice floppy brimmed hat, with feathers, and then buckled on his great boots.

It wasn't the most comfortable or practical outfit, but it served its purpose. He opened the door and strode out on deck.

Hundreds of eager faces, some camouflaged with charcoal and fat, turned and stared at him. They had already organised themselves into squads. They knew the drill, sneak ashore, check the coast (harbour) was clear, then light up a few lights, break down a few doors, find anything worth hauling away.

"Alright boys! Go for it!" Garim yelled, waving his arm towards, he hoped the harbour.

Silently, by group, they lowered the great boats over the side, oars lying within them. Soon, eight boats gently pulled towards shore, Garim, hitched a ride on the last.

The clouds a dark inky black mass, curtained the stars from view. The oars dipped and rose, dipped and rose, a slight splash, and drip, being the only sound.

The men were eager, some already had weapons drawn, others clasped torches, unlit, the whole bay in almost pitch darkness, and yet not a sound.

Darker against the darkness, the buildings of the harbour began to loom, first a little away, then closer, closer still, and then they were around them, above them and to the side.

Soon, in barely minutes, they approached a jetty. Still, firm, the wood sound, despite its abandonment. They tied up, mooring the ships boat, and climbing carefully one after another up the jetty.

Garim, Captain Fortune to his men, climbed up there too.

Not a sound not a light, the jetty slippery, with moisture.

"Okay lads, lets have some light." He said.

"Already Captain? Are you sure?" The young sailor asked.

"Yes, I think I'd rather see it coming as not." He replied.

The sailor struck a flint and steel, the spark flared, flamed and the torch soon blazed. It cast its light, maybe twenty yards around, and dimly further.

Cursing sounded from the other wharves, followed momentarily, by other torches lighting up. The boats had put in equally spaced out, along the harbour, and their light, dimly invaded the port. All was still quiet. Nothing moved but the pirates.

Other boats were in port, all were sunk, some protruded above the waterline, others were just shadows below.

No salvageable craft here Garim sadly observed.

The landing parties all advanced, leaving lit torches, bound to posts on the jetties, at intervals. The city and its port, was now more alive than it had been in years, little did they know.

Ferd the leader of the squad Garim had rowed in with, looked at his Captain, with concern.

"We have seen no living thing, yet. What if we are going to be ambushed?" He asked.

Garim, drew his cutlass, tying its ribbon round his wrist. He wasn't going to lose this sword to the deep, or the shadows, either.

He stepped forward.

"Well, follow me." Garim said.

Follow they did. The wharf was abandoned, long abandoned. He crouched, causing his followers to crouch and gaze around too. He however, looked down, the slime, the silt, hadn't been disturbed for ages. No one had walked this way for years. Where ever the encampment was, or had been, it hadn't used the wharf, or harbour.

He stood up, the men behind him rose too, a little more slowly.

"Take care on this planking, no one has walked this way in years, it slimy, as hell." Garim spoke out loud.

He then stepped forward, slide a little, straightened, and marched, a little more carefully, off the jetty, and out into the harbour side street. One or two of his scouting parties had also got that far. Some had lit up torches. One was noisily beginning to break into a storehouse, axes being the preferred tool of choice for that endeavour.

Ferd drew level.

"Enemy, has gone then Sir?" He asked.

"So far, that seems possible, just, be careful. I'm going further in, here give me a couple of torches." Garim asked.

He took three from the bundle, held by a lad at the back of the squad, lit one, resheathed his cutlass, and shoved the other two, in his belt.

He followed the street around the bay, looking for roads heading inland, he found three, almost straight away.

Pausing for a moment, he chose the middle way, and marched along it, watching and listening for any sounds of life, or unlife.

Nothing, just a dead city. Rubbish, and bones lay around. Debris from collapsed buildings lay, choking side streets, and alleys. If this place had been an encampment, there was no signs of it. Ahead, a great space opened up.

Garim slowed. It wasn't just a square. He walked closer. Oh the city square had changed, even in the light of his torch he could see, the edge.

A great, huge dark pit, had been dug, a ramp lead downwards, winding around the edge of the pit, down into the depths of the earth.

Garim stopped, the smell that arose from it was nauseating. A wind blew, cold, surprisingly cold, his torch fluttered, sending crazy shadows, flitting around, somewhere below, a rock skittered.

Clouds moved a little, then a little more. The moon, hiding its face from the world all evening, and most of the night, snuck a glance at the lands below. In its silvery light, Garim saw the walls of the great citadel, just across from the pit.

He saw the figures solemnly marching on its battlements. Again he heard the skittering from the pit, something was there. He felt fear, ice water ran down his spine. He backed slowly away.

A shadow, there was a shadow in the shadow of the pit, a shadow that filled the shadow, with a deeper shade.

It was rising, every now and then dislodging a stone or pebble, from the pits side. It wasn't using the ramp. It was too big. It was looming out of the pit, as though it was just stretching.

Garim walked backwards a bit quicker. This was an unexpected development. The shadow, now was as high as the battlements behind it, it was turning, turning, and then it stopped.

Two bright star like glints shone, high up on the shadow. They moved. Garim turned to run, except his legs wouldn't work. He crumpled down, and prayed.

What gods were left? Would they hear him? If they heard him could they do anything? He gave up. The shadow thing was staring down, down at him. It was amused, it was savouring his fear, relishing his despair. He thought of Adan, why didn't they just stay on the farm?

A bright light flared behind him, the shadow loomed up, drew what for all the world could be a paw fashioned of pure darkness, up ready to smash down, down on him. It was angry now.

He was caught up, from behind and dragged away, through light, and nausea, to a dizzying marble precipice. He was standing, well struggling back up to standing, on the edge of a marble precipice, with a low balustrade, also, of carved marble, shapes of dragons, and nymphs cavorting, being the main subject.

"You're alright now." Said a deep masculine voice.

He turned. A scruffy, bearded man, in inadequate furs, muscle tone abundantly displayed, stood behind him.

"Adan? By the gods! Where are we?" Garim shocked, and full of wonder, gazed around.

"Officially, we are in the Passions, Palace of the Wrath of Thunder, not my choice, old Kershaggulumphie has a sense of humour, and the casting vote." Adan offered, by way of explanation.

"This is the Upper World?" Garim stated, amazement written over his face.

"Well, you were praying, and, for some reason, you'd found your way into the presence of the Devourer itself. A bit careless, really. But, you know, for old times sake I thought I ought to get you out." Adan spoke, smiling.

"Can we move away from the edge?" Garim, somewhat nervously asked.

"Of course." Adan replied, guiding him into what turned out to be a rather austere marble temple.

"You live in a temple?" Garim looked surprised.

"Technically, I don't live at all. I've kind of shuffled off the mortal coil, and now, well, apart from supernatural guest appearances down below, which it seems, I now have to save up for, I'm stuck up here. This is it for me. It sucks doesn't it." Adan sounded depressed.

"What about my men? What's going on down there?" Garim asked.

"Go back to the edge and look, you can see everywhere from up here." Adan offered.

"I guess, they are probably all going to die." Adan offered.

"What!?! Come on! We've got to stop this!" Garim shouted.

"There's little we can do. I was duped, my power, came all from the Hammer, an old relic, an artefact I picked up, a few years ago." Adan looked sad.

"Well, look at you now, you're a god!" Garim shouted in frustration.

"Apparently, yes, I am, but the weakest one in this world. The Hammer changed me, gave me power, but it was all a trick, so I've been told, and now, the Hammer is down there, in the hands of, well, a dubious Count, and I don't want any more to do with it." Adan looked sad, and angry.

"So, your letting my men die?" Garim said coldly.

"Nothing I can do. I'm not lying to you, I thought I could hold that thing, bound by own will, until, someone found a solution. I thought I was helping, and now, I realise it was just a sideshow, a distraction, apparently, I was some spiritual fatted calf, being readied for the slaughter. Well, I've opted out of that." Adan muttered quietly.

"Send me back. I'll die with my men." Garim angrily retorted.

"What would be the point of that?" Adan asked, he'd found a chair and sat down. It was a really nice ornate chair, with a side table, likewise, previously not there, or not seen. Next was wine, with glasses, likewise from thin air.

"Send me back." Garim said.

"Pull up a chair, and have a glass." Adan replied.

Garim looked, there was, from nowhere, a matching chair, just beside him. He sat down, it felt real.

"What are you doing?" Garim asked.

"This is a world of thought, the gods, well, what we want, becomes 'real,' up here anyway, not like the strange land of summer thing, I had going on a few years back." Adan murmured.

"I don't know what you're on about! I don't want wine, I want to go back and fight beside my men!" Garim, was almost pleading.

"Look, Captain Fortune, this is your lucky day, I have saved you from certain death, along side your men, and all you say, is that you want to go back there, to certain death, by their side. Well, I can't do that." Adan sipped some nectar.

"I'm not drinking that stuff. I'm sorry, whatever you were to me once, you aren't now, and I've heard the stories, you never eat and drink on the 'other side', old times sake, or not." Garim frustration filling his voice, stood up to leave.

"Well, then, I'm going to find my own way out, if, you won't help." Garim shouted.

"Just avoid, the dark paths, if somewhere looks broken or twisted, don't go there." Adan advised Garim's back as he left.

Garim halted, and turned around.

"You'd know about broken and twisted!" He turned away again, and walked out.

Garim pondered, how did one set about leaving, a world of the mind?

Adan watched him go. He'd changed a lot in recent hours. Literally, he'd lost his giant size. He was now a more normal five foot eight. He'd lost some of his strength, physically, and mentally, he was reduced. It was the Hammer, it had built him up, and now it was gone, he'd fallen back down, except, the divine energy still flowed within him, and he was receiving more. Kershaggulumphie, as good as his word, had set him up with temples, priests, even worshippers, and a tiny trickle of divine power followed.

The few things he could do, burned energy, an energy he could only replenish slowly, he had to find ways to make it count, but he had no idea what to do.

The Magi had been right, the Hammer, that was an elder magick, if it was actual magick, not something else, some art unknown. He walked back to the precipice, glass in hand, and stared down, there was the Hammer, where he'd left it, otherwise the Counts Hall was clear. He could step down, seize the Hammer, and be back in moments, and then what? He would be its tool again.

He shook his head, sadly. An idea crossed his mind. There was something else there, down in the castle of the Count, that he could find a use for.

Chapter Forty Five – Perils of a Princess.

Nirnadel sat on the wooden bench, a lamp outside, just beyond the floor to ceiling bars of her cell, mounted on the wall, her only light. Across the way, another cell, floor to ceiling bars, cell door, in the bars themselves. More cells, to her right and left.

Rhian, sat despondent, in the cell opposite, and then her grandmother, in the cell just to Rhians right, her left. She had seemed cheerful.

"Everything will work out in the end." She had said, an hour or two earlier. Why she believed this, was anyone's guess, but she seemed quite optimistic.

Rhian, had stood near the bars and whispered across.

"It's the power potion, the blue glowing bottle? If the Count wants more, he has to do business with Lyra. No one else can get it. Don't worry, he won't dare do anything, stupid."

Nirnadel, looked about her. The Count had already done something stupid. Ten Grief had escaped. He would come back. He would see it as an opportunity to score points with Xagigg, rescue the Princess, bring the villain to account, and expect her to be grateful.

"Can't we escape?" Nirnadel had asked.

"Yeah, let's escape!" Rhian had enthused, sarcastically.

"We're safe here." Lyra advised.

"We'll escape, when, and if, we need to." Lyra continued, with an assurance, that startled Nirnadel.

"You just going to whistle up a key then?" Nirnadel asked.

"Don't doing any whistling, until you really mean it." Lyra said, smiling.

Lunch was served. The slightly embarrassed guards, brought food, and wine. They also asked if they were cold, and if they would like extra blankets. Nirnadel quickly realised, they didn't fully get on, with their master. The Count, was weirding them out.

The guards, actually, didn't care less about the Count. Rumour had spread across the land, and had reached Navorny, like summer lightning. The Bone Legion was on the march, and it was headed this way.

Not one guard wanted to be in any fight against the Bone Legion. The other implications had sunk in too. No one, or practically no one, was guarding the border.

They all knew, the peace they had enjoyed was over, and dark days were coming, and their Count had brought them to this sorry pass. Some of the servants, had already slipped away, fleeing that morning, heading east to the stronger fortifications of Heidelheimberg.

The militia, not requested by the Count, was already drilling, in the square of Navorny, the strange Maquettemen, firing their maquettes, with great billows of smoke, flashes and bangs, at targets, practicing their aim, their loading drill and all, secretly wondering if their alchemical magick, could stop zombies. Secretly fearing, their magick would fail, and they too, would be raised to join the Bone Legion, to serve forever, perhaps, in undead bondage.

Pikemen, there were too, and archers. The archers, felt little need to practice, they had already drilled, for years. The Pikemen, went through the motions, their long spears, double bladed, with vicious prongs, pointed sideways, just below the head. No one wanted to be on the receiving end of one of those. Again, zombies, probably didn't care that much about spikey sticks.

The militia knew it. No one wanted this fight.

The Count himself didn't seem to care. He was angry, everything had gone wrong. He had three, very important guests, now in his dungeon, an artefact, he could do nothing with, two undoubtedly angry Mages, on the loose.

Oh, Hunbogi had been caught, by the sleeping draught. He'd had gloves placed on him, so he could not gesticulate, a ball gag, so he could breath, but not cast spells. Hunbogi, had been watched, like a hawk, he'd awoken, and within moments had vanished, leaving the gloves, the gag, lying on the floor of his cell.

He had also lost the gnome. She had been out, a very short time, and had portalled out, immediately, she had come round.

The clairvoyant, never passed out at all. He just sat there smiling.

"Good, good." Had been his only comment.

He'd left him, in his guest room. This medium, seemed quite content, to wait for whatever happened next.

Erik, he'd thrown out the castle. He was last seen heading towards Heidelheimberg, what he could tell anyone, would not matter.

The Count had already had the Mayor of Navorny, wringing his hands in fear, like an old woman. Why had he taken the Princess prisoner? Surely he could let her go? The town could not stand against the Bone Legion.

The Mayor, ominously, had said:

"Perhaps, we should just let the Legion past, after all, this is not our fight."

He'd lost his head then, and yelling some quite dark and terrible imprecations, he had the Mayor thrown from the battlements.

This was a mistake. He'd sat on his carved wooden throne, and gnawed on his knuckles.

He tried to relax in his laboratory, but, he could make no progress without power! The bottle, the glowing blue bottle, the distilled essence vital, the strongest power source available, was missing. His servants had searched, high and low, it had gone.

Somehow Lyra, had spirited it away, or, one of the other guests, had done so. After the dinner, he'd taken it personally, up to his lab. He'd set it down, by his notes, his charts, and log books. He'd locked the door. This morning, it was gone.

Everything had gone wrong.

"My lord." Karles, his butler, addressed him.

"Yes, what is it?" Count Bruno Orvull glared.

"My lord, the guard, they have deserted." Karles reported, impassively. Karles knew it was his duty to remain, professional, under all circumstances.

"They.......what?" The Count sat back, aghast.

"I think the Captain, said something about, no money was enough reward, in order to die for a, ahem, a rather descriptive term, which I expect would seem wholly inappropriate, to your dignity, and station. Anyway, he then left, with his men, probably for the city. He, ah, left the gates wide open too."

"Oh, damn them!" The Count glared again. He was done for.

"What became of that wretched faerie dog?" He asked, after a moments pause.

"Oh, he was seen heading off to town." Said Karles.

"Good. I'll be in my laboratory." The Count, stood, and walked behind the throne, to a small door, and a spiral stair, up.

Back down in the dungeons things were quiet.

"You know, we haven't seen anyone for hours. I hope they haven't forgotten us." Nirnadel, forlornly sighed.

"Don't worry, at some point, they'll set us free." Lyra smiled, her confidence undimmed.

Karles, looked out the window. He was gazing down at the town, thro a clear pane in the stained glass of the great hall of the Keep.

The town was buzzing with activity, and the fairground was clearing. The wagons of the gypsies, the people of the road, or some such, he had forgotten, what they referred to themselves as, were leaving, but they were heading, yes, as he watched, it was quite obvious, they were heading for the Castle.

He smiled. What had the Count expected would happen? He turned away, and proceeded down to the dungeons. He would find the keys, open the cells, and await the new 'masters' will.

Chapter Forty Six – Developments.

The Wizards Workroom, round, fine granite, grey-black, fine fitting blocks, many feet thick, high in the towering spire, of Alurici's mountain hideaway. A staircase, curved, fine rosy wood, hardened, beautifully carved in whorls, and arabesques, stretched floor to ceiling, with a small landing, before curving away to pass into the floor above.

Turning clockwise, a hearth, likewise stone, this time blackened by smokes and fumes, roared, heat and light radiating outwards, bathing the figure, robed in white, jewels of power glowing, runes glistening, leather apron, and metal mask.

Fine sconces, jutted at regular points around the tower, magickal light glowing forth, vying with the hearth blaze.

"There now, that should be about right." Said the figure, lowering a mould, long and flat, brown, and a bit lumpy, upon a great pitted, and scarred workbench.

He paused a minute, and then taking up a hammer, and a small chisel, carefully began breaking away the mould. Silver shone forth, brilliant even in the yellow-reds of the hearth fires glow.

This was alchemical silver, or star of silver, the finest silver possible, at least within the middle land. In other worlds, other dimensions, other silvers might exist, but here, and now, this one was king. Especially for binding spells.

A few more taps, and then some careful brushing, and then gentle wiping, and the silver rectangular plate lay exposed, gleaming. Embossed upon its surface, the designs, runes, and sigils, Nirnadel, had drawn upon that scrap of paper.

Alurici had recognised some of the markings straight away. Runes and sigils of binding, ancient and arcane. Other symbols, he did not recognise, but, he felt it was safe to assume, they belonged to the same ilk of magick, just magick unknown to his lore.

Rarely would he ever have dreamt of creating something unknown, unproven, untested. Flying blindly into the unknown, was not how he did business, or research either.

This was one of the very rare exceptions, one of the few times he would break his own personal golden rule, if you don't know, don't do. This rule had saved his life on numerous occasions in the past. He hoped it would stand him in good stead in the future too.

Except, now he had the binding focus, he needed the magick word, the name of bondage that would lock the creature away, hopefully forever. He suspected he knew what that word was, or at the very least what it sounded like.

One other thing bothered him. He was a research Mage, well, Arch Mage, in fact. The idea of confronting an ancient Elder Horror, such as a Great Big One, really did not appeal to him.

He needed a stooge, he caught himself, he needed a hero, some schmuck, some worthy, who would bravely, and blindly rush off to almost certain death, on the off chance he might save the world.

Hmm. He pondered. The obvious candidate, Hammer Guy, had wised up. That was Hunbogi's fault, admittedly they were both communing deeply with the spirits that evening, but Hunbogi could have been more tactful, or indeed crafty in parting godling from ancient relic.

Now said, new god, was out of the action, and wised up, making his own plots and plans, whatever they turned out to be, someone else, would be needed.

Someone heroic. Someone daft, someone fierce and brave, with enough wit to cast a simple spell, someone with the gift.

His misogynistic heart quailed. He could have the perfect heroine! But, great quests always went to the men folk, not women. It was traditional. You wouldn't catch a great Mage bestowing world shaking responsibilities, no matter how suicidal, on a mere woman, let alone someone who was barely out of her teens.

He counted the options again. There was always Ralph. He smiled. A middle aged fire sorceror working for a robber baron in a far off land. He might do. There was Captain Fortune. He'd heard of him. He was lucky. Luck was a brilliant thing for hero's to possess.

Thing is, Captain Fortune might be so lucky, he'd dodge getting lumbered with such a quest. Also, he knew no magick, not did he have any gift for it.

There was Nirnadel. She was a trained Necromancer, an abhorrence in any right thinking world, and she knew a little of the other magick arts.

Why not get all three?

All three, he thought. Yes, he would try that.

Carefully, he placed the silver plate, into a leather sleeve. This needed to be protected. Maybe he would travel with them part of the way, he could make some excuse to duck out, as soon as things get too hairy.

Chapter Forty Seven – Bits and Pieces

"You know it really is very kind of you to let us out, and settling us down into the guest quarters again, is well, not needed." Lyra warmly, and wryly addressed Karles, who in full Butle, had taken control of the castle, temporarily, at least.

"I understand, my lady, your kinfolk will be arriving shortly, and I'll be happy to extend the hospitality of Castle Navorny to them likewise." He continued, smiling deferentially.

Fudge had reappeared, and was allowing Rhian to fuss his ears. He clearly felt the honour was due, and was prepared to put up with it for special occasions.

Nirnadel gazed west and south. She was pensive. If the Bone Legion was coming here! What about the frontier? Sad, to think that the frontier, had once been thriving farmlands, and the highways to the great civilizations of the South.

Now, in ruins, and presumably some kind of assault would come, now the Legion was away. The Count, had apparently hidden up in one of his towers, the one it seemed, that he reserved for his experiments.

Dark and horrible they would be too. She had heard of the type. Pale young men with clammy hands, dark ringed eyes, and the weirdest obsessions. Who knew what perverse things went on up there. Actually, she rather wanted to go and take a look. She was a Necromancer after all, dark was her domain.

Except, was it? She had come to realise that her father, had had some very unusual ideas about parenting, and home education. Maybe, she shouldn't be a Necromancer? Maybe she should take after Rhian, learn how to throw a knife like a champ, and settle down to casual robbery, trade and travel. Or perhaps, she should train to be like Lyra, whose arts had enslaved faeries, for decades.

Maybe, she should try and be nice? What was nice? The whole of her world seemed to revolve around arbitrary power structures, people owned stuff, because their ancestors did, people did stuff, because their relatives did. People did stuff to other people, because, that was how things were done. Do unto others before they do unto you. She'd read that somewhere, or been told that, by someone, possibly Rhian. Was this really all there was to life? Perhaps that was why people like the 'clairvoyant,' or 'medium,' whatever he was pretending to be, sold out so readily to the Devourer.

I mean why not? If you are at the bottom of the heap, just plankton in the great food chain, why wouldn't you jump at the chance to be a shark?

The Clairvoyant, had not been found. She suspected he was with the Count, planning something nasty. She wanted to go look.

Well, it was a good excuse, she knew she was just making up reasons to see the Counts laboratory. She'd had her own laboratory and library at home, well, back at the Palace in Graeffenland, and sometimes she missed it.

Would she ever go mad, so buried in her studies of the obtuse and the eldritch, that she would vanish down the rabbit hole, perhaps never to return?

She wondered if that happened to people anyway. They spent so long obsessing over the littlest things, that those things rose up and ate them, converting them into just metaphors, allegories of some principle, or bizarre stereotypical idea, rather than thinking human beings.

She shook her head, she shouldn't think this way, it was too, philosophical. Still, she was a princess, and a member of the People of the Wagons! She was a winner. Of course, by definition, winners meant losers. No team effort, come first, or lose. That all sounded so wrong.

She didn't feel like a winner. She felt like she was waiting for the other shoe to drop.

A flash of colour, caught her eye, and looking down, she could just make out the upper part of the gatehouse, and the road, winding away from it, down towards the town. Many wagons, some brightly painted, were heading up the road, possibly already at the Castle, and its courtyard.

"You know, I think the family is here." She said aloud, glancing back to Rhian and Lyra.

Rhian looked worried, Lyra just smiled.

"That's nice." Lyra offered.

"I know this is a big place, but there's only one road in and out, no field for the horses either." Rhian stated calmly.

"It's only for a little while though, isn't it? I mean we're not staying here any longer than we have too, are we?" Nirnadel felt her spirits sink. What in the world did Lyra want? Money? They had enough. Contacts, influence? The Count, would soon be in trouble, the townsfolk knew full well, that he'd murdered the Mayor, they would be here for justice on their own account soon enough.

"Well, we can't all stay." Lyra said, smiling mischievously.

"You are not serious, there is no way I'm staying here! Anyway, that stupid Count, will be history soon enough. In fact we should probably go up there and sort him out right now!" Nirnadel almost , but not quite shouted, at Lyra.

"Do you want to live the rest of your life, trundling around in one of our Wagons?" Lyra asked, in all seriousness.

"Why wouldn't I want to?" Nirnadel retorted.

"Well, because you could have so much more. Like a Castle. This Castle, for one." Lyra mused aloud.

"I don't want anything to do with the Count, and he will probably be facing justice any time now." Nirnadel scowled. It was not like her grandmother to be so irrational.

"No, if you want the Castle, when the Bone Legion gets here, just tell them to hold it for you. No one is going to argue. How do you think Xagigg, your father, got his Crown?" Lyra smiled.

"Mother, that was different." Rhian interjected.

"Really? He just got voted mister popular then?" Lyra grinned.

"No, he picked the crown of Graeffenland up, after, the usurper died." Rhian muttered.

"I am not having this conversation with you again." Rhian continued walking to wards the stairs.

"I'm going to make sure things stay calm and civil below, I'm sure they will, but they need to know we're all safe and sound. Okay, just safe then." She shot a glance back at Lyra and Nirnadel.

"You know I enjoy the simple life." Nirnadel whispered across to Lyra.

Fudge had chosen that moment to wander in, from possibly another looting session in the kitchens. Perhaps the crumbs, were from the previous day.

"Why does he do that? He is house trained." Nirnadel asked.

"No life is simple, every thing gets complicated. The only difference is how much control you can have over your own circumstances. Power is control, even over the little things." Lyra replied.

"Right, I'm exercising some control right now, I'm going up that tower, and seeing what our dear Count has been getting up to!" Nirnadel turned and marched for the little set of stairs, behind the carved wooden throne.

"Fudge! Go with her!" Lyra shouted.

"If you're not back in twenty minutes, I'm sending a search party." She added.

Fudge dutifully bounded after Nirnadel.

The other faerie dogs, they had a pack of them still, friendly loyal, fuggly beasts that they were, would be out there taking up positions around and inside the Castle, scaring kitchen staff, and watching out for trouble.

They were tough, scary beasts when aroused to anger, or just hunting, one would be enough. Fudge's yellow eye and orange eye glittered up into the stairwell, of the spiral staircase, heading up to the laboratory of the Count. He'd already taken a look earlier. It was his duty, and last night, he'd scouted out every inch he could sneak into, and for all his size and maddening colour scheme, he really could sneak.

It was like people pretended he wasn't there. They wouldn't look at him, and sometimes made strange smells and noises, or froze, looking in some other direction, until he'd left the room. He didn't understand it. Still, they didn't stop him, or get in his way, so, it wasn't much of a problem.

Nirnadel, had started out stepping high and quick up the steps, but as the stairs dragged on, with no apparent landing or doorways, she started to trudge. She really was getting high up the stairs. Every time she looked down, Fudge seemed to be sitting waiting.

Finally, she stopped.

Fudge nudged a wall. She looked down. She hadn't gone very far, and yet she'd been climbing the stairs for ages. She stepped back, up a step. Fudge and her distance to him stayed the same.

She swore. Illusion!

She'd been walking to nowhere.

Fudge nudged the wall again.

Alright, a secret door. Very clever, Count.

She paused, actually, this Count was more dangerous than he appeared. High quality gnomish alchemy, magickal illusions, she couldn't afford to underestimate him.

She gazed at the wall, and raised the sight. The lighting changed, except there was a concentrated patch, a pattern on the wall.

Not a secret door. A road block. An illusion simply to stop her climbing the stairs. How did she know this? She thought back, back to her library, oh gods, was it that simple? A prank, not really even a spell, except it was a very basic enchantment, and it had worked on her.

She raised the rune of dispelling in her mind, quickly negotiating it's pathways and thought forms. The patch exploded, soundlessly, sparks of arcane light flickering away. She lowered the sight, and looked up.

There it was, barely a yard or too further up. A simple wooden door. She must have walked in place for ages.

She swore, again.

Up she went, Fudge trotted behind. His expression, a cool impassive neutral, his eyes fixed on the door.

She reached for the door and stopped. She pulled back her hand. There's was bound to be another trap.

She lowered the sight once more. The whole door glowed. So many spells had been laid across it, it was more magick than wood.

This was silly.

She brought up the dispel rune, paused and waved Fudge back, shielding her eyes, she completed the spell.

The spells unravelled like a catherine wheel. She dropped the sight, it really was quite bright.

She stepped back, a few paces, going back down the stairs.

Pieces of the door started whizzing down the stairs. The wood itself, so enthused with charms, was now disrupted, and through long attraction followed the dispersing energies.

Finally, a clink and a tinkle, attracted her attention. The door knob and the mechanism of the lock, hadn't fallen to the floor.

She advanced. Fudge pushed past her.

"Wait." She said.

Fudge ignored her, advancing a few feet before her, into the room.

Light, daylight was plentiful, floor space was not.

The laboratory was full, tables, workbenches, stools, chests, shelving, creatures, bits of creatures, crackling electrical contrivances, of no apparent function, glugging test tubes, and bottles of strange liquids.

Nirnadel smiled. It had atmosphere.

"So, you've come at last......" Said the Count.

He stood, dressed in black and purple, a surcoat, griffins rampant, either side of a small crown, and portcullis. Blackened chainmail, showed beneath, at shoulders, and wrists.

"What are you talking about?" Nirnadel almost laughed.

"You have come to wrest from me my great secret!" The Count shouted.

His face twisted, and he snarled.

She stared at him, so this was what crazy looked like. Fudge growled, low and warning.

"Oh, you brought your pet? Well, I have pets too! Vivo animus! Attack! Attack!" The Count laughed, almost maniacally.

Fudge looked at Nirnadel, and then stepped back. Things, were approaching, crawling, and flopping, slowly across the floor.

Mostly, they looked just like hands, some with a bit of an arm attached too. There were also feet, they sort of wriggled.

Nirnadel gaped at them. They weren't zombie parts, they were, somehow still alive. They also, moved really, really slowly. She stepped around them. Fudge nibbled one experimentally.

"My creations will destroy you!" The Count yelled, backing away.

"No, they won't." Nirnadel spoke. This she felt, was an entirely accurate assessment of the situation.

Something nagged at the back of her mind.

The Count turned. He grabbed a ceremonial long sword, its blade scraped, little sparks glinted off the metal work. He turned back.

"Well, I'll kill you myself!" The Count continued.

Light dawned, Nirnadel brought the patterns, and runes of the word of Command, to mind.

"Stop." She said, flatly.

The Count froze, his face a picture of amazement, the sword lifted high above his head.

Fudge crunched something, it was distracting.

"Put down the sword." Nirnadel asked, reasonably she thought.

The Count, mouth lolling open, lowered the sword, his fingers loosened, and the blade slipped from his fingers. It clattered on the stone floor.

"Go down stairs, to your dungeons, and instruct whoever is there to lock you in." Nirnadel stated.

The Count, rigidly, almost mechanically walked, down the steps, and away.

Nirnadel watched his back as he walked away. She followed, slowly.

From the shadows, the medium, his darkened eyes bandaged, watched them both depart. Fudge eyed him carefully, whilst chewing.

Nirnadel vanished down the stairs. The medium stepping out from the shadows, raised his hands. Fudge dropped something that squirmed, and wriggled. He growled.

A door below, slammed shut. Fudge stood up. The medium, slowly stepped towards the window. Fudge padded forward.

Stretching an arm out, and smiling, the bandaged figure, opened the window. He stepped towards it, never taking his subjective eyes, off the faerie dog.

He turned and leaped. Fudge, surprise not being one of his greatest weaknesses watched him go, impassively. He turned back to the mobile sweetmeats.

Lord Drool had listened to this exchange with fascination. A sort of horrid, cold, wonderment. He stared, as always, up. The talking had stopped. There was a breeze from the window, and the sounds of snuffling, crunching and smacking, came to his ears. He wondered if, the creature would ever reach him?

Chapter Forty Eight – Death and Destruction.

Kenovass, its new fortifications, glistening in the late afternoon sunshine, it had rained earlier, the guards, in their red, and yellow livery walked, still in oilskins, along its walls. They gazed out, south and east, across the misty barren fields.

It had been a warm day, nothing moved, nothing stirred. The city itself was quiet. The people, many had left, going west, temporarily, they hoped, some, meaning never to return.

The departure of the Bone Legion, was a big deal, even the gnomes, had drawn back, waiting for further orders. The people, mostly had headed out too. Cold eyes watched the ramparts, secretly, watching, waiting for the signal to move.

The day wore on, evening closed in, and, then the fun began. It began slowly, a clinking noise, a rustling, a slow shoosh, and then, in one corner, a paving slab, gave way, sinking, suddenly, and then slowly, into the ground.

The careful observer, would have seen the hole, slowly, expanding. Pale hands reached up, drawing pale bodies skyward. Arshan's Horde had arrived. Quietly, they clambered into the streets, strange agglomerate creatures followed, multiple arms and legs, and other, less distinguishable appendages followed.

All as silent as the grave, gradually filling the streets. A cry arose, as the first guard spotted the invaders.

The cold eyes, watching impassively, would have grinned if they could. A cold arm rose, dead lungs blew a rusty horn. Rutger Tostwic, General of the Bone Legion, drew back his lips in a rictus grin.

Out from the houses, doors flung wide, by long dead hands, spewed forth the Bone Legion. It had gone nowhere. Xagiggs orders had been explicit, take the bait, be the bait.

Arshan's Horde continued gushing, now through multiple holes in the paving of the streets, and fighting ranged the whole length and breadth of the city.

The living populace, mainly the garrison on the walls, hunkered down. A few fires sprung up, the gnomish weapons, intended for field operations, were a bit heavy handed for urban warfare.

Rutger Tostwic, once Marshall of the Realm of Graeffenland, briefly its usurper King, and now, in his afterlife, General of its army, wearing his slightly rusty platemail, skeleton fist emblazoned on its front, drew his sword and stepped out into the fray.

This wasn't how he'd pictured his afterlife. He hadn't really believed in the gods, monsters, or heavens and hells, but this Zombie existence, wasn't so bad. He supposed he'd deserved to be punished, some kind of hell would have been appropriate for his crimes. He had done, many terrible things in life, and, the existence as a Zombie General, leading an army, potentially forever, was a punishment, but also, perhaps, a reward. He enjoyed soldiering. He always had. He'd enjoyed fighting, he still did.

You got used to being a Zombie, it was just like the hardships of soldiering in a way. You did without. You forgot about the things you didn't have, until you were on leave. Except, as a Zombie, you were never on leave.

He swung his sword, dismembering two possessed creatures. He'd got better. Before he'd passed, not so much away, thanks to Xagigg, but into his new, unlife, he'd been getting slow, rusty. Now, all his old skills, had come back to him, with a clarity, he hadn't had before. Nor did he tire, his sword swung, and he danced, a step here, a swivel there, a pirouette, figures dropping, all around.

His blade was a delight. It had been turned up, in the Northlands, that independent kingdom as was, north of Graeffenland, sharing the same island, but not the same masters.

It had been found, half buried, with the bones of its crushed last owner, amidst the ruins of Evehollow. It was magickal, it was possibly cursed, it was named Heartseeker, and this it did, speedily, from any direction, starting high or low, there was only one way the blade would go.

It was a gift from Xagigg, who had confiscated the weapon, giving free membership of the Bone Legion to the hapless souls who had found the blade. It was cheating, but Rutger didn't mind, he was a good swords-zombie? An extra edge, in battle, was worth having.

The battle raged, rage being exactly the right word. The Horde, as single minded as the zombies, fought like men possessed, which, in fact they were. The zombies fought like well oiled machines, fires spread.

Pausing amidst his recreational slaughter, Rutger noticed, the possible snag to their counter trap. Zombies didn't like fire.

Fire was, on the whole, one of the few ways zombies could be finally despatched. There were other ways, but they required more effort. The Horde wasn't making use of fire, itself, but buildings were starting to collapse, catching defenders and invaders alike.

This was not Rutgers preferred strategy. Field warfare, massed ranks, this was his bread and butter. Fighting room to room, street to street, attic to attic, was not his accustomed milieu of melee.

Still, they were winning. He was sure.

The gnomes, had gone along with this plan. They had alerted the General to the tunneling, many months before. It had been so quiet, no sorties, no attacks. At first they had believed Arshan's forces gravely depleted, which, though also true in many ways, was also an underestimation.

The Horde, the gnomic long range scout service, had assured them, was almost spent. Just a few tens of thousands remained, out of the original hundreds of thousands.

This was more than enough, potentially, to overwhelm, the remaining lands of man, hopefully, they would finally expend themselves, here.

A signal flare went up from the walls. Another force had been spotted outside the walls, heading north.

The gnomes, their war mechanicals, the thirty foot high mechanical 'men.' piloted by two gnomes each, wielding great fire sphere throwing enchanted rods, had been holding back, waiting for some counter thrust like that. Rising from where they had been camouflaged, shrugging off the leafy netting, the war machines marched forward, quickly covering the distance. Magickal fire bloomed, and flew, striking the enemy as they tried to run northwards.

The sun, falling low behind, the trees, cast the shade of evening, across the terrible, heaving scene. More fires erupted, more buildings collapsed. People who had refused to leave, fled or hid, or ran amidst the confusion.

Squads of the Legion, pikes shouldered, or presented, blocked thorough fares as yet unsullied by the riotous battle. Other squads pressed forwards, pushing the fighting mass, containing it where they could.

Other squads, crossbows readied, had taken positions, where they could, over looking the battle. Volleys of bolts began to rain upon the massed enemy, which fell, like wheat before a scythe.

The Horde fell, shrinking, as its strength expended itself.

Ten Grief, standing in his accustomed tower, gazed down on the destruction. It was nearly done, the last battle, the finish of years of siege, years of stand off, he could find himself the library of his dreams, his own laboratory, and begin a happy life of academic seclusion.

He looked east, the night was coming in. He looked again, shadows, don't pad. He stared. There on the horizon, not far enough away, a great deep darkness, deeper than the dusk, deeper than the night. A great leonine shadow, with two great glowing stars for eyes.

It walked, sixty, eighty, a hundred feet tall at the shoulder, it padded, crushing the ground beneath its feet. It strode, nonchalantly, calmly, straight towards the city. Straight towards him.

Cold, like ice spread through him. It could see him, it knew he watched, it was coming for him, for everyone.

He watched the Devourer draw near to the city, all thought of spells, charms or enchantments, falling from his mind, he gibbered in fear.

Chapter Forty Nine – Questing for the Beast.

White bejewelled robes, were not generally considered the best adventuring gear. Alurici, had early on, incorporated self cleaning, and deodorising enchantments into them. He did have a moment though, having to unpick one enchantment, when blue white, actually turned the robes a light cyan colour.

As far as whiter than white was concerned he was happy with basic matt white, no bright dazzling colours needed.

Several of his power jewels, were simply dedicated to maintaining the crispy freshness of his apparel.

He'd had no luck with boots though. For some reason, that area of enchantment had eluded him. So, he'd found a good faerie cobbler, fine but expensive boots.

He stood there, amidst the colours, the strange echoing musical noises, the odd scented winds, and waited.

He did not have to wait that long. He escried Garim, in his Captain Fortune garb, wandering aimlessly lost amidst the pathways of the higher world.

He had simply portalled, not teleport this time, but the slightly different dimensional door opening, between worlds. He'd stepped onto the pathway, just a little ahead of Garim's route.

Garim, walking along, would be with him shortly, and there he was, despondently strolling along. He was lucky. The Higher world was dangerous to those with a bad attitude. It tended to respond to peoples emotional states, especially the pathways themselves. A nice happy path, could spontaneously fork, and the unwary traveller could find themselves rerouted, to somewhere darker and more fitting to their mood.

Thusly, amongst the erstwhile 'mortal' dwellers of the Upper World a new phrase had been born. To fork, to get forked, and to go fork oneself. These phrases were generally considered terms of abuse.

Garim had encountered several dozen forks, but randomly guessing, he had picked the right fork each time. He would have been described as 'forking lucky' back in the day, but Kershaggulumphie, did not approve of cuss words, and Adan, erstwhile god of thunderousness, actually had no servants in the Upper world, so the phrase had fallen into disuse.

Garim stared at the white robed figure.

"So, who are you then?" Garim asked. This was the first person he had seen, for hours, and the white robed fellow looked like a Mage.

"I am the Archeus Magnus, Alurici." Replied the white robed figure. He felt no need or requirement for lying.

"You don't know the way out of this place?" Garim asked scratching his red fluff.

"I do indeed know the way out, and I can help you get revenge." Alurici said, a thin smile spreading under his white beard.

He gazed into Garim's eyes.

"I have quite a list, which 'revenge' did you have in mind?" Garim enquired.

"If it involves a certain egomaniac on a cloud back there, it can wait." He added, quickly.

"No, it involves something big, something bad, something that consumed, half your crew." He smiled again.

"Only half? Well, I'm glad some of them got away." Garim's throat constricted. Dark thoughts crossed his mind. I suppose they all think I'm dead too. Maybe that was for the best.

"Yes, well, there is a way, you, and possibly only you, can help destroy, or, imprison that terrible creature. Your men would expect nothing less." Alurici enthused.

"So, what is this way? Can we leave this mad house first." Garim asked.

"Yes, yes, here, walk thro there." Alurici, had gestured, a glowing portal appeared.

"Really? You first." Garim said, smiling grimly.

"Okay." Alurici, stepped thro the portal.

Garim, hesitated, considering his options, and then shrugged. He stepped thro.

The other side, was a great stone chamber. Lit by lamps, oil he guessed, several dozen. People, dressed in blue livery, stared at the two as they stood there.

"I understand we're standing in Castle Navorny, and that princess Nirnadel, is here, somewhere. I want to talk to her." Alurici stated, smiling broadly.

"Yeah, well, now show me the way out." Garim asked, adjusting his floppy hat.

"Wait, you want your revenge, don't you?" Alurici turned to stare at him. A servant looked at him sideways.

A few minutes passed. Karles appeared, wrung his hands in mock consternation.

"Please, follow me, gentlemen." Karles advised.

They followed, out into the great stone corridor, to the magickal moving room, and up, into the heights of the building.

Karles stood to one side, as two very gypsy like men, their colourful bandanas and gold jewelry, very strange, especially compared to the formal blue of the Butler, held open the doors.

Alurici walked quickly through, and paused, Garim just to one side. He had recognised the style. These were People of the Wagons, and the faerie dogs, of various sizes, shapes and dispositions, their glowing eyes boring into them, brought back some fearsome memories.

Garim shivered. Someone had a knife at his back.

A tall, grey haired gypsy, stood up. He'd been sitting on an old wooden throne. He smiled.

"I would be called Pierjin, and the ladies of the house, can't be speaking to you right now, but I can. What is it you too most magickal gentlemen my want?"

He smiled, and fingered a dagger.

"Nirnadel's dream drawing, I know what it is, and how she can use it." Alurici, smiled. He'd counted a dozen faerie dogs.

"My drawing? I wondered what had happened to that, and that wretched blue bottle, did you take that with you, somehow?"

"Eh? No! May I sit? Perhaps, without, so many hounds?" Alurici asked.

"No, we're family. You can sit though." She waved, and one of the gypsy's brought up a chair. The dogs eyes followed him as he moved to sit. He placed a leather case on the table. He opened it.

Nirnadel moved forward, standing just beyond the table, opposite.

"So, what have you got for us?" She asked.

"Your page, your Codex, it's a binding spell. Here is the focus. I've produced the focus in finest alchemical silver. No need to thank me. I want the world to keep turning too."

Alurici smiled.

"Binding enchantment? How's is it activated?" She asked.

"Well, that's something you need to find out. Can you not remember?" Alurici grinned.

"There it is. Just get to the creature use the focus, with the word, you think of it, I'm sure, and the threat to the world is over!" He declared.

"Oh and this gentleman here, wants to help you." He added.

Garim, stared at Alurici. Nirnadel stared at him, he looked to her, like a gaudily dressed pirate.

"What are you supposed to be?" She asked.

"I am Captain Fortune." He bowed, swishing his hat, off in a sweeping bow. He couldn't run for it, not yet. The faerie dogs, Pierjin, he knew these people, he met them before, years ago, and miles away. Nothing to do but play their game, for now.

"You really are a pirate!" She grinned.

She had met pirates, merchants of extremis, in Vondrbeorg, about a year before. She didn't like them at all.

Pierjin just smiled.

"We know you! You escaped the Woodfolk, killed some of them too, somehow. Why should we let you live?"

"I didn't kill any of them, I just ran. Do I look like I could kill them?" He replied, trying to stay calm.

He adjusted his hat. One of the dogs was sniffing his leg.

He remembered them. He remembered being dragged from a horse by them, back to the gypsy camp, all those years ago.

"Old times. I would be grateful, to help Nirnadel fulfil her quest, in any way I can." He tried to sound sincere.

The dog had sat by his foot and was staring straight up at him.

It was eyeing his crotch. He was certain. He began to sweat.

Nirnadel held the metal plate in her hands. It was highly magickal, it rang so many bells, struck so many chords, it was so close to her dream-vision. Just the word of the Shaman, it rang out in her mind, "Codex". Was it "Codex" she heard? Or was it "Koh Dekks."

She smiled. She thought she knew.

"Well, you're the expert, why don't..." The question died on her lips. The Arch Mage, had gone.

Garim saw Alurici teleport away. Typical, he thought. Sets them up, and leaves them to it.

"Well, I suppose we ought to find out where this creature is." Nirnadel, reached over, taking the leather case, and placing the silver pane, back within. She clasped it to her.

She looked at Pierjin.

"Are there any gnomes in town?" She asked innocently.

Chapter Fifty – Confrontations

Adan sat staring at the glowing blue bottle. It was like, so very like the bottle he'd drunk from, by the cave, in the woods, so very long ago.

He opened it. It smelt like ozone. Of course he'd never smelt ozone, it just smelt of storms and lightning. How appropriate he thought. He drank. Energy coursed through him. He felt supercharged. He finished it.

He sat back, thought for a moment. He should now see what could be done. He walked back to the balcony, and gazed down. The middle land, spread out before him, zooming in and out of focused, as he looked at different points.

Hmm, he thought. I want to see, lines of influence, magick, other forces. He tried shifting his perceptions. Different coloured lights, sometimes streaks, pools and whorls, dance before his eyes. There it was, the Devourer, so easily recognisable after all these years, it was romping through Kenovass, crushing houses, buildings, streets, walls, and people. It was thoroughly enjoying itself. It was savouring its victory.

Anger rushed through him. What could he do? He saw something else, a dark purple string of energy, going up. He followed it with his gaze, and stared harder.

There, above the Upper World, there was an above! That was a shock to the system, other places, other worlds. One of them, seemed to connect to the Beast itself. He stared, his gaze zooming in, passing through the veils of energy between him and who?

He stared harder. A desert, a pyramid, a hall, dimension twisting and wrought with extraplanar energies. A figure, nut brown, and covered with blue tattoos, sat cross legged, deep in meditation.

His eyes snapped opened. Their gaze met. Adan had never felt a will like it, it was more powerful than his, it bore down upon him, brought him to his knees, quite something, considering who and where he was, now.

Their minds wrestled.

In the world below, Nirnadel and Garim stood by Elbie. She hadn't gone far, and had returned, almost suspiciously fast. She had in fact been assigned to shadow Nirnadel, but she wasn't going to let on about that.

She had made enquiries, and had heard straight away, where the dread creature was. There was no doubt and the information was not regarded as classified, more catastrophic. She had memorised the coordinates, needed for portalling (well, for the gnomish version of that magick).

Taking a deep breath she looked to the others, they nodded.

She opened the portal. They stepped through, into a nightmare.

Smoke, flames, screaming, terrible bellowing roars, smashing noises, shouting, the cacophony was limitless.

"Oh, by the gods!" Nirnadel cried, wiping smoke from her eyes.

"Only dark ones." Elbie spoke quietly.

Tramping noises rushed up and passed. A squad of Zombies, still fighting, no morale to break, determined, rushed to engage the horror. The ground was thickly covered, littered with crushed down debris of all descriptions.

Nirnadels gaze followed the charging squad. She shuddered. What she thought was just a cloud, a patch of dark sky, was the creature, rampant, movement undulating through it, as it stamped and reared, over the ruins, and the remaining defenders.

One of the gnomish war mechanicals remained, spitting fire, from its enchanted fire rods, and then it was swept away, one paw of darkness, and it was dashed to pieces.

Garim no longer felt like being brave.

"What in the world can we do here!" He shouted over the din.

Nirnadel pulled out the silver pane, and held it forth. "Codex!" She yelled.

Nothing happened, the clamour continued, riotous havoc drew closer to them. They stepped back.

"Is there something else you should do, you know to cast it?" Garim asked.

Of course, she thought. She hadn't cast it. She stared at the sigils, the runes, and the patterns, embossed upon the silver panel.

Focussing on the symbols, she presented the device again.

"Koh deks!" She yelled.

The creature paused, it turned, two great stars in the sky, stared down upon her. She presented the focus more forcefully.

"Koh deks!" She intoned.

Its will bore into hers, and she pushed back, flinging her energy into the focus, into the binding spell.

She wasn't dead. She felt surprised. She was wrestling with an alien horror of ancient eldritch dreadfulness, and she was holding her own. It also wasn't stepping on her, which had been her first concern.

Something though, something was boosting the creature, it was getting fresh strength.

Garim stared. He had drawn his cutlass, it was pathetic. It wasn't even a pin to this horrific creature. He stood guard, watching for enemy troops. Maybe some were still around. The creature seemed to have been trampling everything. Not really that smart.

Feet were running towards them, he turned, and there was a muscled warrior, his eyes only part dark, as he liked to think of those who made some kind of deal with, the Devourer, or was it the Devourer, they'd dealt with? That huge beast didn't seem talkative, more like someone's pet.

This figure, had a scimitar of considerable size and weight, in his strong gnarled hand.

Garim rushed to meet him. Steel met steel, and whirled away.

Slice met thin air, steel met guard, sparks flew, the figures rebounded off each other, then lunged to clash again.

He was strong this man, and fierce. Garim slipped, and as luck would have it, the scimitar whooshed above his head. He lashed out, his cutlass, backhanded, hit just behind the man's knee. He cried in anger, and pain. He slipped backwards, landing heavily.

Garim rolled to his feet, cutlass between him and the downed warrior, who was already rolling around, into a kneeling position and drawing back his arm, to throw.....

Garim lashed out with his cutlass, the scimitar, flying from the warriors hand, was clipped by it, and spun, harmlessly passed Nirnadels head.

She was still locked in mental conflict with the creature.

Adan, locked in his own battle of wills, could feel his foe distracted. By the gods, (he would have laughed at himself for that, had things been less serious), this fellow, was not only crushing him by inches, he was fighting someone else too, down there in the middle land.

A light began to flash, and pulsate in the weirdling chamber in the pyramid. A blue cabinet appeared, its doors opened, three figures stumbled out.

Chapter Fifty One – In the Pyramid.

It had been a bad couple of days. Jaeson Smith had had bad days before, but these last few were different. True, the city was dark, all cities were dark, it was the people who made them that way, Hell, after all, was other people.
He longed for the simplicity of a cheating husband, or a cheating wife. The business partner whose skimming the take, the simple nastiness of everyday life.
His life had been simple. Now, here he was, next to one fruitcake dressed as monk, or as a priest, and another, who sounded like a Britisher stage magician, he dressed like one too.
He was always talking to himself.
At least, Jaeson hoped the dude was talking to himself, he was doing it now.
"Oh fiddlesticks! Somehow, we have been knocked clear off course! Some kind of forcefield, very strong one too. Still, if I make a few adjustments, I believe I can get around it. Well, or through it."
The man was dancing around his glowing coffee machine. The coffee had been good too, he felt more his old self. His old self wanted to go home, have a shower, reload his gun, put on a change of clothes, and eat Italian. He liked

Italian food, it comforted him. No, it didn't remind him of home, but it filled, it warmed, its flavours, sometimes generous, sometimes mild, entertained, but in an undemanding way. Yes, he wanted Italian.

He wanted wine. Lots of wine. Wine was good therapy.

This strange man, in his theatrical costume, wasn't taking him home. This was not good.

"I want to go back to Boston. I don't know how you pulled this stunt, but you're going to reverse it." He offered this by way of friendly advice. He patted his gun, still in its holster.

"Yes, yes, all in good time. I do wish you wouldn't fret so!" PAM commented. He was fixated on his dials, and knobs.

He manipulated this, fiddled with that, tapped another, and then looked up.

"Yes, just one stop, and then I'll see about getting you both home." He smiled.

"Alright, you better not be yanking my chain." Jaeson Smith.

He stood, near the doors. He considered trying to force his way out. The room swayed. They were moving, doubtless on some kind of truck, or other vehicle. So that was how they made the changes of scene. He had wondered. It was obvious really.

"We're nearly there. Hold on it might be a bumpy landing!"

The central glowing column ground to a halt, its lights twinkling slightly.

PAM through another lever, the doors whirred, and gently opened.

"Thank you, this is my stop." Jaeson muttered, and got out.

He caught his breath. He was in, or under, or within, a pyramid structure. It towered around him, in cyclopean proportions. He looked around. Green tendrils swirled by or in the walls, some of which, seemed to be glass. The pyramid, was half aquarium, half sandstone edifice.

"This isn't Boston." He said.

A figure, half turned towards him. It was a man, nut brown, blue tattoos, distracted look upon his face, but he addressed him nonetheless.

"You defy the gods, and all that's holy!" Said the cross legged figure.

PAM, and the priest had come out too. The priest seemed to be praying, very hard indeed.

"My dear fellow, what are you playing at?" Asked PAM.

"Leave this place! Or I shall slay you! Horribly!" The strange man said.

Jaeson Smith drew his revolver, he had plenty of bullets left. He'd reloaded, earlier.

"Now, now, I'm sure we can all settle this amicably like reasonable men." Said PAM.

"Then die!" Yelled the crosslegged man. He waved, a wall distorted, and a great green tentacle floundered in. It was wet, it grabbed Berythus. He screeched in horror!

The tentacle began to withdraw.

"Stop that! Don't be horrid! Call off your creature and lets sit down and talk!" Yelled PAM looking anxious.

Bang went Jaeson's revolver.

It's bullet, not used to the unusual dimensional arrangement moved, at first slow, then fast, oddly speeding up, then slowing down. It even rewound at one point.

Jaeson wondered what herbs the old herbalist had sold him last. He also wondered if he wanted more, or not.

The cross legged man seemed to have no idea what a bullet was or perhaps was too distracted to notice.

It closed slowly, inch by inch, with the man's temples.

Jaeson was fascinated.

PAM had run, and was hanging on to Berythus's legs, the tentacle was slowly dragging him towards the transparent wall.

He was screaming and yelling.

The bullet reached the old shaman's head.

He seemed to recognise it as a threat, at last, but in that fraction of a second, he seemed powerless to move.

It hit, drilling slowly through skin, bone, brain, and suddenly bursting into speed, and exploding out the back.

Jaeson liked dum dum's.

The tentacle released, as the pyramid wall solidified.

"Let's go!" Said PAM.

They returned, quickly to the blue cabinet.

It vanished.

The pyramid crumbled.

Chapter Fifty Two – Down to Earth.

Nirnadel was on her knees, the effort was killing her. The creature seemed invincible, its strength limitless.

Garim remained behind, and Elbie stood beside her, watching out for enemies.

A cry sounded behind her, Garim had jumped back, startled, a cold hand, hard, bony, had landed on her shoulder. She dared not look. Strength poured into her.

She stood, not daring to look behind her.

The creature's will snapped, it crumpled, it diminished, shrinking, the focus snapped out of her hand, growing larger, floating down towards the ground, a hole, opening, deeper and deeper, the creature sucked down like dark smoke, the silver pane, hurtling after. It was over. The creature was imprisoned. They had won.

She looked behind her. Gold Crown, tatty grey robes, once fine, once richly brocaded, sunken eye sockets, glowing purple gem set into the forehead.

Her father, the Lich King of Graeffenland stood before her.

"You never called. Whatever happened to the mirror I gave you." He asked in a light whisper.

"Um, I lost it." She replied quietly.

"Really, the first diplomatic mission I send you on, and you go missing. I'd have torn my hair out with worry, except, well, the hair was the first thing to go, and worry, of course. Why would I worry?" The old Lich grinned. He couldn't do much else.

"Return to Graeffenland with me now, you're needed." He said.

"Um, only, only if you swear you'll teach me how to teleport." She replied, firmly. She had just saved the world.

"Maybe, I'll think about it. You are very irresponsible you know." Xagigg muttered. He waved his bony hand. Air rushed, and they were both in the dark, dusty shadows, of the throne room of Graeffenland.

Elbie and Garim stared at each other.

"Can I have a lift somewhere?" Garim asked.

"Oh, where?" Elbie asked.

"Eghior. I sort of left a ship near there." He replied.

"Okay." Elbie said, concentrating, she knew those coordinates.

The portal appeared, they stepped through.

In his tower, Alurici, quietly powered down his monitoring enchantments. Things had gone so well. He couldn't have planned it better. The world was saved. The damaged bits would slowly recover, the gaps in reality would heal, he supposed. He could get down to studying bananas, their cultivation, he felt, was of major importance.

Up in the Upper World, Adan had stood, he'd watched the last moments of the shaman Zonthas. He felt sad. Such a great and ancient being, come to such a sorry end, too bad.

He noticed, with curiosity, Libraria's Hall was reforming, belief was rebuilding it. Someone believed in the power of books, and the Upper World, responded.

There was that blue cabinet too, dropping off a thin distraught looking man, in monks robes. He'd vanished into the palace, when it had appeared solid enough.

He looked around. Time he thought to redecorate.

Yes, he thought, it may be the palace of the passion of thunder, or whatever Kershaggulumphie had named it, but it would be decorated as the palace of the hot sunny summer beach lightning, and it needed to be as authentic as possible. He started installing palm trees.

Away in another dimension, the strange anomaly faded away, the starship had ceased tumbling, and the last crew person, her heart still heavily beating in her chest, moved the various remains of her fellow officers, in body bags into the hold. The ship was on auto pilot, and she needed shore leave. She went to her cabin and collapsed. The data discs, all filed away, were someone else's problem. As she closed her eyes to sleep, she wondered if she would get any bonus for this trip.

The uncaring Metacosmos whirled on, unabated, for now.

Other Titles, available from Amazon, and all good book stores.

Dragon / The World Unseeing:
First in the series, two Heroes quest for their fortunes, and get tangled up in more than they could ever have imagined.
ISBN: 978 153 2786 570

A King in Graeffenland:
The Kingdom in turmoil, and a Crown up for grabs! The second in the series.
ISBN: 978 151 8710 643

Princess of Bones:
The perils of a Princess, and a road trip to the ends of the Earth! Plus a looming Apocalypse.
ISBN: 978 151 8711 107

Metacosmoclypse:
Can the World of Graeffenland, and the whole multiverse be saved? Will the Gods find a way? Will the Mages and Priests find the answer? Will it really be down to an ex princess, and her family to find the elusive solution? The answer may lie within.......
ISBN: 978 151 977 9373

Once A Knight:
Sir Tarquin dreams of Knighthood, adventure and true love. Well, two out of three ain't bad!
ISBN: 978 153 464 2607

Hand & Eye:
The Worlds should be at peace, enjoying everything that has been hard won, over the last few years. Except, an Ancient Sorceror, has other ideas.
ISBN: 978 153 755 6536

Jaeson Smith, Private Eye:
He's back in his own novel! More spooky, Lovecraftian shenanigans in 1920's America!
ISBN: 978 153 992 9161

Printed in Great Britain
by Amazon